Dr Tenace

©Yves Bernas 2014

Cover pictures based on the wood engraving by

Camille Flammarion, from his book:

"L'atmosphère: météorologie populaire",

published in 1888.

This novel is dedicated to
my son William.

Many thanks to Kathrin
for her encouragement.

Contents

1. Morgue 15
2. Sarah Schein
3. Anna Haridana
4. Tennis
5. The Who
6. Falkennest
7. A photograph
8. Atomic density tomography
9. Autocorrelation
10. Parallel infection
11. Dog burial
12. Banking
13. Marrow road
14. The coachman
15. Ma
16. Back home
17. Zeppelin
18. Random death
19. Guignol
20. Jolly Roger
21. Son of a bitch
22. Resonance
23. Jealous eyes
24. Stolen Tenace
25. A little liquor

26. Reflecting on waves
27. Dickerdon
28. Gunter
29. Russian jumps
30. Leaning out the window
31. Falling off the window
32. Wild dogs
33. Snap
34. Retouche
35. Smoke to Heaven
36. Sequencing
37. Supper for tea
38. Standard deviation
39. The greylag goose
40. Juan Almeida de Barros
41. One way street
42. Madame Lavenue
43. Resuscitation
44. Happy birthday
45. The party
46. Escargots de Bourgogne
47. Valerian
48. Papa
49. Kosher Tenace
50. Just the two of us
51. Good old Edmund Rosegarden

Chapter 1: Morgue 15

As a doctor, you are interested in life, you fight for it and rejoice when you've healed, when the heartbeat is regular, the cheeks are pink and the eyes shine with hope and not with fever. After you've signed his authorisation to leave the hospital, you walk the patient to the door and say:

— I never want to see you here again Mr. Barns, you promise?

As a surgeon you're usually sad when you did not manage to save someone, like the young boy whose parents brought him in so late that his appendix burst and produced the lethal peritonitis. You're not sad because you messed up and were a bad doctor, 'cause you surely weren't. You're sad because someone died in front of you and you couldn't do anything about it. Perhaps this is why so many doctors have a couple of drinks more than the rest of us. It's a hard job to clink glasses with the dead. James Tenace was a doctor, but he wasn't sad when someone died, he was interested. He had the professionally compassionate look on his face, so common to undertakers. He had always wanted to be present when someone died. He had even given instructions to the nurses to call him when someone was about to kick the bucket. When he came, he entered the room quietly, got closer to the dying person, caress his cheeks, maybe thereby smelling what was still left of the breath and coveting, would take both his cold hands and peer deep into the fainting eyes. He would then sit down on the chair next to the bed, still holding the dying person's hand to avidly scrutinise all around his body in a frenzy.

To say that Doctor Tenace loved death is probably too much, but decay, especially mental or soul decay fascinated him. He was hypnotised by the last minutes of all sorts of living creatures struggling with death. He loved their panic, their trembling, their eyes at a loss, looking one last time around the room to see if they still knew someone, before this sudden calm would invade just before it was all over. This is when he would stand up, bend down over the corpse and possibly rejoice, holding the stethoscope, that the heartbeat would never be irregular again.

I always wondered what kind of physical pleasures such events triggered in his body, because afterwards he always looked sweaty, compulsively excited, and his eyes would glitter like engaging swords in the subdued room before he would routinely order the nurse to take the corpse to:

— Morgue 15 please!

Tenace had not always been like that. On the contrary, he used to fight for life even when most of his colleagues had already given up. It's not clear what changed him. Some say it was a love affair, one that actually had not quite reached this stage.

Chapter 2: Sarah Schein

Sarah Schein was a Jewish beauty, dark curly hair, extremely vivid and mocking. Arrogant and elitist, she would despise a man as soon as possible if she could detect the slightest hint that he would not be up to her expectations and these were certainly great, all the greater since it might have been the only greatness she would ever achieve.

But Doctor Tenace had been fascinated by her in his youth, her eyes shining like the hearth of her soul. Her smile mocked the entire world and she was so sure of herself, like one can only be when one has had a perfect childhood. Her parents had loved her so unconditionally, in a glimpse of divineness she would never forget. She would radiate back this divineness at the most unexpected moments, even through the narrow doors of her smirk.

Poor Tenace fell for that, not only the quick mouth and the dark locks, her childishness and insolence; that was the sunny side of it, but he fell for the impossible, the perpetual challenges she kept on giving him, all he had to reach and change before she would finally let him have her. Tenace started to believe in this promise of a later paradise, in another life, and started to get used to the idea that happiness was not for now but for later, once you're dead. Perhaps this is why he was so fascinated by death. He had renounced to be happy in his very life and was ready to endure the challenges and rejections, eternally waiting for the moment when she'd finally say yes.

His life had shrunk to checking a daily list of to-do's and the only, but great, pleasure in it was when this list was done. He was so used to things going wrong that he could not enjoy things going right. They were a bad sign, the sign that it was going to go wrong again. This is why he enjoyed and preferred when things went wrong, end of story. It was secure, nothing could get worse and that was good, so good that he could relax and rest in this dead end.

But what Tenace didn't realise is that in Sarah's mind, even this other life was definitely not meant to include him. When he reckoned that, it was too late; he had already started to hate her.

For Tenace, life was exterior to human beings; it visited them like the wind, blew over streets and houses and in a twinkle, it was somewhere else, leaving people at their windows, complaining, "It's dead here!"

Chapter 3: Anna Haridana

These were his thoughts as he was looking out the window of his office at Falkennest, a medical institution specialised in trying to get patients back from the coma they fell in after surgery or accident. Tenace opened the file on his desk: Anna Haridana. Anna was the worst case, no sign of life except her breath. She had a poached eye which she had never bothered to vitrify. Perhaps if she had had the money she would have had it replaced, even with gold, since her father was Russian.

Tenace read "Married to the painter and lacquerer Miguel Sofrer since 1958", then further: during the trial it was not completely clear either to the judge or to the General Attorney or even to Anna's public lawyer, who was the accused and who was the culprit. But since one of them was dead and the other one about the same, none of these wigged officials was very much troubled by this uncertainty. Why Robert Stank, the Attorney General, insisted on Anna's presence in Court was a mystery, since she could neither understand nor hear the questions posed by the court, not even the final sentence. She was just a flabby packet on a wheelchair disrupting the sudden silence of the high-ceiling church that served as a court room with her hoarse breath. If he could have, Robert Stank would have ordered the coffin to court.

The circumstances of the accident -should I say murder- are unclear. All that is sure is that Anna and Miguel were found lying on the round perron after having both smashed through the second-floor window of the dining room and flown to the ground screaming. Who pushed who is unclear. Miguel died instantly. The neighbours, Mr and Mrs Rütli, said that a fight about money had been going on. They testified that they have clearly heard Miguel accusing his wife of haven stolen money from him for years. He is supposed to have yelled at his wife just before the fatal flight:

— 200,000 Francs in that bank account! How on earth did you get it? If you weren't so fat and ugly, I could guess how you got it.

This is when she grabbed the knife. Though small, it was glittering in her hands just like her eyes, and Miguel knew she was going to kill him unless he stopped her. But he was much angrier at her that she had been stealing from him than he was that she intended to kill him. Money was more valuable than life. He stood up, rushed at her, not caring about the knife, just longing for her throat. He clawed his hands around her throat, screaming and pushing her across the room, holding her gullet, his arms so stretched that it seemed to keep the knife away. Most probably it was because the knife was too short, since it was an oyster knife. He began to shove her around the room with a strength and determination neither of them suspected him to possess. He kept on looking into her eyes and perhaps he saw in them that she still loved him and was never going to kill him, but then again why did she steal all that money? These were the fateful seconds of his life; he did not have time to answer his questions. He did not have the patience anymore. He had asked himself these questions over and over again, forgiving her everything, her moods, her unfounded accusations, her animosity, her verbal abuse, her contempt, her refusal and domination. But this time, he'd had enough. He had come to the conclusion that the solution was this stained-glass window representing the dome of the Universe according to Flammarion. He did not even feel much when she stabbed him with that oyster knife; perhaps he thought it was the door to heaven. And anyhow he had his eyes closed and was thrusting her. He moved like a bull rushing to his torturer. She was imploring him with her eyes, but somehow it seemed that she did not care either. Whatever would come, if it was his way to show her his feelings, whatever feelings, at least feelings. Their voyage lasted an eternity and they went through the stained-glass like the milkman through the door. The window exploded and they stopped screaming for three seconds, honouring the silence, and then there was a big thump, like a big pat on the back. That was it.

Tenace closed the file and his thoughts drifted. He remembered his father saying:

— I'm 54 and I'm done with my life. Ain't that good, the next years are free, no duty! Duty is an excuse for not doing what you want! Tenace was afraid of not being afraid to die. He kept on thinking that if you're not afraid to die, death would come and get you. There he was, abashed and not caring to survive, indifferent to death. He thought, it could come when it wanted. At the same time this very idea scared him because he thought it was like lowering your guard. Accepting the possibility of one's own end coming any second, wasn't that the ultimate wisdom and freedom? He could not totally adhere to hat and kept on thinking he was somehow spitting at life. Maybe the answer should have been to want something, to really want something extraordinary, instead of surfing like a parasite on the organic waves of life. He also thought if you refused to live, you'd get another life, and that thought suited him because he wasn't pleased with his, where he was born and how his life had started.

Tenace placed the file back on his desk and looked through the window. Old Yvonne, who looked like a turtle, was being walked by young Maja. He fancied Maja, a young nurse, short blond hair, blue, slightly mocking eyes, sporty, joyful, 200 percent alive and always humming a tune like she would bring babies to bed.

This story was too close to his; Anna Haridana could have been his mother. A tear drop was about to be conceived by his lachrymal glands, when, probably, the satisfaction of being alive, at least for the prospect of a dinner with young Maja, made his cheeks spread apart to press his lips together in a smile of solidarity for the living.

Chapter 4: Tennis

The music of a tennis match arose from his past, so did the green lawn they were sitting on to watch it. Well, he didn't really watch it, he watched the buttocks of the spectators, and some of them had their wallets sticking out. He must have been nine. He walked behind them and took one of these wallets. He had stolen for the very first time in his life. And as if it had been a routine of his, he knew he should not carry the wallet with him, and immediately headed for a tree to hide it. The poor victim must have been fourteen or so, a young blond boy named Paul Eyre, who he thought was too handsome and too happy not to have his wallet stolen.

The handy thing about his strategy was that he could then run to the tuck shop whenever he wanted and buy sweets with the tuppence and thruppence coins of her Majesty. He was smart enough not to overdo it, and only used the inexhaustible resources near the oak tree with caution. He got through it, well nearly. It seems that some suspicion was raised when, having had enough of the undeserved treats, he claimed to have found the wallet in the wood near a tree. The suspicion even took the shape of an accusation in the mouth of this 13-year-old curly-headed midget called James Bear. He remembered him solidly planted in front of the dark red brick wall near the kitchen, defiant and indignant:

— You found the wallet where you hid it! Because you're the thief!

Then the rhythm of the tennis ball faded away and his father's voice came out from the woods behind the court and the woods turned into the living room. He could then read these terrifying words on his father's lips:

— Where has that money gone again?

And Tenace would tremble inside because he knew that he had, though very rarely, reiterated the wallet trick, at least in its main points, with his father's wallet. And though he had the trick from his mother who he had surprised pinching some of the magic notes from his father's wallet, he could not avoid feeling guilty, feeling it to be the cause of their divorce, as his father had also discovered that she had stolen from him for years. Though she definitely did most of the embezzlement, Tenace secretly blamed himself for all, their ensuing divorce and her tragic death.

Kids are like that: they take the blame on themselves for ever and ever, and the story of Anna Haridana reminded him of his own story and Anna of his own mother, except his father didn't die then. This time the tear drop made its way to the light.

This is why he paid particular attention to Anna and visited her more than any other patient. He had even personally accompanied her to the trial and brought her back after the bewigged spazzes were done. How much he hated lawyers and judges! He despised them. They were professional liars who had learned all the tricks about hiding and turning the truth around to defend any one and any cause, applying their finely-oiled machinations to bleed hearts and purses with no remorse, no empathy and no feeling for justice. This is about the only point he agreed with Hitler on a land with no lawyers, except that Hitler probably saw lawyers as the Resistance to his corrupted "judges". Of course, Tenace knew that there is nothing more dangerous than that feeling for justice. It is precisely in its name that the worst atrocities are committed.

He was therefore somehow relieved that any Joey Smith lawyer would just follow his paragraphs, if not like a Swiss watch, at least like a Bavarian cuckoo clock, and issue some absurd statement by the end of the trial, as timely as the clock cuckoo utters his cry. Right then, Tenace's cuckoo clock uttered three o'clock.

Chapter 5: The Who

Tenace was excited, he was among the top three doctors to get the governmental mission of the century: the Definition of Death. DOD was the job. This was just his cup of tea, his hobby, his cherished theme, cut out just for him. He was going to get the job, he felt it, he knew it, he wanted it.

— Dead is dead, it's clear cut! thought Tenace the Child, remembering when his mother had died. He had wanted to look at her one last time and as he had gotten closer to the coffin to see what a dead mother looked like, his Dad had opposed him:

— Why do you want to see her?

As if death was only a grown-up thing.

Death was clear cut, a real cut in his twelve-year-old heart. He remembered how it bled, on the bench in the town house park, for days and days after her death.

But Tenace the Doctor knew it wasn't clear cut. When are you dead? Certainly not when the heart simply ceases to beat or when you stop breathing. When then? When your encephalogram is flat? When your temperature is below 15 degrees centigrade, or when everybody you know has forgotten about you? The existence of this uncertainty interval was precisely what organ traffickers were taking advantage of. Their clear cut in the flesh robbed the organs away in a flash, rendering the matter suddenly very certain and dear. This is why the government had launched this project and this is why Doctor Tenace, who was eminent in this field, had received an invitation to apply for the job and had applied.

If he did get the job, he was going to decide who was dead and who wasn't. Wasn't it like playing God? He liked that. Of course there was a knock on the door at that moment and of course the messenger brought him a yellow letter with the official stamp of the Ministry for Health. Oh, how Tenace's heart pounded! It pounded like the heart of a writer opening the answer letter from his editor. Will he, Tenace the Doctor, be allowed to publish his Law of Life and Death in the great Register of Medicine and thereby most probably escape his own law?

He sat back on his chair. He could have rushed to the envelope and torn it apart to either voluptuously read his nomination aloud through the walls of the entire clinic or read in a desperate mumble the usual apologies:

—- We have read you with a particular attention but regret to have to inform you that you do not quite match our very special needs..., bla bla bla! Don't hesitate to run for our next office...

— Thank you Margot! He finally uttered, not realising that Margot was already bringing other letters to other occupants of some neighbouring offices equally at odds with their own hopes. He wanted to throw a last glance at Maja that would give him the necessary kick to open the letter. The virtue of short glances at beautiful young girls is magic. Suddenly elder men start to sing or whistle and they have no clue why they do so. Only the wife guesses, and for no other reason than jealousy, she kills that ephemeral flight of joy by some dreadful sarcasm, so that the love bird drops dead in the kitchen, in all kitchens of the world. Tenace was in his office and he appreciated it. Maja wasn't out there anymore. He didn't open the letter.

Chapter 6: Falkennest

The familiar blue van drove up the alley. Falkennest had a new pensioner and as Tenace had always done, he would go down and greet the newcomer personally. Something must have been rejoicing him extremely, because he had that funny look on his face that only young boys have when they're up to something very stupid.

— Good afternoon, Mrs Van Brandstaetten! Welcome to Falkennest. I am Doctor Tenace, in charge of this place, but most of all, in charge of your well-being! And he giggled cheerfully, not even looking at her but throwing a dirty smirk at the male nurse operating the crane that lowered the wheelchair Mrs Van Brandstaetten sat on.

— Mrs Van Brandstaetten, you can call me James, but only if I may call you Walburga! He said with a false smile and reached his hand to hers.

— She's degree five! muttered the nurse, trying to hide his dislike of Tenace. It wasn't so much the false teeth that made Tenace's smile so false but some kind of creepy prospect that oozed out of his professional doctor mask. The only part of Walburga that moved was her grey locks, which the wind gently caressed.

— Fantastic, you are wonderful! added Tenace pressing her hand against his heart with both hands.

— Get her straight to room 15! He yelled at the nurse and walked down the perron onto the main alley of the park.

He suddenly had the urge to walk, actually to run, but his back ached, so he accepted the compromise. Something was creeping in his stomach. Wasn't he doing the right thing? Why did that stupid nurse grin at him with such contempt? These treatments were no experiments. It was the only way to get these comatose patients back to consciousness. Who cared whether it was legal or not? Great scientists always broke the law, even their own law.

He was a Professor and a Doctor of Medical Sciences, originally a gynaecologist but now specialised in brain surgery, neurosurgery, anaesthesia and reanimation. As the Head of the Falkennest Clinic Faculty for treatment of comatose patients, he would most probably be imminently nominated by the WHO for leading the soon-to-be created IDDT, International Definition of Death Team. Such a definition was urgently needed for the eradication of organ trafficking related murders.

It was his favourite subject and he secretly regarded himself as the premier specialist on soul matters, near death experiments, and, should he confess: soul transfer? This was the crux of his vocation but he could not print it on his business card nor impress any female with it.

It was not that nurse's look that was going to make Tenace stop. He had stopped too many times in his youth. He had stopped running when mum had called him. He had stopped crying when Dad had yelled at him.

He had stopped eating his beloved chocolate ice when that bitch at the nursery had wanted him to go lie down. He had stopped fucking when Sarah Schein had not wanted to, stopped drinking when he had studied for his damned exams, stopped talking when his father had commanded it. No! No! No! This time he was not going to stop. His heart pounded, his entire body was about to explode at the remembrance of all these interdictions piled up from the bottom of his stomach up to his gullet. Still pacing up the alley, he started to hit the oaks with his stick, like a teacher his pupils' fingers.

He suddenly remembered Gaby, the tomboy, that obnoxious hoyden who wore a black and white cap à la Belmondo, except that she was a romp appointed as an "éducateur" in a French holiday camp. She had them all lined up on the stone wall between the dry fields out in the middle of nowhere because none of the 8-year-old boys wanted to say who had pulled some little girl's nickers down.

Belmondo had then ordered them to pull their own pants down, showing their willies to the crows while she would walk from behind and smack each of their buttocks with her callous hand like a field marshal on troop inspection. And Tenace the Child was touched for the first time in his life by feelings of injustice, shame and indignation. If he could have gotten Gaby's soul right now, he would have transferred it into a rat before squeezing it to death with a stick yelling No! as he was doing right now to a slug in Falkennest's park.

Chapter 7: A Photograph

Ralf Weber liked his new black-pointed shoes even though they had just started to hurt, squeezing his toes together against the shoe cap. The leather soles were slippery, but the shoes reminded him of his time as a student, where, employed in a shoe shop, he'd spent most of his time listening to LP's while rearranging the shoe boxes, his back facing the customers, instead of turning down the volume, which chased them away.

— How is your twinkly wonky doodle doing today, Mr Randy Vous? Oh, your name isn't Vous but Wu. I'm sorry, I didn't study Chinese; should I have? You're not worried are you? We are just going to take a little picture, a family picture Randy, 'cause we're all a family, Randy, a nice one!

He gave Randy a pat on the back through the waxed cloth of the wheel chair. The pat was a bit too rough to be a friendly one, and Randy's head jerked forward, but Randy didn't complain. Randy Wu had served in Vietnam, so he was not a weak sister.

— Hey Randy! Does your name spell Wuss? And Ralf Weber let out one of his dirty corporeal laughs.

— You're no Wussy, Randy? And another pat on the back. This is when he heard someone in the park scream "No!" He recognised Tenace's voice. As if struck by lightning, Ralf Weber's hand stopped dead a few inches away from Randy's back this time, and he quickly slid to Elsa Piolet.

Though he had intended, for the picture of course, to pull that nasty white hair out of her nostril with his bare thumb, squeezing it against his index, the echo of Tenace's word had still enough strength to make him renounce it.

— My lovely little goat, I'll leave it there. You're pretty enough today. Hope it'll shine.

Then he rolled Mrs Van Brandstaetten next to Haridana, so that she'd be close to the centre of the picture. Ralf was afraid of Mrs Van Brandstaetten. It was not the imposing gold chain and bracelets topped by the vivid Chanel red on her lips that impressed him, he was simply afraid of newcomers: What if she was a checker, one of those Gault et Millau-style testers converted to hospices and asylums? And though Ralf's impulse was to wipe the red off her lips and confiscate the jewellery, since it was against Falkennest's social policy, he postponed it, awaiting a clearer assessment of her state of consciousness. He would then proceed, but with the whole strength he had accumulated through his restraint, like a long-awaited tide.

His eyes drifted towards Tenace's hunting trophies: two deer heads, a bear head and a couple of other animals. He wished the patients had been stuffed too, since those padded faces looked definitely more alive than the patients.

Ralf Weber heard the distinctive pace of Tenace behind him.

— Get Harridana's face up, I want her to look at the camera. What did you load it with? Tri-X pan?

This was not a question but an order, and Ralf nodded. He hated Tenace's quirk to straighten the heads and the inert limbs attached to nylon strings hanging from the ceiling. God knows what Tenace was doing with these pictures anyway and why he insisted on using a plate camera. He remembered Tenace's answer a year ago:

— They're ideal subject for photography with a plate camera. They don't move, you can close at F8, take advantage of the fine grain of a 50 ASA film and leave the shutter open for an eternity, catching second after second all the particles of their soul to engrave them in the chemistry.

Ralf remembered remaining perplexed at this answer, but now, a year later, he understood a little more, especially after having peeped at Doctor Tenace's manuscript entitled: *On a field theory of consciousness*.

The pictures taken under these conditions were scary, particularly the black and white ones, exactly as if they had caught the soul. Ralf had witnessed himself trembling while watching them, especially the positive glass plates that Tenace had been experimenting with for a while. He was struck by the astounding crispness of their looks, and much to his surprise, they all looked much more alive on these photographs than in reality.

Perhaps Tenace was right. Accumulating the "soul particles" over such unrealistic exposure times made their feeble life radiation that we call coma, suddenly cross through accumulation the threshold that defines life.

When everything was about ready, Tenace bent down behind the camera under the black felt and looked through. He came out again and impatiently complained:

— Pull the curtains together! I don't want to see the nylon strings! Ralf, who had pulled the ugly orange curtains apart precisely to let the sun shine on the strings to counteract the flashlight and make the nylon strings less visible, pulled them back together. As if Tenace had guessed his questions, he uttered:

When the flashlight hits the strings, it's better they're lit from behind, but today we don't use flashlight, Ralf. Tenace pressed the button, the shutter opened, and in that silence where no one moved, he counted up to 30. He released the trigger, the shutter closed again and with a grin of satisfaction, Tenace pulled the tray comprising the exposed plate out of the camera.

Chapter 8: Atomic Density Tomography

It was years back that Tenace had the idea. He was still a student, and as a student you question everything, and particularly all that is sacredly given as wholly true by any of your imposed spiritual fathers, beginning with your own. Tenace's father was an atheist, an atheist of the most stubborn species, and he had started to work on his sonny as soon as the latter could talk. The poor kid had learned very early in his life the tricks and bits of rhetoric you need to fool anyone with your own rubbish.

Little sonny Tenace would entertain whoever wanted to listen to him on the bus trips organised by the school or during the holiday camps he was so often dumped at. On economy or religion, or the necessary infinity of space, with the argument: if it's finite, what's behind it? He'd explain market law to flabbergasted, chubby football fans wondering what kind of alien had landed on the seat next to them. And tiny Tenie made it, or thought he did: The girls in the front looked at him, his 10-year-old's energetic face, accompanying his words with the adequate unforgiving grimace of a Hyde Park speaker, his hands sweeping the air like Roberto Benzi to the music of his bullshit, while his heels would stomp the floor below the bus seat in front of him.

But the girls would still be looking, and this is what confirmed Jimmy Teeny the tiny that his father was right to argue and grin, to wag his hands as if they were the tail of a horny dog, spitting endorphins-loaded saliva instead of drooling slobber.

So God did not exist! These girls were the proof, and his father was right, and tiny Teeny walked in the footsteps of his father like any toddler would do, until he finally gathered that daddy did not believe in God only because God had told him not to! Daddy Tenace was obedient, and obedient to the currents he had chosen to belong to, probably because of the war: materialism, Marxist-Leninist materialism. And when your master tells you not to believe in God, you just don't, even when later, in an instant of weakness, as you must prepare yourself to close the big shop and your master has become God himself, you say you don't believe in him and that's because HE told you not to.

But Tenace was no longer tiny, nor was he teeny and he had definitively rejected the idea that consciousness ended with your death, with the same old stupid fatherly argument: If it ends then, what's next? Though it did not make much sense there. But then again, who really cares? Should it make sense? Sense is an illusion you only care for when you've got all the rest and nothing to do. Do you care about sense when you're in intense pain, when you die or when you crave to kiss a pretty, unknown mouth that you don't even want to listen to?

So Tenace had decided at the age of 21 that the soul outlived the body, period. He did this as he was climbing mountain like a guerillero with his friend Ronnie Chair, carrying a backpack radio transmitter broadcasting illegal programs from tapes playing on the tape player mounted on Tenace's shoulders, and let me recover my breath. "Radio Che" was back on Campus and surroundings, and no radio-goniometry was fast enough to locate the revolutionary climbers. That was good so, because to become the best scientist, the most talented doctor or the most effective capitalist, you have to have had been a god-dammed good revolutionary in your twenties or at least a taxi driver in New York.

So Tenace, although his Uher Report 2010 was weighing hard on his reddened clavicle, had decided to believe that the soul existed independently of the body whether or not it weighed 21 grams, whether or not you could see it, whether or not it was dark matter, invisible moulded cheese or hyper-violet light. Well influenced by his four years of physics before he converted to medical sciences, he postulated the theory that whatever the soul was made of, it was only able to connect to the body under certain circumstances. What he was interested in was not the connection itself, which was the study of all the philosophers and writers throughout history, but it's reconnection and disconnection, birth and death.

In other words he focussed on observing reincarnation and disincarnating, and since he had a very small budget at that time, his focus remained purely intellectual, just like Einstein's when he focussed on the restricted relativity theory. Tenace came up with his theory that only when the body is in a certain atomic state, a soul entity, be it energy, dark matter or intergalactic fart condensation, may connect to or disconnect from the body. From then on, his project was to study the whole body at atomic level at the capital instants of life: birth and death.

This is why, if you study the registers at the Margarita Central Hospital where he served 5 years, you will notice an important number of dubiously-justified tomograms of foetuses in the womb at various stages of the pregnancy, all ordered by Doctor Tenace in persona. Of course the Hospital did not care, because someone had to pay for the machines. Of course Tenace did not find any answer to satisfy his demoniac curiosity. Not only was the resolution of these prehistorical tomograms too low but, should it be true that the soul walks into the foetus flesh, at what time in the pregnancy then? And even if he had by any chance hit the right moment, how would he on earth recognise it? But creative scientists don't always bother with such details, they just go ahead. One can be lucky that Tenace had a plan, some don't even have a plan, like Fleming and his penicillin.

Anyhow Tenace held on, *nomen est omen*. It was in his garage- he had long sold his beloved 1938 Jaguar XK- that he had created, with pots and pans, and after numerous ifs and ands, his Atomic Density Tomograph (ADT) which gave such dense imagery that there was no room for tinkers.

That cost him his wife. Sarah Schein could not take it, week-end after week-end, savings after savings, and worst of all, it was all that Tenace talked about, his bloody ADT. She left him one morning with the dog. Though it is not clear if Tenace concentrated on his ADT because he already could not bear Sarah any more, just like sporty husbands spend their week-end mending the car, or whether Tenace was so into it that he took no prisoners, which wasn't that bad 'cause Sarah was definitely not the type to be taken prisoner. The poor dog, his name was Badger. He was the first living creature ever (after the dead rats Tenace had picked up on the channel's bank, near the flat boats) to enjoy the honour of being scanned at atomic level. This took place when he discovered that the dog's alleged hip dysplasia had actually turned into bone necrosis and since Tenace was close to broke, he shot him on the spot with a good dose of potassium and also took a snapshot of his death in his tomograph at atomic level.

Chapter 9: Autocorrelation

Even with his super-duper tomograph, Tenace found no trace of a soul leaving. The only departed souls he noticed were the ones of his wife and his dog. He fell into a deep depression and started to hang out at the village's taverns. And as if chance was nothing but a meticulously designed plan, he heard the conversation of two mathematicians, most definitely drunk at the neighbouring table, and one, probably the more sober of the two, mumbled this very philosophical question:

— What do you do when there is no signal? When there is just noise, random and deceiving nonsense, just fucking bullshit?

The man, who according to the owner responded by the name of Lebel, started to shake his buddy angrily:

— Bullshit, like the one you've been telling me for the last hour, what do you do when your own encephalogram is flat, no signal, no meaning no results for 3 years and your boss asks why?

And the man started to weep, and Tenace felt a big ball in his throat and he could have wept just as well except he was too curious about the answer. Then the other man, who wore a ginger beard and looked more like a woodcutter, burped, and Tenace thought he was vomiting but he wasn't and between two hiccups he pushed Lebel on the shoulder and spat out these words:

— I'll tell you what I'd do Lebel, burp... Auto... burp... correlation, burp... He repeated one last time, waving his finger at the waiter who had gotten closer to the noise:

— Autocorrelation! The waiter did not have time to tell him they didn't serve that, as the man's head dropped dead on the old oak table. Tenace's heart started to pound, blood rose to his pale cheek, his eyes lit up like life itself, he screamed, stood up, kissed the comatose woodcutter on what was visible of his forehead and disappeared into the snowy night of December.

He had drunk all his William's Pear on autocorrelation that night, scribbling equations and other cabalistic signs from his first life as a physics student down on paper. He had a goddamn hangover in the morning, but he knew where to go and that made up for the hangover by far.

It is not the locus here to provide a detailed explanation about the insight Tenace had just gained through the rather short conversation at the pub, but a few tips to the novice, though not indispensably necessary for him to feel at ease with the present narration, would certainly help him to understand the feelings of immense hope and ecstasy that Tenace suddenly experienced. Autocorrelation, or how to detect meaning out of chaos? How to bring life to what merely appears as silence or signaletic death?

Imagine someone tells you something but is so far away from you or you are both in such a loud environment that you can't hear it.

If by any chance this person repeats regularly, let's say each second, the word LOVE again and again, like the beat of a heart, you will still not hear it. This person can speak this word during his entire life, but you will never hear it. However, if you should record this apparent silence or noise, cut the signal into bits of one second each and add their acoustic signal over and over again, and if the word LOVE was always be pronounced exactly the same way, there is a big chance, that after having added it a thousand or a million times, your impaired ears would finally hear the word LOVE, because it would suddenly be a thousand or a million times louder. It would stick out from the noise, like Berkeley Physics students would say. Actually there is another step to the recipe to really please the gourmet lingua of a mathematics student of the Zürich Polytechnikum. This step is that he should not so much add them but multiply them, over and over again.

With such a method you could probably hear someone saying: SHIT on the other side of the planet, provided your microphone is delicate enough to pick up such a word from the other side of the earth.

What did this spacey autocorrelation business have to do with detecting when the soul walked in or out of a body? You'd have to be a former student of these top universities to envisage fooling yourself with the prospect of such a connection. Well, Tenace was such a student and he did it: His idea was based on a law of nature, actually the very corollary of autocorrelation, namely that a state or situation does not really exist for just one split second, be it a nano- or a microsecond, but repeats itself at a given frequency in order to get the seal by the Norms Institute of the Universe: "It exists!"

In other words, once is not enough, or like the Germans say: one time is no time. Translated into Tenace's soul theory, it meant that the state in which the body was able to receive or let go of the soul did not occur one single time but repeatedly, at a given frequency, for a certain lapse of time. It would allow the soul to become aware that a body was available for walk-in or that the body was available for walk-out, just like an acoustic modem used to repeat its horrible scream before it would shake hands with the internet server.

To conclude, for the bored and impatient novice, all of this means that Tenace suspected a certain periodicity of the readiness of the body to let go of or to let in the soul, just like females are ready for mating. He could find this period by systematic trial and error on the high-definition tomographic videos of the dying body or of the growing foetus. He would find out which "word" it was "saying" when it died or was born, that is, what the tomographic takes looked like when they highly correlated in time.

This is the conclusion Tenace had arrived at, some point down the William's Pear bottle. Unfortunately, he realised in the same split second that he needed a tremendous amount of computing power to process the gigantic amount of data his ADT would spit out, in order to autocorrelate Death or Birth. That gave him the final knock-out for the night. His forehead banged down on his white desk next to his Mac, just like the woodchopper's at the Inn.

Chapter 10: Parallel Infection

Strangely enough, when Tenace woke up, as the sun invariably fulfilled its duty to irradiate the planet with its pinky snowy light at its well-known periodicity, Tenace had the solution to his unsurmountable problem. He had to infect as many computers in the world as possible with a tiny virus, whose unique task would be to process a distributed computing task on the host, using the host computing capacity, and send the partial results back to Tenace's computer.

This was not new; this was called parallel processing. The biggest computers in the world were made up of hundreds or thousands of computers connected to each other in order to parallel process. What might be new, though it is very doubtable, is to infiltrate private computers without the consent of their owners with little programs called bots (stemming from robots) so as to borrow part of their computing power to perform alien tasks. This is precisely what Tenace had in mind when the sun made him raise his right eyelid like a crocodile thinking about breakfast.

Tenace had come a long way since the moment he did not believe computer viruses existed. He remembered buying one of the first books ever on computer viruses, thinking it was just a journalistic joke bred from total technical ignorance and amateurism. He had come such a long way since then that he was in the position to design such a bot, no question, and he loved programming. The only thing that worried him at that very moment, when his second eyelid went up and he wondered in parallel whether he still had some coffee grains in the cupboard, was how on earth he could spread the goddamn cyber-bacteria fast enough to get the power of a secret CRAY 1000 megacomputer before March the 23rd, the date at which his credit would run out and he'd have to get another one?

And since Doctor Tenace was not applying for patents on any of his alleged technological or medical breakthroughs involved in his Frankenstein-like enterprise, there was very little stuff with which he could impress and convince the bank to lend him more money, except some more tangible results. Tenace was lucky that the bank director Walter Luetzi was about just as crazy as he was. They had met on a binge as students when the latter was going to St. Gall's School of Economics. Luetzi was just as bad as he was, divorced, too, so he had time now to pursue the meaning of his life, a super duper Kalmann Filter to predict stock values, meaning which he was generously, equally sharing with his other meaning of life: Booze, Sex and Vinyls.

By the time the espresso coffee had erupted like the Stromboli in its aluminium top reservoir, Tenace, who had not stopped thinking, even during his sleep, already had a solution for that second problem, which you have probably forgotten about and I therefore allow myself to remind you of: How to spread the villain, the computing power thief? This virus, which would inevitably slow down the host computer it had infected at the speed of light, at the very moment when all its power was needed.

Tenace visualised HER avidly licking HIS strawberry ice cream up to its creamy topping, contaminating the YOUPORN screen with the cold it radiated, so that the screen would freeze at the most thrilling instant, thereby frustrating the million impatient husbands who could not synchronise their molecules anymore with the bytes enlightening the screen's pixels.

Such a villain it would be! And precisely that effect gave Tenace the third decisive symbol of his triptych. He would spread the naughty one over porn sites. Who was running a porn site on the side, thinking Uncle Tenace did not know about it? Who else but innocent Ralf who had never done anything really naughty in his life, and who at the age of 35 was still "sage comme une image". He would first spread it through the site Ralf was unduly running from the premises of Tenace's Institute. And Tenace, who had the peculiarity to never react in a hurry, was particularly thankful to himself to have shut up when he discovered a month ago that Ralf was running such a porn site from the office's computers, and thereby making quite a bit of pocket money with it.

Satisfied and eager to go on, Tenace had to spit out the coffee: the rubber seal was burned and you could tell by the taste of the coffee. Tenace walked to the shower and though the shower had mouldy sealing rubber strips that perfectly matched the orange-tiled shower floor and the chalky plastic curtains, he sang happily, in his strong Swiss German accent:

Oh! Je voudrais tant que tu te souviennes, des jours heureux où nous étions heureux, les feuilles mortes se ramassent à la pelle et les souvenirs aussi".

Chapter 11: Dog Burial

Though he had a hangover, Tenace was a man to stick to plans, specially the plans he had made up himself. He was extremely tenacious in all he did and this is precisely what had brought him so far. He would just hold on and never let go, nomen est omen. Well, he did let go once and that was when he let go of Sarah and that was an incredible task for him, but he'd had to. She would have eaten his guts all the way through till she could have stuffed him with straw and hung his headed bust as a trophy over men in the hall of her villa. Of course she would have added horns to the skull to make him even more a mythical animal from the land of her fantasies and it would definitely better render the reality of their marital life. So even though the breaking up of their marriage was a kind of defeat to Tenace, who liked to lead things to their end and could not stand going back or losing, Tenace managed to decree it a victory.

He had led the thing to an end, to avoid the end meant by the priest and the mayor: *Till death do you part!* Which, sadly, so often means the end of one, induced by the harassment by the other. That was not in the Bible. It took him some months to see his divorce as a victory, but he eventually did.

Tenace's plan for this Saturday was to bury the dog. The dog he had murdered or "relieved" in his super-duper tomograph. Its death was weeks ago and the poor thing would have rotted away somewhere to the disgust of the fleas, if Tenace had not put Badger in the morgue of his Institute. He had been lying there, very well-conserved, for six months now, and that was enough. It was, to be honest, not very hygienic, even for the dead, but that was only a fake reason; Tenace had some kind of intuition that he did not want to face: he needed one more free drawer in the morgue.

Tenace decided to have breakfast at Falkennest and get on with the job. He jumped in his beige Mehari, which still smelled of stable and horse shit. He had bought it from a horse tamer and the goddamn stink was about as tenacious as he. But that car was good on snow because it was so light, the French military say. Where Falkennest was erected, there was often enough snow to make the smell of horse shit enjoyable.

For a reason known only to himself, he walked in through the kitchen. Most probably he didn't want any one from the medical crew to see him carrying a big white bag from the morgue to the back of his car. The Mexican cooks might see him, but he didn't care about that. He hated Mexican cooks, not because they were Mexican or cooked badly, but because they were so bloody loud and always listened to that South American music over and over again at a volume that could compete with Ralf's punk shoe shop. So he gave a nasty look at Ignacio instead of telling him that he didn't like his music. The poor guy looked away, scared. Though a couple of butter Gipfeli accompanied by a cup of coffee was most certainly his bodily priority, he started heading for the morgue.

In the staircase he unexpectedly decided to walk upstairs to the computer rooms. The door was half-open and to his interested surprise, he could hear a female voice moaning, followed by the grunting of a male counterpart. Tenace, who thought some of the younger staff were having a good time, smirked, and discreet as he always wanted to be, was on the verge of stepping back, but curiosity or perhaps jealousy traitorously tackled him. Who was it? Was it Maja? So he walked in, to realise by the light thrown into the subdued room, that someone was watching porn on a computer. By the amount of the scrunched tissues he suddenly spotted under the desk, the person must have been there often, or long enough. The person? This was a rhetorical question because from the minute Tenace realised what was going on, he knew who it was. He could surprise him, but he wouldn't enjoy the power of humiliating him.

He could see him recall the blood mobilised elsewhere back to his usually pale face, and make it blush. The way his tiny eyes, ashamed, would then try to look at him from underneath, like a beaten dog avoiding the hits. He imagined how the wounded sparks in them would kindle the fire of his long dragon tongue, spooled in his stomach, and make it throw up and reach for Tenace's mocking eyes like a giant lizard's tongue at ants, to blind him for ever to what he had just seen.

So Tenace slowly retreated on tiptoe, soon enough to still enjoy his self-made magnanimity, slightly eroded by his equally self-made, frightening speculations. He was not the kind to blackmail or bully either, he would get all he needed from Ralf, just like he'd always done and he needed no trump for that, at least not yet.

He walked past the three refrigerated glass closets sheltering the computers, through which you could see those inevitable LED garlands. They looked like broken-toothed rows of a smiling mouth munching the necessary bits and bytes to control the "autojector", which was how he secretly called Falkennest. He then went down the stairs straight to the cellars.

Tenace had always been utterly disgusted by Bryukhonenko's dog decapitation experiment, probably as much appalled as the Soviets were proud of it (they were also proud of roasting Laika the dog-cosmonaut as its rocket fell back to earth). Bryukhonenko had designed a heart-lung machine that he had called the autojector, cut a poor dog's head off, connected it to the autojector and showed that the dog's head still lived apart from the body. As if this was not enough, he had stopped the machinery for 10 minutes, showing how the dog's head would die, and then, and this was the crux of the film - which was not at the 60th page of the script but at the end, contrary to Syd Field's theory - he had resuscitated the damn thing at the eleventh minute by turning the heart-lung machine back on. Tenace thought such an experiment was superfluous and just showed, once more, the cruelty of humans.

He had put his own dog in his ADT and killed him, but that was to relieve him, wasn't it? Suddenly doubts overwhelmed him, and as if to try and shake them out of his body, he started to walk like a soldier, stomping the floor to the rhythm of his denial, he could have raised his legs to a goose walk if his abdominal muscles had gone along with it, but they didn't. He headed to the morgue, troubled, realising he was no better than Bryukhonenko, and he squinted so as to lock this fact into the necessary realities. He unlocked the door of Morgue 2, walked to drawer 23, unfolded the corpse bag rolled under his arm pit and pulled the drawer out. Tenace was good at blinding out all emotions, as many surgeons probably are. Life must go on. He looked at his dog briefly, stroked its head gently and said:

— You were a good dog. We're all someone else's good dog! He shoved it into the white shroud and threw it over his shoulder. He met no one on his way to his Mehari, not even the Mexican cooks. Lifting the car's plastic back shelf, he dumped the bag between the shovel and the sled which lay on its back like a dying cockroach. Then, just before stepping into his car, he was moved by a sudden sense of rebellion, threw a mischievous look at the building and shouted at the windows, louder than the music:

—- Yes, I bury my dog, it was in a human morgue! We all have to bury our dead before we die ourselves. It's no good to keep them in the cellar. It's high time! He laughed and closed the plastic door of his car.

It was a five-minute drive and the Mehari did well. Then Tenace pulled the sled on the snowy path through the woods for a good 300 meters at the rhythm of his mountain shoes cracking the wet snow. The white bag was tied up to it with rubber bands, like on a bicycle rack, and the poplars saluted the fallen scapegoat of mankind.

He stopped near a big silvery one 30 feet away from the path and started digging. The soil wasn't frozen. When he finally started to sweat, he was done. He undid the rubber bands, opened the bag and tucked its rims around the dog's neck to free the head, like bedding a child. Since it was its last sleep, it'd better be comfortable. He then pulled a flask out of his jacket, drank half of it and, spreading the dog's lips apart, baring its teeth, he poured the rest into the canine's gullet.

— To all the bunks you did, Sonny! And he lifted the flask.

— Cause you ain't gonna do no more! He kissed his muzzle, heaved the front of the sled, and the bag whooshed into the hole. It might have been the spirits in the flask but Tenace hummed on his way back, the shovel on his shoulder dangling to the rhythm of his tune:

I'll die on the other side of a road,

poor and forgotten,

like a dog in the mud,

I'll die with tears in my eyes,

Eaten by the birds.

I'll die on the other side of the road,

poor and forgotten,

from all the words I heard,

but not for those I said,

too weak to bury myself,

but I'm in no hurry, no hurry.

Chapter 12: Banking

— Boy! You're just as mad as me. Christ! You know what? We don't know what to do with ourselves anymore.

Walter Luetzi held a box of cigars in front of Tenace's hypnotised face, but Tenace just picked up one of the Rothhändle cigarettes bedded with the real males. He wasn't a banker, he was a banker's client. He put his whiskey down. Walter went on:

— First, we play with dinky toy cars and cry in mum's breast, then we play with real cars and kiss our wife's breasts and then we go back to our cars, except there are no cars anymore. Tenace, who just spilled half of his whiskey trying to light his cigarette with the pistol lighter on the table, countered:

— We never leave cars, we are the universal plumbers and you know why? We think that's why females love us, but I'll tell you what, they don't like us to be plumbers, actually they hate that, they just like us to do what they want. It's a sort of revenge for their narcissistic wound, accumulated over centuries... Walter coughed and interrupted:

— What are you talking about, narcissistic wound.

— Yeah! They get old, and we're not responsible. They get all wrinkled and loose. It must be hard to get floppy, since they were so used to being admired, desired everywhere by any man, even when carrying a 24-toilet roll pack out of the supermarket and suddenly... that's the narcissistic wound you know. So they start bossing us around to make up for it, to try to convince themselves that they're not old and ugly, that it's all like before, when they were young and beautiful and we did everything for them... They start shouting around, hitting around, wounded to death by time, secretly challenging our patience just to prove their value on the universal meat market. We clink glasses with younger ones but whine invisibly, walking home late at night. They call it the climacteric syndrome and it's supposed to be hormonal, but I don't believe it!

Walter dried off something in his right eye and mumbled:

— Their own bloody fault, loving their looks like that! Do you know that women spend one and a half years of their life in front of the mirror? Think about all the years spent in front of a mirror by all the women in the world in history! You end up with a billion years and that doesn't count the ones who don't have a mirror. No wonder. We ain't like that, we grow a belly and we like it, goodness gracious!

— Yeah, and when they've bossed us around long enough, we leave and play with cars again, except our cars are much more expensive and they don't look like cars anymore.

— Yeah, and they see that as betraying them - how dare we play with bigger cars. How dare we have another project in mind than getting a hard-on at the sound of their tune like a tamed snake?

— Oh stop it, Walter!

— Don't you think Sarah left you 'cause you were working on your tomograph? 'Cause you were trying to become immortal without her.

Tenace, who was starting to get nervous, said, although he didn't want to agree:

— Yes, she did, and I need some more cash to become immortal, Walter.

Tenace did not listen to Walter's answer. He was drawn again into the labyrinth of his scientific thoughts. He knew from his readings in cosmological physics that matter could be characterised by a bunch of fields, electromagnetic, gravitational, weak nuclear, the strong nuclear attraction of Femton, Akashic, Zero Energy, you name it. He had the intuition that all these fields were interlocked and that a signature of part of them was enough to characterise the entire state of living matter. However he did not believe that the field at the surface of the human being would be enough to characterise it, contrary to what Maxwell's equations implied. Tenace wanted the repartition of the electromagnetic sources in the body and dreamt of electromagnetic holographs.

When he came back to Walter, it was to hear:

— Another 300,000 for your soul dirigible then!

Chapter 13: Marrow Road

It had rained again and the narrow road could be slippery. The car was surely made for it, but Tenace didn't want to provoke the Gods, not in this matter at least and he could not claim that only they knew how slippery clay could get.

Sharp rocks dangerously coveted the tyres. Their colour reminded him of shark teeth, especially with these graceful rivulets of red clay that slowly drained to the earth, entrained by the rain water that had mixed with it, like the blood of an ingested prey. But Tenace was grateful to this threatening white, because he could at least see these rocks. It was not like this winter on this very road where they punctured his tyres in the middle of nowhere, in the middle of a freezing winter night when you could not change a wheel 'cause the damn jack would sink in the snow instead of lifting the car.

Maybe it was the Gods again who sent him this van packed with four removers who gently lifted the car while he would change the tyre, but this time, the white rocks on the side of the road did not hide in the snow. Tenace's side vision, which appeared to be directly linked to his hindbrain or reptilian brain, left him all the freedom to enjoy the view of his beloved mountains, beloved because they were the setting of one of his recurrent dreams in which:

He would be driving this road, when he would suddenly get intrigued by the fact that someone with a similar car to his would be driving a similar road at a similar speed and height on the other side of the valley. He was aware even in his dream, that in reality, there was no road there. He would stop the car to get his binoculars from the boot to have a closer look at the other side of the valley, and as he would stop the car and get out, he would notice that the other car had also stopped. His heart would start to pound, he would rush to the boot, get the field glasses hidden in the emergency kit and aim them at this car on the other side.

And he would see a man who looked just like him standing by his car and watching him with his binoculars. He would be extremely excited and would free one of his hands and start to wave it to this other man and the other man would look more and more like him and would wave his hand back as if this mountain was just a huge mirror.

This is why he loved these mountains so much. Perhaps he loved them so much that he dreamt about them, whichever. One day, he swore to himself with a smile that he would go there for real and meet himself on the other side of the mountain, even if there was no road there.

It all looked like a glossy black and white photograph which the early dusk turns anything into, and Tenace admired the scenery. He felt happy and confident, he had secured the financing, even for the case he would not get the Definition of Death job.

The yellow envelope was right there, in his pocket, and he still had not opened it. He had carried it along for days now, like a bill that no one wants to open, so afraid of the amount to pay. But Tenace was not afraid of the content of this letter.

Tenace the Magician was secretly trying to influence its content. He was secretly convinced that its content was not yet written and that it depended on what he wanted. He decided on the outcome. Tenace, who already knew that it was in life like in quantum physics, where the outcome depends on how you observe, wanted it to be the same with the letter in the envelope. He waited till he was sure the answer was the one he wanted before he'd open the letter, and this time was about to come.

It started to rain again, the wind blew stronger, and he sensed it in the steering wheel, then there was thunder and the lightning gave the last polish to the silver halide picture.

It is in that moment that he thought of Sarah again, Sarah here, Sarah there. He would even see her jumping from behind the trees on the side of the road in front the car, black and white Sarah, Sarah the Witch, lunging out of the bushes accusing him, her finger pointed at him in the eternal night of the forest, of all the crimes she could think of. It didn't matter what she was accusing him of; it never mattered to her. He was just the eternal culprit, guilty of everything. You name it, it was him.

He turned on the windshield wipers but

Sarah's face did not disappear; it jumped again, right and left. The face was screaming:

— You, you, you betrayed me! How dare you? How dare you leave me after all this abuse on my side? This abuse was love! I loved you unconditionally. This is why I allowed myself to treat you that way, so badly, because I knew you didn't! It was despair!

Then the face disappeared in the woods. Tenace's heart pounded; he was sweating again. He felt like stopping the car and resting for a while, but he didn't dare, as the Witch would come back again. She would open the plastic door and tear him to pieces in the mud. He thought he had fever, and he must have had. There was no vodka in the glove box. He had to carry on driving, like he had to carry on driving the night they married. He should never had married her. Suddenly his back ached, his left hip hurt like hell, just like after the wedding, and then it was his right knee. He could not sit; he could not press the pedals. He started to panic - this disease was not going to come back again. This disease which filled the marrow with water. No! No! He started to shout, to yell this witch away, back into the night of time. He needed air, the road was getting so narrow, so quick. He found the strength to press on the gas pedal, but his knee hurt like hell. He could hear its bloody bells.

The tree branches were smashing his peripheral vision; he should not stop, although he felt an incredible force trying to stop him, to attract him like a powerful dark magnet into the woods, but he knew he shouldn't. A commander sitting in his brain like his super ego was ordering him to keep on driving. The road had turned into a tunnel, like birth, her remembered birth, and he had to keep on, stick to it, be a man. But something in him was telling him to stop. Of course, he should stop and take a good look at himself on the other side of the valley, where it is always greener. He'd just go and get his binoculars in the trunk and see if it was really himself who had just stopped his car at the top of the mountain on the other side. It was his chance to get to the bottom of it, and his guts were telling him to stop, have a look. It might be where he really lives! But his little commander in the back of his head was pulling other strings:

— Don't you dare stop. There is no one there, it's a delusion. Drive, drive!

And Tenace hesitated and was barely breathing as he looked at his face in the rear-view mirror to ask himself what he should do. But he only saw this terrorised face of his that didn't know any better and was itself asking him what to do.

Then suddenly, as too often happens when you hesitate long enough, something decides for you and perhaps this is what Tenace wanted. He heard a blast and felt the car limping like a wounded animal hit by a hunter's bullet. He felt an acute pain in his back, his marrow reminding him of his sorrow. The rear left tyre had burst. Holy Shit! He was terrorised, and the car was undoubtedly telling him to stop.

Tenace stayed prostrated at the steering wheel, not even daring to get out. He looked at the other side of the valley and saw that the car there had stopped too. He was sweating and his temples ached. Something was telling him to stay in the damn Mehari, which he did. He thought he would just wait till his heart stopped pounding, then just step out, go to the boot, pick up the spare wheel and the jack and change the wheel. That was the only natural thing to do. So after he had looked at the moon, suddenly free from the clouds, he pushed the plastic door and stepped out, deeply convinced he was just going to the boot. After his first step in freedom, he realised something utterly powerful was drawing him towards the woods. He did not go to the boot - he started running into the woods right away, as if attracted by a supernatural force. Tenace ran; his heart was getting in the mood for a marathon. He ran after her. He knew it, as after a while he was crying her name: Sarah! But Sarah did not answer and Tenace ran like a madman in the forest.

Chapter 14: The Coachman

He ran, but he realised that what he really wanted to do was to scream, and since you can hardly do both at the same time, he stopped and yelled. It was a terrible scream, that came from his guts, from below his guts, maybe from the ground, the underground. It was a long shout for these two words: go away! and it lasted very long, the time to empty his lungs. His face was unrecognisable, totally distorted by the pain, the anger, the misery of his memories, and his eyes were screaming along. He took some air in and screamed again, and this time he chose a frequency that matched his chest better because it sounded even stronger and more harmonious for the circumstances, like a well-matched resonance chamber.

Tenace started to see her again and tried to punch her. Bang! A right one on the right eye and he would see her face move back from the hit, and bang! another one with his left punch, and he would shout again. This time he yelled:

— Leave me alooone! Have you not haunted my nights often enough? Haven't you reproached me enough? Haven't I given you everything? He screamed another long "go away" like a wounded wolf. Suddenly it took hold of him again, he jumped like a jack out of the box and started to run after her.

— I'll get you, IIIIII'lll get youuuuu! I'll strangle

you against the tree. And he started to punch the faces of her that he kept on seeing right and left, then he stopped, stared at a large branch on the ground, sweating and puffing, his mad eyes blinking, his arm stretched. He suddenly fell on his prey compulsively uttering:

— You wanted me to creep at your feet like a little dog while you were drilling my guts with your screams! You wanted that final victory!

By the time Tenace was saying that, he was already at her throat on the ground.

— I should have been your little worm, your little slug, should have surrendered to you under your long leather boots on the kitchen floor picking up the garbage bag from the bin! Is it that what you called love?

He was now clearly strangling her and shaking her from right to left on the wet leaves.

— And I nearly did it! I nearly accepted this last piece of dominance of yours, accepted to be guilty of everything, take it all on me so that you'd be happy at last. So happy that I could be happy with you at last! I nearly did it. Perhaps this is true love, perhaps I should have tried, the total sacrifice!

Tenace had now rolled on his side, beside the branch. Then he sat on the moss and stared through the trees, sobbing like the child he had been, knocking down his own soul to become a man. This child was coming back to the surface, was literally exploding in his body and tearing apart all his defences. He was just a fountain of tears sinking deep in the ground. Oh! How he wanted to sink in the ground, to have the earth press and caress his breast, his limbs, his stomach. He started to fall to the side, rolling his face in the moss, stretching his arms towards the tree. He wanted to become earth again. This is death, he thought, and it is nice, and his heart ached and this wasn't nice, then he sat down on a fallen tree and smeared his face with mud.

This is when he realised that to be a man was to love and cherish the child in oneself, the one that had just come out of its living grave, where it had so long been buried, to say hello to this whining elder man. This is when Tenace embraced himself, and his eyes full of tears, mumbled to himself:

— I love you! Forgive me! I'll never betray you again!

And Tenace went to the tree and embraced it.

Only then did Tenace notice the presence of the coachman, although he should have noticed it earlier because the coachman was carrying a gas light. The coachman mumbled:

— Go! The devil will get you here. Go!

Tenace looked at him and shivered because the man in his black felt jacket and hat looked like the devil himself. The man looked down on Tenace with contempt and said:

— You just keep this to that branch boy! Keep it to that branch! The man turned around and left.

When Tenace got back to his car, he felt at peace.

Something had relaxed in his soul, freeing him. Perhaps it was all these endorphins released by his beating and screaming, but it felt jolly good. He was about to get into his car when he looked at the other side of the valley. There were some lights, so he took his rifle out of the boot and aimed at the lights through the rifle's telescope. He laughed and put it back in the boot. He had just seen the man who looked just like him standing near his car, with a rifle pointed at him as well, then the man also laughed and put the rifle back into his boot.

Chapter 15: Ma

Sarah liked it neat and clean. I mean her apartment, where she was manically tidy. Dirt or dust panicked her, at least when she had nothing to do, because when she was busy, order did not matter anymore, but only what she was doing. This contradiction did not seem to bother her, only the ones who lived with her, because of course, when she was in her tidy mood, everybody there had to be tidy as well. I mean as tidy as she would have liked to be herself. But she wasn't living with anyone anymore. Perhaps that had something to do with it, with her moody tidiness.

Her flat was not big, possibly 70 square meters, but it was sunny and that was a good reason to like the flat. Sarah was not small, but she would not be begged into a basketball team for her size either. She was rather thin and somehow thewy, though it would only partly show, since her outer flesh was as soft as baby flesh.

Sarah had never really worked, and she had not worked when she was married. During the divorce she had managed, with the help of a good lawyer, to get her ex-husband to pay her rent *ad vitam*.

So, she had nothing to do except to water her plants on the balcony, pester about - when not at - her ex-husband, sort her huge collection of shoes all piled up like a brick wall inside their immaculate boxes behind the bed and polish each item of her collection of bags, which all looked like huge purses. She preferred the largest one, because whatever she fancied putting in it, she could put more of it and perambulate like a steady Dutch woman down the streets in shoes far too large for her height. The shoes matched her "Gisele" type feet that she hated so much because she looked like a duck, she'd say.

She would hold the bag ready to swing it like a secret weapon in the face of any passers-by, especially lost husbands who had not caught the unambiguous signals which radiated from her fierce teeth to stand out of her way while she shopped on the main street.

Sarah was sipping her glass of *I can't remember what*, because it is difficult to remember her drinking or eating anything. She was scrutinising the horizon, which, unfortunately, modestly consisted of a busy street. She probably expected someone to come down that way. The street was noisy, in particular the bass noise made by these impossible trucks and buses. Their diesel engines would shake not only the glasses and cups in the cupboard but also the thin walls of the cheaply and recently built apartment. It isn't cool to live in the middle of a construction site.

Then Bob appeared, eating what looked like a sausage in a bun. He had just bought it outside the tube station. She smiled, probably it was her only joy in life, Bob, her son who had just turned 13, her beloved son, not yet a man but on its way, at least as far as his looks were concerned. But Bob looked like his father and Sarah would always shiver and lean back on her chair when she'd be reminded of it either by what Bob said or by any of his inherited idiosyncrasies.

Bob was still far away, his face half hidden by the food queuing up his mouth, so busy he'd not even bothered to get out of the way of the flood of people rushing to the tube after work.

And that reminded her of when Bob, a couple of years earlier, had gotten beat up in the train 'cause he had been eating a doner sandwich. The guy who had beaten him up had asked him to stop eating. Though Sarah hated when people eat in the train especially doner, or worse, Chinese takeaway, because of their stink, Sarah managed to feel sorry for her son, as he told her that upon refusing to put it away, the punch of that guy squashed the doner on his face and it went all bloody from the nose bleed.

Sarah was proud of her son, now he was strong, determined and held that smirk on his face that so much remembered him of James, but this she wouldn't admit it. The sun was behind her son and Sarah had to squint.

She turned around and put her glass down on the orange kitchen bar. She didn't like orange because it reminded her of the seventies. She did not like the seventies because in the eighties when she was a kid, the seventies were out, but her parents did not have the money to swap to the eighties and she was ashamed of it. This is why she did not like orange. But then again, the trucks down on the street matched the eighties when her parents lived on the main road and the lorries would ramble through the living room at any time of the night and day.

She started to think about James and how much of an asshole he was, had always been and will always be and how stupid she had been to fall for him. Then she remained prostrated, looking through the tiny kitchen window over the grey roofs covered with sheets of lead.

A male pigeon kept on nagging a female pigeon near the gutter. She wanted to open the window and throw something at it to force it to leave the female alone. This is what she should have done, she thought, but she just stared at them through the pane. Maybe it's because she did not have anything to throw. I think she just preferred to feel guilty at not standing up to her own convictions.

Somehow she liked guilt; it involved her. It was the only emotion that she could self-trigger and it was better than a void. It was her way of seeing the world: she'd get a knot in her stomach and feel guilty as a whole. This little guilt about the pigeons would tie her up to the infinite net of other knots of her little or bigger crimes and they'd all ring back.

— Yes, confirmation there! She would reason as the ringing would resonate in her breast. She is the same old bitch, true to herself, and that was at least something to be proud of, and the masochist in her would rejoice. Actually this is not true, contrary to common belief. It is the sadist in oneself which rejoices in abusing itself.

Of course this delicate pleasure, which only she knew about, would really blossom when guilt managed to concern someone else, and she made sure it did often enough. Then all the subtleties and skills of years of experience in moral torturing would come into use. This is when the guilt filter in the Photoshop Suite for real life did a fantastic job. James could write a book about it, and their son a novel. So she remained there, absent from her body, immobile and silent, probably meditating on what she thought to be the only one to know about. The doorbell rang. Bob dropped his bag next to the couch table. He hugged her briefly, and then, as usual, years of the past whirled in a flash in his head. He started to breathe with his tummy like he had learned in his meditation books, to stay cool.

Hopefully she was not going to tear his father down again. Hopefully she would not start to whine and complain. Hopefully she would finally be a woman, the mother he had so badly needed all these years. I don't know what she said, I only know that after Bob had finally taken the needle off the landing track of the record, just after Nikto's last song: *"I don't like clichés!"*, that he said to her:

— Ma! When are you going to stop being a little girl?

Chapter 16: Back Home

Tenace was shivering. Changing the tyre had taken so long. As he parked the car in front of the veranda, along its had-been-white wall, he could distinctly hear the phone ringing. There was only one person who would call at this time in the evening, and he was not going to answer. He walked to the entrance door, feeling heavy, paralysed. He tried to cut the air separating him from home with his eyes, to make a connection with the door handle, like Spiderman throwing a rope, so as to prevent that kind of wind, the melancholia wind, from blowing him away. He forced himself to walk, one step heavier than the next, towards this anchor he had compelled himself to throw, to avoid drifting away towards the infinity his cul-de-sac life awaited him with. He had never wanted a home and preferred to live in hotels. There he was, eternally blocked at his own door, dreading to step into the empty house that had become his fortress of loneliness.

But then again, he rejoiced a little, realising that he might well be alone, but he could relax. He did not have to fear any voice ordering him to put the cup in the dish washer or to look for something HE had allegedly lost.

He could just stretch his arms and legs. The space around him belonged to him. He could roll on the bed and the contact of his body with the bedspread generated a flow of warmth through his breast. He was free. This is when he started to dance, without music, without booze, without girls, all alone at his place at half past eleven, shaking Marrow road and the Woods off his spine. He fell on the bed, sweaty and exhausted. The four triangular holes at the tops of the sheds made them look like a severe country constable, but did not prevent him, this time, from falling asleep.

Chapter 17: Zeppelin

The ellipsoid was nearly finished now. It was 30 meters long. It was composed of 9000 tiles, all printed with 3D printing technology, an appropriate manufacturing technique given the variety of curvatures of the tiles. The inner surface had then been polished so that it would be able to become a perfect mirror when coated with silver. Thanks to the high precision of the machining, the tiles were all perfectly aligned.

They walked in, and Tenace let the banker go first. As Weber wanted to follow him, Tenace cut through, reminding him who was the boss here. There was a table inside the ellipsoid, and strangely enough there was a candle on it. The table was more of a lectern. This is where Dr Tenace had been doing some of his writing in the last weeks. This mirror ellipsoid had been one of Tenace's dreams since youth.

As soon as he had got acquainted with the geometrical properties of the ellipse, a little seed had started to grow in the back of his mind, with no particular purposes. It was his passion for mathematics. All these cabalistic signs that only a small percentage of the population understood, fascinated him, especially as most of the time, he suspected, and later knew of all the power behind them. From Gauss to Einstein, mathematics were the best proof for magic. You first write signs on a blackboard and then they come true, like Apollo 8 or Hiroshima. When Tenace the Small One obediently wrote the ellipse formula and drew one with the help of a string stretched out between two pins, he had no idea that his attraction to this geometrical form would lead to one of the most amazing machines in medicine. He just loved the ellipse. He loved the fact that it described the trajectory of a satellite around a planet. He loved that all waves of whatever source emitted at one of the foci would all reach the other focus.

It is reasonable to admit that when Tenace designed his HD tomograph, though he had other alternatives, possibly cheaper and definitely less cumbrous, he opted for the ellipsoid, for purely aesthetic reasons. This hidden and irrational love for certain choices, not necessarily the optimum parameter like volume or price, is what gives us the passion and energy to carry on, and Tenace knew it. He knew what kept him going.

Since neither the banker nor Ralf was even remotely acquainted with the magic of Physics, Tenace played this little joke on them: He walked them to one of the foci and since their mouths were at approximately the same height as the focus, he told them to whisper something, and promised them they could whisper as low as they could, but that he would hear it. He then walked to the other focus.

Ralf began, and spoke so low he could probably not even hear himself:

— How can you trust this madman? He swallows tons of money that you will never see again.

That struck the banker right in the heart. He went pale and looked at Ralf, trying to figure out whether the malicious grin on his face was caused by his joke or by a gift of divination. After some blood had flown back to his face, he answered in a whisper:

— You never see the same money, Mr Weber. Thank God, it's always different.

Ralf wanted to have the last word by saying he hoped it wouldn't be less money, but righteous as he was he couldn't step over the triviality of such an answer. This is when they both nearly went deaf:

Not only had Dr Tenace, standing at the other focus, perfectly heard those whispers, but he took the opportunity to shout back at them his anger. One can be sure that for the banker and Tenace's assistant, due to the same feature of the ellipsoid that enabled Tenace to hear their whispers, it was just as loud as if Tenace had shouted right in their ear.

What Tenace said is irrelevant, because its loudness impaired their understanding it. The banker had grasped a couple of words like "wanker" and "sell some shoes". This time it was Ralf's turn to go pale. The banker walked to Tenace and managed:

— Utterly convincing James. I'm impressed.

At this time, you could not tell whether he was just being polite, like bankers usually are, or whether he was convinced of something. Tenace smiled, and looked at him, admiring his impeccable suit, but mostly his absolutely perfect mixture of politeness and hypocrisy, aware that the scorpion of perspicacity could raise its ugly tail at any time and sting him to remind him you can't fool bankers so easily. He went on:

— I'd like to personally complement the training of my apprentices, since in this case, not everybody has been such a good student as you, Walter.

He slightly turned towards Ralf and with a sudden twitch of his lips, added:

— I'm afraid I'll have to somehow reiterate the experiment from another point of view!

A sadistic glitter escaped then from his eyes in a flash. He looked like a mischievous child on the verge of playing some nasty trick. The banker, who obviously wanted to divert the growing tension between Tenace and his assistant, asked:

— So as far as I remember your explanations, this device replicates the field at the one focus on to the other focus and the advantage of this replication is that you can have all sorts of sensors at this other focus because the space there is empty, as opposed to the first focus, where you have your patient lying?

— Fantastic, Walter! I am so impressed that you remember my explanations and can summarise them in such a brilliant and concise sentence!

Although it was not his intention, Tenace noticed once more that flattery works. Even in the subdued light inside the ellipsoid, he could observe a slight blush on the banker's cheeks. He turned to Ralf:

— This is just brilliant, Mr Weber, don't you think? How is it to work for a genius?

Ralf, who had not quite recovered from the blast, answered, feigning a whisper:

— No! It is completely stupid, a waste of time and money! Mr. Tenace does not even know what kind of sensors he is going to put at his second focus, which is why he did not deal with this aspect. He preferred to "relocate" the problem somewhere else. If he could have relocated it to New Guinea, he would have.

Ralf started to get very vivid and moved to the first focus, he then slid the footstool towards it, and making big circles with his arms all around the top of the stool, he said:

— Why not put the sensors right there around the body? I might not be from MIT but there is plenty of room here, plus I'll tell you what Mr Luetzi, all these reflections on all these mirrors, they cannot reproduce the field as cleanly as it is here in the real field!

Boy, that stung Tenace right in the heart like a gigantic wasp sting would have done. Because it was bloody true and Tenace knew it. He knew his choice had been an aesthetic one but he had thought he'd be the only one to know. That son of a bitch Ralf was blowing the whistle right in front of him and to the most inadequate person, his banker. Oh boy, that justified by far this little complement of training that Tenace had in mind. It even deserved a punishment. Tenace hesitated; it might just be a coincidence. People sometimes inadvertently discover the truth, but not even realising they hold the truth in their hands, they throw it away for someone else to pick it up. Tenace was definitely going to pick it up and bury it somewhere, very far away from his banker.

Instead of showing anger at the very pertinent impertinence of Ralf, he seemingly sided with him:

— Excellent Mr Weber, absolutely excellent, especially from someone whose only education has been to sell shoes in a main street boutique! And turning to Walter:

— He is damn right, it would have been cheaper, smaller and less prone to aberrations, but this, my dear Walter, looks much more impressive than the claustrophobic box Mr Weber is suggesting to surround the patient with. This has style, elegance, this is a symbol, a trademark, a piece of architecture!

He was getting excited and you could see his eyes glitter with passion as he accompanied his words with a firework of saliva drops which shone in the light of the flood lamp.

— This is a synergetic fusion of art and science!

Have you ever heard of marketing, fashion, design? Do you think people would believe in Dr Tenace's HD Tomograph if it looked like a super-sized deep-freezer full of ugly cables and tiny blinking lights?

For some reason, Tenace had an especially strange look when he spoke the word deep-freezer.

- We're not in 1965 anymore, and Star Trek is over. DO I HAVE BIG EARS? he shouted.

The banker looked at the assistant in a state of alarm, and Ralf smiled at him in a flush of satisfaction, his whole face expressing: See, I told you!

Tenace was getting going and completely ignored the effect he was making on Walter.

— Medicine needs design! Have you been to the dentist recently, Mr Luetzi?

The banker suddenly got very pale again. It was not that he had not gone to the dentist, although it is perfectly comprehensible that such a question could have such an effect, especially when you know something has to be done down there.

— I'll tell you what! Go to Zigowitch on "Banhofstrasse", marble, stainless steel, very chic design all over. I'm sure the dental seat and table is designed by Philip Stark. It's all show but it builds trust, elementary magic, Mr Luetzi and don't tell me you don't know that, Mr Luetzi, as a banker.

He laughed and Luetzi didn't have anything to say because this was also goddamned true and truth always leaves a cloud of silence after it explodes. Tenace walked to the lectern where the candle stood and started to carry the lectern back to the second focus.

— Fortunately, Walter, in this case the €500,000 is not only for decoration. There is a fundamental advantage with this "design" (he grinned when uttering this word).

Stumbling slightly, he finally let the lectern down and kept adjusting first the lectern, then the candle. Both the banker and the assistant were perplexed and hooked by Tenace's sudden twist. Ralf thought that the first focus would be a nice place to listen to Tenace's explanation, and walked there. Tenace went on:

— The advantage is that with this "design", you can slip inside the body!

He had this particular look on his face as he was saying this, as if slipping inside a body was something particularly desirable.

— Since the field is nearly a replica of the field inside the body, bringing sensors there is like bringing them inside the body. You are inside the body, do you understand?

Tenace was accompanying his words with gestures, pointing his index at an immaterial body. Ralf wasn't sure he understood but he surely heard it good and loud. Then all of a sudden, Tenace lit the candle. Ralf Weber screamed at the other focus, holding his jaws and his face was distorted by pain. He was blowing air in and out hastily, puffing air out of his cheeks:

— You burned my tongue! You bastard!

Tenace was satisfied; the punishment had been meted out. He ignored Weber, and turning to Luetzi, said:

— Inside the body you see.

The banker was convinced, it's not clear of what. Tenace's scientific competence or the determination he could read on his face.

It seems he did not really want to know.

Chapter 18: Random Death

Randy's heart was feeble and beat erratically. He could hardly breathe since he had water in his lungs. He was about to die. Sister Julie, as instructed in such cases, had been on the lookout for Dr Tenace. She had been looking everywhere. Dr Tenace was not to be found. Sister Julie was British, with curly greyish-blond hair, about which it was difficult to say whether the curls were natural or hand made. Given the delicate silky skin that covered the thousand muscles of her very attractive face, the locks must have been handmade and according to the usual salary of a nurse at Falkennest, the hands that crafted those locks were most probably her own. Julie Mortimer wore rose lipstick, which was rather unusual for someone of her profession.

She had all the assets of a mid-Victorian educated young lady except that she wasn't that young anymore. She just looked young. You could also tell that behind her porcelain mask, a fragile and compassionate soul kept vigil. A heart that had not fully managed to blossom, to imbibe itself with the ineluctable tears that life hurt us with, was beating under her erect breast, even if those tears for which we are sometimes so grateful were missing. This heart had not beaten enough for love. It had somehow preserved itself, always at the threshold of the big dive in the shallow pool of feelings in some five-star hotel of her high expectations. Yet it was craving for love. More than one man had wanted to discover what kept those beautifully slanted blue eyes so humid and sparkling with such devilish ardour.

Her body lived up to her face. It was long but not too long, well proportioned, and yet it was the legs that contributed the most to her height. Her muscles gave the body that crunchy look, though they were covered with an indispensable thin layer of soft flesh that luckily differentiated her from these women portrayed in muscle magazines. Men fell for it; the mixture of soft organic warmth and energetic life under it kindled their imagination. Maybe it was the incessant appeal to unlock this craving heart that intrigued men. Men always need challenges.

Julia Mortimer walked back to Room 3. She was noticeably tense but all of a sudden her lifted shoulders went down, the wrinkles on her forehead disappeared, there was a man staying by Randy and by the acoustic colour of his voice, it was Dr Tenace. Tenace was holding Randy's hand but his eyes immediately drifted to Miss Mortimer's legs, like a well programmed target-following radar.

Tenace had always felt when death was around, and this is why he had left the Ellipsoid at 11:43 this morning and rushed to Room 3. Julie blushed as she usually does when Tenace devours her legs with his eyes. Her breath suddenly but very shortly stops, then her heart starts to go into first gear until a definite flow of warmth irradiates from her womb right up to her heart, after which she usually quickly swallows some air as in a hiccup, deliciously wondering what happened. Tenace's mind finally landed on airport JOB, business class:

— We'll have to take him to the ZEP. ZEP was the shortage for Zeppelin, a nickname Tenace's friend and banker Walter Luetzi had given the Ellipsoid in an instant of lucky distraction. There was a very brief spark of fear in Julie's eyes when Tenace said that. It was short, but it did not remain unnoticed, and Tenace roared:

— Don't stare at me like a goldfish in a bowl as if the ZEP was a Gestapo cellar and the HD Tomograph a French Gegene (hand-powered electrical generator used by the French during the Algerian War to torture people). I know it's the Germans who invented the Zeppelin but it doesn't make me Mengele, goddamn it!

Tenace was boiling, the hands of his fingers stretched like the spikes of a lawn rake, trembling as if he was in his last round with Tetanus. Sister Mortimer did not speak more than the goldfish Tenace was talking about. Fear was just climbing up from her crotch to her breast, and was just about to take over the scene of Ralf's story, which she had heard. The image of his burned tongue that had been in her mind was shifted away by the one of Randy's head sparkling underneath a metal dome, like the rotating theatre scene of a Ceske Budejovice puppet theatre staging Dr Frankenstein.

She obeyed, switching the emergency device to battery mode, and silently unlocking the wheel blockers of Randy's bed, and off they rolled to the ZEP.

It was already unusual for a doctor to roll a patient's bed himself. What was even more unusual was that this doctor would hum a tune at the rhythm of the wheels fighting with the gravel and stones on the path that led to the ZEP's dwelling. Julie Mortimer was humming no tune, and for her, the 200m short journey lasted for ever. She was horrified.

As they finally got there, the only feature that made Randy different from a dead man was his ragged breathing and erratic heartbeat on the screen of the electrocardiogram. His hands lay joined together like those of a Saint. His grey curly hair, or what was left of it, was slightly moving at the will of an inexplicable light air haunting the guts of the Ellipsoid. The only noise was Randy's breath, disturbing by its murmur the majestic speech of the Ellipsoid, that is, the hum of the motors moving around the table-bed in a scanning pattern.

Randy's heart was scanned. Tenace was not looking for a heart failure to correct, like a cardiologist would do. The organic state of Randy's heart did not interest him at all; he knew it was fucked and old and that Randy was too old to be worth repairing. What the word 'old' meant in their jargon was that Randy did not have the money for any surgery, given that no doctor in his right mind would go too much out of his way to save a no-lobe if he was not privately insured. Of course this definition of 'old' was not in the house dictionary. You could not say this; you could not even be caught thinking it. Luckily, even with Tenace's machine, no one could be caught thinking anything, at least not yet. This suited Tenace particularly well because what he was now thinking about should not be on any record.

Speaking of which, the delta sigma 3-inch tape recorder was doing a hell of a job. This rather old technology was the only way to record the terabits of information per second that came out of the scanner at a reasonable price.

It had cost him a very humble sum to bribe the keeper at the Ampex Museum in California, the night they stole the prototype. The machine had been one of the first attempts to record video signals back in the fifties. It was in all respects over-sized because the engineers of the Clipax Company completely underestimated the resolving capability of magnetic tapes. Maybe it's not true, maybe the first magnetic tapes did not resolve so much after all. Tenace did not investigate that. What he investigated was how to steal the monster. He and Ralf had visited the museum a couple of times and the strategy they used matched the simplicity of the security at the Ampex Museum. It's hardly worth writing about it. The guy had one vice: he was rather loose on the bottle, especially on Sunday afternoons, since Sunday afternoons are particularly depressing, but mostly since he knew he could doze off after his party the entire Monday morning because it was his day off.

They disguised the booty as an Isotope Separator Canon Control Module by taking the top cover off and painting radioactive symbols all over the mammoth. No one cared about the theft, it is possible that the keeper did not even notice it or did not bother about it or most probably concealed its theft. The only thing Tenace had to do was to have the data interface redesigned to make the monster able to crunch and digest digital.

Tenace was holding Randy's hand, on the lookout for death. He would stay hours like this, trying to feel it, expecting it and trying to guess when it would come, as he had done in his younger days when he served in hospital. The same frantic state of physical excitation was taking him, all senses alert, watching a dying person's lips and hooked to their silent final speech.

Tenace wanted to predict death to the second and this, minutes before it should come. Tenace wanted to discover the signature of death, like a radar system detects in the reflected signal the particular pattern that betrays a Rafale or an Illiouchine. This is why he recorded all the fields he could for a dying person, hoping to fish out something characteristic from this ocean of data that his Clipax II would write down in silence behind the wall.

Tenace would wait hours, trying to guess the forewarnings of death as if he would not trust the calculations to be made by the gigantic world-wide computer he would be stealing the CPU from.

There were good reasons for him not to trust them, as the program was not yet finished, not only the program but even worse, the entire mathematics behind it was not yet completed. Tenace was recording the data for later evaluation, just like some State Security Services (SSS) record conversations of their citizens for later use in case of…

The ECG had gone a little erratic. That did not seem to bother Tenace too much, he just watched

Randy's nostrils. When his face gave signs of unrest, Tenace's concentration rose. He looked at him, like a TV predicator faking an instant of bliss between two phrases, while knowing perfectly that one of the cameras was zooming on him. Except that Tenace's bliss was real. Then Randy's heart calmed down again and Sister Julie came in. As if answering an unspoken question, she said:

— I thought you needed some help, as the ECG was in the red on the monitor.

And as Tenace did not show any sign of impatience or anger, as she had feared, she dared the question that had been in her mind for months:

— Why are you so interested in predicting the exact moment of death Dr Tenace?

He looked at her like someone weighing the pros and cons of the truth. What he wanted to scream was:

— Because I want to catch the soul and put it in another, healthier body!

Maybe she guessed his thoughts, because she turned very pale before Tenace had even opened his mouth. But Tenace only said:

— Because I'm paid for that, sweetheart!

And he smiled, uncovering his perfectly aligned snow-white dentition, which he had gotten done at Zygovitch three months ago. I have been charged by the WHO to establish a norm definition of death. This is badly needed to prevent criminal doctors (he insisted on criminal in a very sleazy manner) from fishing out organs such as the liver, kidney or heart from people who are not quite dead, you see, and who could very well recover. Isn't that a noble task?

Miss Mortimer didn't say a thing. There was something strange in this man, she felt. And then suddenly the ECG went wild. The man rocked right and left, his hands escaped Tenace's grip and slid up towards his own throat. Tenace was jubilant and his eyes were getting lubricious. Sister Mortimer got hold of the defibrillator and started unwrapping the two huge electrodes. She caught Tenace's look, and Tenace's hands fell on hers like handcuffs.

— He's too old for that, sweetie!

Miss Mortimer shrugged with horror, then opened her mouth to scream but no sound came out of it. But she managed to free her hands. She pushed Tenace so strongly that he fell beside the bed. She then pulled up Randy's pyjama top and laid down the two electrodes on the hairy left part of the breast. That's about how far she got. Tenace had picked her up from behind like a 12 year old girl. She had by then recovered her speech and yelled:

— You can't do that! You can't let him die for your madmen experiments, you WEIRDO!

That was the word she should never have said. That was the word which triggered in Tenace an avalanche of reactions that looked more and more like a chain reaction. He was not able to think anymore. His ex-wife had used this word with him often enough and he was not going to take it anymore, not even once. But Mortimer didn't realise anything; she was just obsessed with her view of things, she carried on:

— You took the Hippocratic Oath! You can't kill him!

His hands slid inadvertently onto her bosoms and there she needed to catch her breath, and then he added:

— I'm not killing him darling! I am just letting him die! Finally letting him die his natural death!

Julie Mortimer looked at him like a small child who has to give a toy back. Doctor Tenace dried the tears in her eyes and suddenly stared at her rose lips. The frequency of the ECG beeps went higher, and the man was suffocating. Doctor Tenace looked at her lips, and in the background at the dying man. He seemed to be in an ecstatic state. The ECG suddenly stopped, just at the very short instant when he had his eyes closed. When he opened them again, Randy was dead.

Chapter 19: Guignol

Ralf was utterly upset. He was worried the flame had not only burned his tongue but that it may have left some irremediable lesions in his brain. He could not remember how he had approached the focus of the ZEP. Of course you do not have nerves in the brain so you cannot tell if some candle flame is making mechoui out of your lobes. But he did not see stars or asteroids or start to wiggle his feet out of control. He was just afraid that something might have happened. But there are always thousands of things that might happen in life and make you worried, sometimes make you very worried. This is what insurance companies play with. Of course they don't tell you that most of the real cases you've contracted an insurance for are not covered. By the time you find out, they've already cashed in 10 years of your contributions, and if you leave them, you can be assured that it'll be the same anywhere else. So you just stick to it, telling yourself the fairy tale that it was an exception.

Ralf was not really in with the game of dramatizing things. He knew very well there was nothing he could do about it. Most of all, he did not want to start a fight with his employer, especially one of Tenace's calibre. Perhaps Tenace was right after all; he should have held his tongue and it would not have gotten burned.

There he was again making friends with the enemy. This was typical of Ralf, withdrawing his fangs to lie down like a dog on the carpet. Finding somewhere in himself a justification for the abuse made on him. Accepting he was a piece of rubbish that could be tread on and deserve it. Ralf was there again, where he had sworn to himself a few weeks ago to never again approach. Ralf submitted himself to his boss. He admired him for having the guts and cruelty to harass him. He was strong and fearless and he himself, Ralf Weber, was just a piece of shit. He preferred any kind of order, of hierarchy, even if he was on the lowest step of the ladder, to uncertainty and chaos. He preferred to be behind the shield than to be the shield itself, the boss, the captain who daily scrutinised the immense sea of hazards the ship could encounter. He preferred to hide behind others' backs even if they squashed him with disdain like a slug against the walls.

So Ralf was happy, at least part of him was happy that little man in his head who constantly tells him he is despicable. This man was happy and this man was a very good friend of Tenace. But the other man in his head, the one that had just been told off, the one that had dreamt that Ralf would stand up to him, this man was bruised and didn't like it at all.

It was in that frame of mind that Ralf had been finishing the shooting of the newcomer's welcome picture, for the thousandth time. This time, he had attached nearly every arm or leg, every movable part of the body of all of the pensioners with the correcting strings, as many as there were available pulleys. He had spent hours tweaking the heights of each limb to obtain the best picture composition. Probably it was a particular act of devotion to Tenace, an art of begging for pardon for having forced him to abuse him and taken the unnecessary risks to put him back on the right track of obedience and worshipping. Because deep inside himself, Ralf Weber didn't want freedom, respect and responsibility. Deep inside, he wanted to be hit, to be shoved into a cupboard under the stairs like any naughty English boy would be.

He had already taken the picture, the best he had ever taken, and then a second picture better than the first one. He had even gotten the video camera ready. Up on the stage, dominating the friendly assembly of allegedly brain-dead oldies, he smiled, proud of his achievement.

This is when his smile twitched. His body went out of control for a second, his jaw muscles bit something invisible and immaterial between his teeth. He grunted and stretched his right arm down to his thigh like a supersonic robot. It only lacked his raising his legs in a goose step, for him to, possibly, have laughed at himself. But that didn't happen. He suddenly felt an indescribable hatred towards these indifferent and shiny scrouts who looked like huge vegetables in a shrubbery. He remembered how he had to clean their bottoms. He remembered their helplessness and that reminded him of his own helplessness. He hated it and he hated them. If there had been a machine gun on this tripod instead of a plate camera he would have shot them all. He did not want to end up like them because he knew he was already like them, though 30 years younger. He saw no way to derail himself from this lethal track he was on, that we all are on. Whoever designed the game of life was bloody cruel. His brain was oozing droplets of sweat through his skull and they dripped down along his orange skin pores.

Ralf stood up. He looked worse than Jack Nicholson when he was raising the axe on his son. He walked to the control cabinet like a mechanical soldier and sat down at the big desk board, watching the scene like the light technicians of a theatre play do. He moved some of the sliders and it made Haridana raise her right arm. He repeated this a couple of times and then set it on automatic.

He then tried the big ropes on Mrs Van Brandstaetten. She was harnessed, so the lifting was stable. Ralf looked at her with the grin of a child burning the wings of a fly with a lighter. In contrary to the fly, who would drop on the kitchen floor, Van Brandstaetten's feet had just left the planks. She started dangling right and left, probably an effect of an unequal length of the two strings on the harness. Ralf jubilated: Finally life in those corpses! Finally movement! He then activated the knee strings and lifted them one after the other to the beat of the music. Life, that Dr Tenace had not managed to bring back to those organic bags for years; he, Ralf Weber, the little shoe seller on the main street, was bringing it back. The no-lobes danced! He could not stop. He crunched a tomato between his teeth and the pulp splattered all over the sliders. He then put the knees on repeat mode and went to the other patients until one by one they danced like string puppets in a morbid serenade that would wake the God of sleep himself.

He then stood up and went to a small cupboard attached to the wall and reached for a bottle of spirits. He poured himself a long drink of mescal as if it were water, and kept on watching the show he had initiated.

This area, which used to be the theatre of the hospital, was equipped not only with computer driven pulleys that originally pulled the strings of genuine wooden puppets up and down, but also with sophisticated lighting gear and sound system. It even had a video recording system. Ralf went down the steps with his glass in hand and started to dance with Mr Gruenling.

"*Gruezie Wohl Frau Stirnima!*" was playing for the third time in a row. Everything looked like a wonderful party, except for the faces of the guests, dead and absent as ever, and no machine in the world seemed to be in a position to revive them.

The central rope of Mrs Van Brandstaetten's harness broke and she fell on the floor. Ralf heard the noise but he was too busy trying to push the daily newspaper into Mr Gruenling's pocket to notice:

— Care for a little read, David?

The grid of pulleys at the ceiling slid along a particular scanning pattern so that now it was Haridana who was treading on Mrs Van Brandstaetten's face with her dangling feet. Poor Eva was short of breath, not because of the dancing but because of the harness. That was Dr Tenace's invention, not for that purpose though, but merely to straighten some guests' backs for the monthly welcome group picture.

At the moment Ralf finally noticed Mrs Van Brandstaetten slowly agonising on the floor, the music stopped. The puppets stopped, and the lights went off. Ralf felt like a puppet himself, hooked to some invisible strings in the dark. Then from the control cabinet, a pair of familiar shoulders emerged, topped with an even more familiar head, and a far too familiar voice roared:

— What the hell do you think you are doing here, Weber?

Tenace turned the light back on again, approached the video camera, turned it off and ejected the cassette. He slowly went down the stairs. The closer he came to Ralf, the more Ralf noticed that the expression on his face corroborated the fake tone he had detected in his voice. Tenace seemed not to be completely displeased with the show. When he was less than two meters away from Ralf, Dr Tenace uttered:

— An interesting way of bringing consciousness back into comatose brains, Mr Weber. Well done! And he closed the box on the digital video cassette with a snap!

Ralf could tell that Tenace had been enjoying himself. He didn't know how long he had been watching the play but definitely long enough to start worrying about Mrs Van Brandstaetten's health. He kneeled down to her and took her pulse:

— Get the stretcher will you!

As they both rolled her to her room, Tenace said:

— I see you are getting into it, Weber! That's very

promising. Next time don't pull the harness string so high you have to let the floor take a bit of the weight, you know. It's too uncomfortable if it puts too much pressure on the skin and it presses some of the veins. It goes on the heart my dear! Look at poor Mrs Van Brandstaetten. What am I going to say to her relatives if they see those red marks around the top of her thighs? Have you any idea, Ralf?

This is when Dr Tenace started juggling the cassette from one hand to the other. Ralf understood, like a chess player guessing all the possible moves of the other after he had played. He looked him in the eyes, trying to guess which one he was going to play. Ralf's move had been bad and he knew it but the game looked like it was going to be an interesting one.

— Don't worry! She'll recover, and I haven't seen any of her relatives since the one who signed the papers, and that was three months ago! Tenace's eyes blinked maliciously as he left the room. Ralf blew at her nose as if he wanted to give her a little treat with the explosive mixture that came out from his highly spirited breath, a compensation for the harmless incident.

Chapter 20: Jolly Roger

Just as his fifth, seventh or eighth sense had barely been able to register anything before, during or after Randy's agony, neither had the Climax II recorded very much data nor revealed any pattern that Tenace could identify as a death pattern.

He did look at the data through various mathematical prisms that the latest TeraMathlab package would offer. Most of the time, the prisms amounted to eclectic attempts to graphically represent the cross-correlations between the signals or transformation of them.

A couple of times, the pattern on the screen looked like a cross between the devil and a skull, to the point of even scaring Tenace. Was it the virus that froze the screen of the game of Life? Though Tenace was quite a bit into magic himself, he could not resort to accepting it as a clinical death pattern. Besides, he would surely have a hard time convincing the WHO that a devilish-looking pirate flag was the signature of death itself.

Talking about viruses, Tenace had already designed the core of the disease it triggered: hijacking computer power. However, Tenace's most brilliant idea resided in the way to spread it. He had quasi-invisibly embedded the code into the data of digital films on the Internet. He had replaced the films on their servers with films which looked just the same but were slightly altered in a way invisible to the human eye. Precisely in this alteration lay the operational code. Tenace had targeted the most popular films as well as the most frequented porn servers.

The entire encrypted code of the virus would thereby be smuggled beforehand into the computers of millions of unaware users, and reside dormant and camouflaged in innocent data such as the textures present in films: sea, clouds, trees, skin, grass, walls. It would be activated by a tiny bit of code, a micro-virus, sufficiently small not to attract too much attention. It instructed the CPU to activate the dormant code by adding the key hidden in one texture to the ciphered code hidden in other textures and then, get on with it.

The demonic code that enabled the calculation of autocorrelations on Zettabits of data would be reconstructed by adding water to earth and earth to sky! Typically Tenace.

It took only 3 weeks to reach the minimal number for a good autocorrelation processing in a single night. That minimal number was big: 500,000. Three months later it was 5 million, thanks to the frequentation of porn sites. Tenace could have resold computer power to the CNRS or NASA. Unfortunately these government-funded research institutions did not exist anymore. The fruits they were producing were not interesting to the political generation in power, because they were not going to be reaped by them but by the following generations. No political class was that generous with its opponents, so these kinds of institutions had long been dead.

Tenace was now about to have some numbers crunched and he was rubbing his hands. Though he had two other cases, Gruenling and Colonel Poultre, he started chronologically, that is with Randy. He was expecting the results for Randy's autocorrelation tonight. The "fulfilment bar" on the screen was showing 99.5 per cent. He was going to change that representation. It reminded him too much of the never-ending installation of the operation system of some well-known software company. The result was expected at 23:12 and it was 22:36. Tenace was excited. Months of hard work were possibly going to bear their fruits. It was the first major step. If you could detect the instant of death, provided there was one, you could then define death by analysing the state of all the fields emanating from the body.

Such a great event had to be honoured and he had a bottle of Taittinger ready in the fridge. But what if there were no results? What if all this work had been for nothing? A knot formed in his throat and his tummy started to ache. He had taken responsibility for a project that he didn't even know would work. He felt like a writer in the middle of his book, not yet knowing how to end the novel, doubting of the value of his work. He suddenly felt heavy. Like Ralf, he also had a little man in the back of his head who was ready to beat him up at the least sign of weakness. This little man, whose only song was "See! I told you!" belonged to the army of tinkers who always said "no", who never dared to hope and who circled like vultures above the daring ones, before crushing down on them when they stumbled.

Tenace had one of them in his head as well. He felt numb, scared and alone. Yet a minute ago he was so certain, so confident. Why was it so? Then he heard this incessant little man again:

— It's only bluff Jimmy! You're fooling yourself just like you're fooling everybody else. It'll come out, don't worry, like it always does, and it will hit you like it hits all the guys like you, who want to be something special, you arrogant little snot. You are a failure, Jimmy! The one who wanted to be an eagle is just a limping duck in the farm. You broke the capital oath, committed the worst sin, forgot to remain modest! The little man in Tenace's head was screaming:

— Mediocrity! Remain what you are, a mediocre little parasite.

Tenace was going deaf, he turned his head to the left and then to the right, looked at the clock and at his hands. He wanted to cut down this radio, to break it with an axe, like when you can't stand the music anymore. When you've heard it over and over again, always the same whining cats. His temples throbbed, and his throat was sawdust. His head was exploding:

— Stop this program! he shouted. But there was no radio to crash, no TV to smash. The radio was in his head. It was the little man's radio and it was broadcasting the most popular program "Fuck yourself up!"

Tenace's head now rested on the desk, between his hands. He was actually pressing his ears to stop the internal chatter. If you could have seen his eyes, you would have seen that he had been crying. He was slowly straightening his back and neck, like someone who had just been hit, by the doubts, by the past and by himself. The mechanism by which he usually recovered from such blasts had not yet been activated. He moved his shoulders around in a circular movement and stretched them, looked at the clock hanging from the external surface of the ZEP like a navigation instrument of the Nautilus. He finally stood up, picked up the phone and dialled 4458. A feminine voice answered and Tenace gathered his spirits. He put on the most energetic and important voice he could, and said:

— Miss Mortimer, could you come over to the ZEP a second?

Tenace opened the fridge and pulled out the Taittinger bottle, which he placed next to the two champagne glasses on the metallic medical tablet. He then looked through the middle porthole of the Zeppelin. There was a glass with a rose in it on the bed table at Focus One. This made him smile as he finally heard Miss Mortimer enter the room.

Tenace turned around and tried to smile again, although all he wanted to do, actually, was to cry. He locked his face, as a man has been told to, and looked like an underpaid clown in a second class circus. "Second class!" How he would have hated this expression if he had heard it, as it reminded him of his mother, always haunted with the concepts of second grade, excellence, wasted life and other elitist curiosities. Fortunately he did not hear this expression. Julie looked at him:

— What's wrong, Dr Tenace?

Clearing his voice, he grabbed her arm as if it were the ramp of a stair. He looked years older with his beard. He walked up to her with the two champagne glasses and said:

— Tonight is a special night.

He was warming up for a little speech, but Miss Mortimer could not keep her eyes away from the bubbly glasses, nor could she prevent herself from blushing as she whispered:

— Dr Tenace!

Her entire body suddenly tensed up and you could see some wrinkles down her neck. Tenace carried on:

— Tonight, I'm expecting an answer to a question I have had at the tip of my tongue for months.

Miss Mortimer was on the verge of fainting, but Nemo did not notice, and went on:

— Tonight, in exactly nine minutes, I will finally know if my theory is correct.

Miss Mortimer turned immensely sad as Tenace poured the champagne, but thanks to her Victorian upbringing, she stretched herself, nearly swallowing her necklace, and exemplary, clinked glasses with Tenace:

To your results, Dr Tenace!

Chapter 21: Son of a Bitch

Her glass shook a little bit on its way to meet Tenace's. She just kept staring at the sparkles, rather surprised that one would clink glasses before knowing the results and ahead of time. For being too early, Tenace had a good reason: he just bloody well needed a drink, and right now. For the other part, that was more complicated. In his way of looking at things, the results could only be positive. The mere fact that there would be results was a positive result in itself. Tenace was that kind of man, open to reality, actually deadly in love with reality. He did not live in illusions; he lived in dreams, yes, but only in dreams that were the forerunners of the reality he would create. As if to answer the question on Miss Mortimer's lips, he said:

— We're a bit ahead of schedule. Proof of my efficiency! And he laughed at his own joke. Actually that was a rather embarrassing side of him. He just cracked jokes basically for himself, not really bothering if they were funny or not. And if they were not funny, this would amuse him too, especially the appalled look on the face of his victims. Tenace was a survivor; he could certainly eat out of a dustbin or even sleep in it if he had to. He watched Miss Mortimer and decided it was not enough of whatever effect he had intended to produce, so he added:

— Ahead of schedule! Another reason to party! The five-year plan in four years! Tovaritch Mortimer!

And he clinked glasses with her, nearly breaking hers, and gulped down the flute as if it was vodka, without even waiting for Miss Mortimer to be in sync. But he did look into her eyes. At least that part of the protocol was respected.

Tenace always respected that part even in cases where there was no protocol at all. Boy, he'd needed that drink! For Miss Mortimer, who still had not taken a single sip of the Taittinger, this was just going too fast, and she was watching the hippopotamus rolling itself in the muddy water with her deer eyes. A scene that would never be shown on the Discovery Channel.

Realising a fraction of his tactlessness by the mid-Victorian look that had come back reinforced on Miss Mortimer's face, and fearing that her nose-up-in-the-air head would bring her out of balance, he disguised his own thirst as an act of higher civility, and gently poured himself another glass.

— Her Majesty will perhaps forgive seeing me compelled to remind her that we "goûteurs de vin" always taste first! And he smiled at his own silly joke, genuinely satisfied with it as he clinked glass with her, and he made sure he would not win the race this time. This is when the computer beeped. He rushed to the screen, nearly breaking the glass as he slammed it down on the shelf. The screen displayed four lines:

512846 knots knit

38967 films edited

Average speed 21.13 petaflops per second

Total CPU time: 2.43 zetaflops

Tenace grinned, and the greenish light of the computer screen made him look like an old turtle on the verge of devouring a fresh leaf of salad. Tenace, who had one of the most refined colour screens, preferred to turn it into an artificial green on black modus. He claimed it was better for the eyes but in fact it merely reminded him of his young days at University, where the IBM monitors emitting that kind of light were the only ones around.

— So I reckon it's a flop, Mr Tenace? inquired innocently Sister Mortimer. I'm so sorry. Tenace looked at her. They both looked each other in the eyes like two poker players trying to guess if the other one bluffs. But Tenace was too subtle to gob that.

— Excellent! I could have cracked this one myself!

Always this utter self-satisfaction, thought Miss Mortimer, but she chased the shadow away quickly, preferring to fully enjoy the effect of her own joke on Dr Tenace.

Tenace was just too proud of having stolen 2.43 thousand million million million floating point operations from innocent computer users around the earth. He had no feeling of guilt at all. For the first time in history, these computers were doing something more intelligent than moving tits on an LCD. This line of thought was a relic of his Anglican education because in reality he had nothing against moving tits, especially if there was no glass pane between them and the arch of his eyebrow.

For the first time in history, these computers were trying to break the mystery of life. Tenace felt powerful; he was an incredible hacker on the side, but he was not going to go down this path of self-congratulation and self-idolatry. He had done too much of that. He stuck to his aim, and shaking off any inclination toward self-adulation, he entered graphic mode to see how much of the 128 graphical representations of the results were actually filled. The first sheet looked like a spectrum analysis and he skipped it with a grunt. The second looked like the surface of the moon, except it looked like the moon had been printed on a jigsaw puzzle.

The fourth one was a Hundertwasser mosaic. He skipped it, obviously annoyed. Then he came to the fifth one. He could not refrain a high-pitched cry. The work of art displayed a row of vertical greyish cylinders almost equidistant to each other but growing from left to right as to look like a Peruvian pan flute, or the top of a pipe organ.

Sister Mortimer leaned her head to the side as some visitors do in the Tate Gallery in front of some paintings, in an effort to understand them. Tenace assessed the distance between the spikes with his fingers:

— 34 seconds, he mumbled. Then he read the time under the highest and last peak: 1253.76 seconds, consulted a data sheet on the desk and screamed a long Yoooooooooooooooo! hopping like a kangaroo all around the room and into the ZEP itself. He started boxing with all of the demons his overactive head had probably conjured. Tenace was mad with joy! No one had ever rejoiced so much at the event of death. 1253.76 seconds lay somewhere between the cessation of activity of the heart and a drop of 10 Db of the average electroencephalography activity.

Something extremely powerful had happened there, that the number-crunching program had found out. Tenace was proud of his insight. He had intuited that before performing autocorrelation on the signal field; he had to combine them through a neural network back-looped on the autocorrelation. Of course, such abstract mathematics was Chinese to most people, including many scientists and mathematicians, so Tenace did not bother to explain to Sister Mortimer what was going through his mind at this time. He just enjoyed the intellectual orgasm he was having and happily noticed that it was spreading all the way down to his feet, tickling his breast and ribs like a good slice of lamb with mint sauce going down with a sip of a ten-year-old Bordeaux.

— Now the door is OPEN! he shouted!

Miss Mortimer did not understand. Of course the door of the ZEP was open; he had just opened it to start his idiotic Marsupilanic dance.

Tenace came back, poured champagne into Miss Mortimer's glass and then, realising there was none left for him, just grabbed her glass, thanking her for having held it. He started to meticulously peer at the 123 remaining potential result sheets on the screen.

The sixth was blank and so was the seventh. He went one by one through all the screens although any other man would have stopped. It was strange because Tenace, who had programmed the rotten thing, knew very well that the program decided itself if a supplementary view of things was necessary or not, according to Tenace's design. It was therefore incomprehensible that Tenace kept on scanning all the result fields although he should have known that if the software displayed nothing on the sixth, seventh and eight fields, it was the end of the results. Period. But such was Tenace: tenacious. Where anybody else would have had a cramp in the ends of his fingers, Tenace still played staccato on the C key of this cybernetic organ.

When he finally arrived at field 128, his face went like a toaster spitting out a ham and cheese sandwich, a toaster which had not really been designed to toast croque-monsieur: The ham stayed in, stuck to the grid by the melted cheese, and so did the bread.

The screen displayed these lines, written with a typo: You sun of a bitch, we'll get back at you!

It was signed: Panier. Tenace's heart missed a rev. He made one of the most horrible faces he could make, as if he had been fetching the remains of the croque-monsieur.

The level of his joy sank by 10 db. Someone was pouring water in his champagne, salty water. He reflected for a while and remembered. It was practically impossible that someone could track the cyberattack. The virus was not sending the results back to his or to any fixed IP address. He was not so stupid.

The results were written in the sky, the sea and the forest of dedicated pictures uploaded on popular picture-sharing servers. To get the results, Tenace just had to download them. No one could trace him. There were millions of users downloading pictures from such servers.

Miss Mortimer did not really understand the ups and downs of Dr Tenace. She kept mentally switching from admiration to contempt, secretly acquiescing that what she witnessed was sheer madness, the equivalent of a flat tyre on her way to love. She finally stopped on this self-pity track with no intention to change the tyre.

Dr Tenace was just out of her reach. She would never understand him, but only follow or tolerate him. In other eras, he would have been burned or lynched as a black magician or heretic and she would have certainly joined the army of good folk throwing the stones. Not that she was mean, but prejudice and most of all, fear and the realisation that there were things out of the reach of their intelligence, always made people terribly angry. They would shout, spit and lynch with all the more vigour when they are miles away to understanding. But what they don't realise is that they are angry at themselves.

Chapter 22: Resonance

The mirrors of the ZEP did not reflect on what they reflected. In the words of Jean Cocteau there is no audible difference between reasoning and resonating, just an orthographic one, and whether a head *raisonne* or *résonne* cannot always be detected. But this is not a privilege of the Frenchmen. Tenace did not much care because to him it was all the same. At this point of his research, everything was waves, and waves stand, propagate, reflect and resonate.

Tenace had done it with a cat, or rather with two cats. Later, perhaps, Tenace's cat will be as famous as Schroedingers's cat.

On his way back from Migro, the boot full of food, he'd hit a cat at the outskirts of Marrow forest. The poor thing had been staring at his headlights like a rabbit affected by myxomatosis. Tenace had slowed down, hoping the feline would move off. He had not bothered to completely stop. The poor thing had managed to jump aside in the last second but not quite quickly enough to avoid the left front tyre of Tenace's Mehari.

The tail and the back of its body had been squashed. If you looked with enough attention and good will you could even see the imprints of the Firestone winter tyres on him. Tenace did not bother to switch to summer tyres in the summer. This revolted all the gas station keepers in the neighbourhood.

As a doctor, he should have shot the poor creature or at least reversed over its head till its skull cracked. That should have been his duty, but he picked up the whining animal and a flame sparkled in his eyes. He looked around and above as to check if the Gods were watching him, and slightly bent forward, carried his prey to the car. The creature still lived. He opened the glove compartment and pulled out a first aid kit, which by the look of it, he must have composed himself, for it included a bottle of ether.

He poured half of it on a piece of moss and gave it to the cat to breathe. There he was, a doctor again. What he had in mind on the outskirts of Marrow forest must have come from the forest itself, just as the cat did.

The first thing Dr Tenace did was to put the cat on the table bed of Focus One of the ZEP. He stuck some ECG electrodes to the injured thing, then rushed out. He came back with Gustav mewing around as if Miss Margot's cat had known that he was going to drown in a bucket of boiling water. Tenace's hands were marked with long bloody scratches, and he was starting to look like the first cat.

He attached his loot to a second table. The ZEP smelled of ether. The wild cat's electrocardiogram was very feeble and started to act erratic. Tenace was anxious. It is doubtful that he was worried about the life's cat per se. He rushed to the table where Gustav was attached, and drew that table quickly to Focus Two. He then went to Focus One and adjusted the squashed carcass so that it would, mirror-like, approximately match the position of the other cat. Tenace then ran outside the ZEP and fetched a tiny LED lamp no bigger than a shirt button. He affixed it to Gustav's heart. Gustav managed to slash a claw of his left paw straight across Tenace's index. Tenace uttered a short "shit!" and contemplated twisting the cat's neck once round. The red light of the button shone on the cat's heart. Tenace was almost done; he rushed to Focus One to enjoy the fact that the red spot of the light was hitting the poor cat's squashed bottom. He moved the table so that the spot would precisely land on the cat's heart.

Suddenly the feeble and erratic EEG of the dying cat changed. The beats became regular and stronger; the cat was somehow resuscitating. Tenace smiled. Tenace had the proof of what he had always suspected: Life was a wave and not only the well-known electromagnetic wave of the heart. If you managed to collect all the waves emitted by a living body and focus them on a dying one, you were sharing life, you were reviving the dying. Not that Tenace was fond of such a collectivism, but he loved to have his idea corroborated by such an experiment. One might argue that the idea was not new. Indeed, similar experiments had been done with heart cells: isolate a heart cell, and it beats for a while then gets erratic and starts dying. Bring a second cell into the vicinity and the first cell picks up life and both tune together: the two cells beat in sync much longer. Tenace had just done the same thing today with cats' hearts and planned on doing it tomorrow with humans.

In the back of his mind, Tenace had a much better idea. What if you just recorded those waves, your own living waves, and re-emitted them onto yourself or onto others? Was it possible to record the signature of life? Was this complex packet of waves not something very close to the soul, if not the soul itself?

He unplugged the EEG, and with the skill of a Krav Maga expert, broke the neck of the poor crippled cat in a split second. It was a brutal but quick death. He wrapped the cadaver up in a green waste-bag.

He was making a knot in the bag when he heard the iron door of the premises of the ZEP creak. Some intuition made him relieve Gustav who, after having stared at him straight in the eyes, uncovering his fangs like a dog, escaped through the window in a flash.

Mrs Margot came in:

— Ah Dr Tenace, have you seen Gustav? He disappeared when I was just about to feed him. This has never happened before Dr Tenace. It's extremely strange!

— And what makes you think your cat might be in here? said Dr Tenace, feigning anger.

Miss Margot started to stutter, discovering the train of thoughts that had led her here. Confused, she mumbled:

— I thought I heard him mewing.

Dr Tenace, who still had the green bag in his hands, said:

— None of this, Miss Margot!

And he handed her the bag, asking her in a tone

that made the question resemble an order:

— Could you please put that bag into the red container!

Miss Margot's eyes opened with fear. The red container? She tried to guess the contents of the bag with her hands, and feeling the small balls of fur and flesh in it, she started to tear the bag apart:

— What have you done, Mr Tenace? What have you done? You monster!

Tenace remained completely indifferent. He did not even try to prevent her from opening the bag. He actually was busy repressing a smile slowly building up at the corner of his mouth. The despaired and horrified look on the face of this old nurse amused him. It was a super-duper pack of emotions bursting out there in front of him. It amused him to see people so destabilised by loss and death.

He had lost so many, and seen so many die and agonise that it left him cold as a frozen Siberian mammoth. Perhaps he was a frozen mammoth himself. The tears and screams of this banshee were starting to get on his nerves. Miss Margot had already managed to pull the cat's head out of the bag, panting like a 12-horse equipage:

— But it's not Gustav, Dr Tenace!

— Who ever told you it was, Miss Margot?

Miss Margot was slowly recovering. After all, she did not love all cats, only her beloved little Gustav. If

Gustav was not the one with the head dangling out of the bag, then Gustav was alive.

By the time this train of thought had arrived at main station 'Head', Tenace was about to turn the last light of the ZEP off, step outside and close the door. He then tried to reach for the bag.

— Let me take care of that Miss Margot! You should not have opened it! Next time you ask me! I found the poor thing outside Marrow forest, in the middle of the road. I thought I could do something for it, but it was hurt too badly, and it died 10 minutes ago.

Miss Margot stared at Tenace's finger, which was still bleeding from Gustav's claw. Tenace lowered his head and licked it. Miss Margot shrugged with disgust and had to let the bag fall. The rest of the crippled body then rolled out of it and one could see its flattened behind sticking out like a tomato panini, as if it wished to show the world one last time what Tenace had done to him.

Finishing cleaning his finger with his tongue, Tenace added:

— The poor thing bit me as I picked it up, I just hope he doesn't have rabies.

Tenace wrapped all the bloody bits together in the remains of the bag, with his bare hands. He dumped the lot into a Gucci plastic bag that a nurse had left. As they approached the red container, they heard something rattle in it, then a furred ball flew out of the opening left by the lid, which was not properly closed.

— Gustav! What are you doing in there? You naughty boy!

Tenace dumped the bag in, grinning.

Though Tenace still had no definition of death or life in the sense that he had not yet identified the signature of the complex wave pattern that it created, he had added two significant features to it.

The first one was that whatever life was, it manifested itself as a bundle of waves of different frequencies, a vast majority of which obeyed the law of reflection.

The second one was that this energy, when properly focused, increased the animation of living beings. His next step was to emit these waves again with adequate emitters, so as to output the signal recorded in the Clipax II's huge memory.

What still frustrated Tenace is that he had no idea of what was really going on. He was like a cameraman at the beginning of cinematography, filming life without understanding it and admiring the effect that the projection of films had on the incredulous folk at fun fairs, except he was not quite there yet. He remembered something from his time at University. When he did not understand something, his friend Georg used to tell him:

— If you don't understand something, just repeat it and repeat it!

Tenace had long thought about this saying and he had even tried it out on many occasions: After having repeated some incomprehensible ideas long enough, you become familiar with them and then you start to think you understand. At some later point, you start repeating it to other people. This is when you are convinced you have understood, and by then you are called a professor. You still have not understood anything. You have just gotten used to it. In repetition lies the illusion of truth and this is the beating heart of the media. Repeat it! It will come true, by the sheer force of your will. This is the keystone of creation, of magic and possibly of science.

Watching the country constables look down on him severely from the window shades of his room, he fell asleep, dreaming that he was trespassing a forbidden zone. He dreamt that his latest experiments had annoyed the Gods. They had sent Gustav down to punish him. Gustav was now two and a half metres long and walked upright on his back legs. He had condemned him to lie down on Focus One of the ZEP while his former ex-wife would lie on Focus Two. Dr Tenace woke up screaming!

Chapter 23: Jealous Eyes

And then the phone rang again. Drrrr...Drrrr... It was the ring of an old phone. Tenace had never swapped it. It was underneath that Yves Brayer's painting representing horses running away along a muddy road on a rainy day. Tenace had inherited it from his father, and the painting was unknown to the public. It was definitely worth a little fortune, but Tenace had no intention to sell it. It hung over the old phone just as it did when he was a small boy in his parents' big house. Was it a metaphor for life? The call made his spine vibrate all the way up to his pineal gland. Electricity it was, and a long way to the phone! Not in geometrical distance though, in human distance, and in such metrics, the distance was infinite. Tenace was never going to pick up the phone. It was trembling, trembling for him, and the wood of the table was trembling too, drrrrring... drrrring... Tenace was tetanised by the ringing. He started to shiver in synchronisation with the two metal cups that served as bells, alternately hit by the electromagnetic hammer that moved back and forth between them. He got up like a sleepwalker, wearing old sweat from the night. How dared she? And the phone rang and rang. It was as if the wooden table rang too, the call, the call he did not want to hear. Was it ringing or was it just ringing in his head like it had done all those years? God damn it! He looked at the horses on the muddy road, were they really running?

Who was calling? It was a call from the past. The past he could not cope with when it was the present, no more than now when it was the past, as if one could never leave one's own track, being eternally glued to it, like a snail. Wherever you go, you remains on your track. And he remembered that old Bob Marley song: "You're running and you're running but you can't run away from yourself!"

Tenace was now close to the phone; he could pick it up and listen to whoever was at the other end of the night. He could, he would perhaps pick it up this time. Who was it? God telling him to stop reaching for the apple? Was it his dead mother who had forgotten to tell him something and suddenly repented? Or was it HER AGAIN?

Her, wanting to tell him something she had never told him, or was it him wanting her to tell him something she had never wanted to? Drrrrrring! Drrrrrring! Should he have not left her? Should he have listened one more time to her lies, taking the risk of believing her and ending up fleeing to his garage where she would still come knocking on the door till he would suffer a heart attack like his colleague's father? Just one more time? Tenace was plagued again with remorse. Should he have endured the abuse till his grave, just to die with the consolation that he had done his duty? Should he honour life itself by daring his passion, daring his folly?

It will not be the illusion of having fulfilled your duty that will appease you on your deathbed. This illusion is what all who feed on you breed, to stay their craving. It will be all those pleasures, kisses and adventures, all those forbidden things that will quench your angst. And you know why they are forbidden? Because of the jealous eyes.

The jealous eyes started to move in the room, from the white walls to the white wooden table. The jealous eyes of the jealous people who always spit the disgust of their own self at you as they throw their disapproving look, trying to stop you. You should never be happier than them, never be more open, more generous, richer, have more success, whatever, but most of all, never be happier. You should bore yourself to death! This is what the jealous eyes meant.

Tenace was going to pick up the phone now because he knew who was calling. He was going to tell this person to go to hell, to let him live his life, to let him love himself, to let him be proud of all what he was, tax included. He was not going to take any more of this, any more of these reproaches and guilt, remorse and alleged shortcomings. There are no shortcomings, only specificities. He reached for the handset. He was going to shout all this to whoever was on the line and that would be it. This would be so strong that the phone would never ring again.

Tenace's eyes went red, his forehead shiny with sweat. Rage was there again, his head glided over the phone, dragging the rest of his body along. Suddenly he clenched his right fist, he was going to hammer it down on the handset and break it in two, just as he had done with his answering machine, using an axe though. The ringing was intolerable. His jaws were now open, drooling, drrring... drrring... He picked up the handset finally, slowly bringing it to his ear, ready to scream it all out. His eyes seemed to inflate for the prospect, but as he finally had the handset against his right ear, the only sound he heard was the dial tone!

This is when Tenace went mad once again. He dropped the handset on the table. Had it just been ringing in his head? Was he the telephone? He went through his hair to check! Would this ringing ever stop? He started to bang his head on the table with his ears squashed by his hands. He goddamn well knew who this was: THE JEALOUS EYES!

The entire wall was full of them, then they detached themselves from it and started to float like soap bubbles would, jingling around the room and then, as the thunderbolt struck, the eyes turned red, like the eyes of the devil. RED EYES! Like in a group picture when you shoot with a flash, except that there were no faces around the eyes. This is why Tenace got frightened.

- Stop looking at me! he screamed, hiding his face with his stretched fingers as if the eyes were blinding him.

But the red eyes would float around and he would see them even through his fingers. Meanwhile his fingers were crooked like hooks and he would start poking the red eyes with his claws.

He remembered what his father used to say when he was a young boy:

— Always look people in the eyes my son; never

look away, this way you'll be a man!

He had done so for a long time until he had started to think that it was impolite. It was just rude to stare at someone, trying to peep into someone's privacy. He had then departed from this strange habit, thinking that if people needed this stratagem to feel sure of themselves, there was something utterly wrong with them. Perhaps all these red eyes were those of people whose minds he had violated in his adolescence, following his father's advice.

Now, looking at them, he felt violated.

— Yes! I am what I am! My vices and my virtues! I am Dr Tenace and I stick to myself!

— I am fucking sick of being judged for what I do or don't do! I will complete what I have started and the hell with you! he added, gesticulating like a Frenchman.- He expected that the red eyes would vanish, scared by his dance, but the red eyes remained and the thunderlight made them glitter one more time in the darkness. The country constables in the shades frowned. Tenace refused to collapse and he screamed at this group picture with flash but without faces. He wanted to know who was behind those eyes, and why these faces hid.

— Show yourselves, you bloody cowards! If you dare to judge, dare listen to the one you condemn! You are the ones who never do anything, who never take any risk, who do not even dare to love because you're afraid. You are afraid of everything, you bastards! You are afraid of yourselves, afraid of the millions of eyes like yours, judging and condemning, telling how it should not be, counting the mistakes and pointing at the shortcomings! screamed Tenace, pounding on his chest.

— And you want to be the worst of them, be on the right side, on the side of the ones who never did anything wrong, the ones who stand in the shade of the powerful. You are dead! Your eyes belong to dead people! You refuse to live, and this is the worst sin. You refuse to be! In the hope of belonging to the chosen ones. You fools! You did not understand the Bible. You should have disobeyed! Can't you see? You can't see with a thousand eyes! Can't you see that God wanted us to be humans, not Gods! He wants us to be, with our vices, our passions, our cravings. This is why he made us vulnerable, why he invented diseases and made us mortals, so that we should live, burn, consume ourselves, and what do we do? We try to preserve ourselves, to not grow old. We try to be eternal, to die healthy! What a mistake! Death was not meant for that. Death was made to make us live, to make us dare, to make us try to be infinite in our finite time!

This is when the eyes stopped jingling. Tenace sobbed, and one more time he addressed them:

— I don't care about you! Stare at me! I am not impressed anymore! I don't give a damn. I have tried to love, at least I thought I did, even if it was in silence!

Tenace cried and then, his eyes full of tears, he raised his head to the painting with the horses on the muddy road and he heard the gallop and the splashes that the horseshoes made in the puddles. Then they faded out and there was just the dial tone in the room and it was the door to the future: He could phone whoever he wanted, all over the planet, and finally leave his own track, like a lost bullet, a bullet that departs from its trajectory to land somewhere else than at its point of impact, perhaps killing someone else.

Chapter 24: Stolen Tenace

Tenace was now wide awake. The constables impassibly stared at him like watchmen. A cat mewed. Tenace had tears in his eyes. There was an anxiety soaring in the air like a rook and Tenace just added a question at the end of each thought, a bit like the Swiss do, when they end anything they say with their eternal "oder?" Or was it hope?

Tenace had the feeling he had been stolen. This feeling had impaired his entire life. He felt stolen like some people felt lost. He was a prisoner of the activity he did, haunted by the question whether what he did was what he wanted to do or whether he had been talked into it, possessed by someone who just played with him with a remote control.

— Do I belong to myself? was a question Tenace regularly asked himself. It was absurd, considering the man. Though he was one of the most focussed people around, he had the feeling that he was not going anywhere, merely flying from flower to flower in a zigzag that made him seasick. When his heart was not 100% committed to what he was doing, his will would take over, and this will could be sometime so strong that Tenace would remain miles away from his heart.

Precisely when the heart was absent, he would be enticed to think he had been pushed there by someone. It endangered all of his projects, because it made him destroy what he had started for the sole reason that he suddenly thought: it wasn't him.

He would then wander around looking for his stolen self. Even this quest for the holy self, which would have been bliss to anyone in that mind, would turn into torture as he would start suspecting he had been pushed in this very search as well.

It was a good defence strategy: Each time a project worked, it was his, but each time it staggered, he had been pushed on to it by someone else. But Tenace was too intelligent to fool himself long with such schlock and soon enough you could see his panache again wagging at the front lines like a dog's tail.

The anxiety that he was living to satisfy someone else's desires persisted though. The perpetual suspicion that he did not belong to himself or no longer had any self because it had been eaten, or stolen by someone else, continued to haunt him with a recurrent certainty that enraged him: How could they have done this to him, dispossess him from himself! Murderers! They took his little soul as if he was a little boy. Through a subtle mixture of verbal terror and love withdrawal, they made him obey them to prolong their own souls.

How is it to make a little boy think that he will never succeed in life if he doesn't do as they say? How is it to rob the self-esteem and the innate self-confidence of children and replace it by the dependency on the approval of parents, teachers, neighbours, colleagues and boss? How is it to live an entire life in fear of disapproval? How is it to go where you are told to go, and even when you think that it's a free choice, you remain haunted by the suspicion that it might just be the only path through the crowd that the crowd left free for you!

Tenace was now pacing back and forth in his room. He felt like smashing the sheds, the same sheds as the ones of his childhood. He remembered that he thought they had been spies set up by his parents to watch him.

Tenace felt a big bubble of tears climbing up his throat. He felt he was never going to be a grown-up. He felt that he was just obsessed with trying to untangle the tethers that his parents, teachers, nasty staff in the holiday camps had tied him up with so that he could never fly.

Deep inside he thought that these people never wanted him to fly. He tried to avoid the thought; he tried to provide the explanation that it was a normal by-product of education.

He remembered how Madame Quiquisi had shouted at and beaten a boy and a girl, both around 10, in front of the entire class, because they had been caught kissing under the bed during a class outing in the mountains. Love was a crime very early in life.

The question always came back: Why didn't they want him to fly? He always came back with the same answer: They could not fly themselves! And for no other reason than this, they did not want anybody else to fly. It was their gift for his life.

They had had no fun. So why should he? And surely it was meant to be inherited by his children as well. It was as simple as that: jealousy. You would not expect it from your wife, from your parents, from your brothers or sisters, from your dearest friends. But wasn't it there that you encountered it the most?

Tenace wanted to fly again, to fly like he had done when he was a little boy, before they had tethered him. He was determined to do it. None of this fear anymore, none of this losing oneself, letting oneself get stolen by ghosts of the past. They were dead. There were thousands like them in the crowd at rush hour giving him nasty looks, reminding him he should not step out, but remain in line like a pawn in their chess game.

Tenace fought, resisting this illness, this self-destructing illness, this self-pity and self-stoning plague in which he had been brought up, the shadows of which followed him and woke him up at night.

Suddenly, behind those sheds, in the midst of despair, of self-loathing and whipping, Tenace had an idea, a spark of hope. He would pierce the mystery of his childhood and it was not going to be with psychoanalysis. It was going to be with science, with this new soul science he was on the verge of establishing.

Could it be that the complex entity that we call a human being, which encompasses emotions, will, desires, goals and past actions, could exist in the mere shape of a complex packet of waves that would beep like a little star in the Universe? That a human being could correlate to a bundle of waves that would travel through the infinity of space and perhaps back? His experiments with the ZEP were a proof of it.

Tenace was convinced there was a one-to-one correlation between the waves emitted and the life of a human being. He wondered whether this correlation was reversible: If one managed to bombard a living creature with the waves it had emitted earlier in his life, would one recreate in his body and mind this earlier state? Was it auto-reversible? And his mind drifted to other questions:

If one bombarded a creature with the waves of another, would the first creature become the other one? Would the consciousness state induced by the waves remain after the bombardment had stopped? Exhausted by all this thinking, Tenace fell asleep again, but this was not before throwing a defiant look at the guardians of knowledge disguised as sheds behind the windows of science.

Chapter 25: A Little Liquor

Tenace had finished the night with his velvet sleeping mask on and a couple of wax earplugs really well plugged in. That was his way to come to rest, though it did not always work. Silence and darkness. When he felt really bad, he would even add a warm bath to it, and he would lie there in his amniotic bubbles, longing to become amnesic. This is how he tried to become the unborn Tenace, floating like a 1m90 baby in the huge womb of his bathtub.

Earlier in his life, on such occasions, he had wrapped a lead belt around his breast and let his head sink in the water, breathing only through a snorkel, door shut, until his skin would get all soft and wrinkled like an old apple. This is until he nearly drowned after he had felt so relaxed that his beatitude had turned into sleep, and water had sneaked into the snorkel right down to his lungs.

Oh! The poor guy, it woke him up better than any alarm clock. He had coughed for 10 minutes on the floor of the bathroom, head down, on his arms, his legs stretched against the wall, his body almost vertical, trying to get the water out of his lungs.

After that dramatic episode Tenace had another go. He bought one of those snorkels with a ping-pong ball to stop the water from coming in. But that was no good either, because when he fell asleep, it was always sideways and the ball never really obstructed the snorkel. Tenace, too afraid to drown again, left that practice altogether, except for the sleeping mask and the wax plugs.

On this particular morning, none of it really helped. Tenace was depressed. It was still early in the morning for Tenace's habits. Something attracted him to Falkennest. He did not quite know what. He decided to have breakfast at the canteen. It was unusual for him, very unusual.

He'd always hated the canteen, as it reminded him of public lavatories. Specific organic compounds trespassed some orifices of the human body, activating similar sphincters to produce similar pleasures. He concentrated on his two croissants, which were called "Gipfelis" in this region. He liked to eat them with jam only, convinced that there was already enough butter below their brown flakes. He concentrated on the Gipfelis, because the stench of some two weeks old "boulette", a German variation of the not less-German hamburger, had headed straight to him, the only human being in this canteen, probably attracted by his heat. Boulettes were characterised by the fact that they were cold, more than well-done, and made from all sorts of meat, including pork.

The stench came from the juice that oozed out of the minced-cadaver ball when it was pressed. This grey juice was full of bacteria, having participated in a macerating orgy of more than ten days before the wretched thing would be considered "à point" by the "connoisseurs".

Unfortunately for Tenace, the connoisseur who was so unambiguously savouring this "delicacy" had decided to sit less than a table away from Tenace.

Tenace envisaged pressing the cleaning man's ginger head down on the flat-shaped meat paste to hear the grey juice come out, but he was delayed by the observation that nothing differentiated the boulette from its future digested form. Neither its look nor its smell. Mustard did not change a thing.

As one of the bosses at Falkennest, squashing a cleaner's nose on a boulette was not on the recipe list.

Tenace did not know what revolted him the most, the boulette or the way the cleaner looked. The cleaner was oversized, like a barrel on two legs. His lips were pressed together in the shape of an upside down "U" and looked like a replica of his short legs at 1/20 scale. The legs were menacingly spread as to unmistakably reveal massive genitals inside the trousers. He looked like a dog.

Tenace finally stood up. As he walked by, he noticed two small bottles of fig spirit, one of which was already empty. Actually, the cleaner did not look like a dog but like a very unfriendly hippopotamus, perhaps even a rhinoceros except for the horn.

Every now and then he grunted and sneezed like a mastodon. Tenace thought the man was ugly and felt so utterly disgusted that he forgot the smelly Boulette.

The man must have been a charming little boy decades ago. Why was it that one could grow so ugly? It was not age, thought Tenace. It was what one had done or not done in one's life. It was frustration, and it was written all over the face and body. Even feeding oneself to the point of explosion would not erase it. Gluttony did not fight death it called it.

Tenace thought he could do with some liquor himself, but he had something else in mind to cheer him up for good, to chase the eyes away, the red ones and the ones of the rhinoceros, the doubts and the bad spirits. Something he had never tried before was waiting for him. Something he had prepared months ago, which he wanted to test right now.

He was in a state of catharsis and depression. He could have melted like an ice cube and become a puddle on the white tiling of the corridor. The cleaner would then mop him up into his bucket or "bookit" if he was from Manchester, squeeze him out of the mop with his huge hands to take his revenge for what Tenace had thought of doing with him.

Tenace wondered why God had made us so different while we were all so similar, particularly in this very craving to be different. He knew it as a doctor and he had seen enough humans despair and die the same way. He did not understand this absurd striving to be different, that made us feel so lonely sometimes. It kindled fights, murders and wars! Weren't we all tentacles of the same huge Octopus! Then again, wasn't any movement a consequence of potential difference? thought Tenace the Physicist. Life could never be peace, retirement. Life was birth and death, brutal and tragic, period.

The cleaner was coming up the corridor now with the bucket and the mop and his huge hands. Tenace panicked. He did not want to end in the bucket and be poured down the cesspit. Tenace concentrated. He grew himself out of the puddle to escape the muddle. He resuscitated and rushed to his office, leaving the cleaner and his huge hands with nothing to do. The cleaner walked up the corridor with bucket and mop and his dangling belly, wafting out the stench of garlic that announced him miles away.

Tenace walked past his office, not even bothering to go in. He walked straight to the ZEP, went to the cupboard and pulled out a 2-inch tape reel with the title: "Tenace, August the 23rd: Happy", all handwritten. He walked up to the big tape player, fed the reel in and fiddled a while at the ZEP control.

He walked to Focus One and sat down on the chair, his head at the focus, like someone getting ready to listen to the 6th symphony of Beethoven: the Pastoral. He closed his eyes and the ZEP antennas array at Focus 2 started to buzz ... Tenace could not refrain a little scream, his body started to convulse with pleasure. It was delicious, it was better than Aperol spritz. The buzz went higher in pitch.

The waves radiated from Focus One to his pineal gland with perfect efficiency, though they didn't enter there, that was a myth. He was enjoying his own self word for word because the signals the ZEP were playing onto him were the signals he had recorded of himself on August the 23rd 2013, when he had felt so good.

Tenace had planned that. He had recorded his own waves when he had felt extremely good, thinking of beaming himself with the record when he felt down.

He had never dared to fulfil the experiment. He did not know why. It takes us so long to finish what we cherish. Most probably, it is because we are so afraid to fail. He felt better. He was uniting with a former Tenace of his, a happy, enthusiastic Tenace. This one was feeding him with happiness: electromagnetic endorphins. Tenace was not only happy because he was getting radio-drugged by his own little liquor: his own self, Tenace was also happy because auto-beaming worked. Because one more time, he had succeeded in proving that the crazy ZEP worked!

Tenace was running on the beach facing the sun. He must have been six years old; he giggled, he had a sea-star in his hand and it was alive. He closed his eyes and he was in the arms of a former flame of his, kissing her, and she giggled too. They were also at the seaside but this time it was in the south of France 'cause the palm trees cast shadows on them. How strange! Tenace thought. This is what I had been thinking and dreaming about six months ago when I recorded that. But this thought was hard to keep because the images were so vivid. He remembered how he was horny about her. Being horny is something entirely self-centred and sometimes it turned the women off because they feel excluded from your horniness. Women want to be the cause personally, not just taxonomically. So they start squeezing their legs together in a refusing giggle. This memory made Tenace a little sad. But this was his own thought now, it did not come from the waves.

He decided to focus on the waves again. Now he was in Switzerland, near Villars, climbing Argentières, and the beautiful sunset threw long shadows of the rocks on the green, while the horses of "Caroline *à la montagne*" were neighing. And suddenly his mother came and stroked his forehead before hugging him:

— How have you been doing, my son?

His mother vanished. He was little Tenace again, lying on the grass in the garden, having his first real reading experience with "Noddy goes to Toyland". He remembered that he had never read a book before and that his mother had told him to just go and read one. So he had gone to the garden with Noddy and had gazed at the sky and its beautiful clouds, alternating between the clouds and the letters until he was trapped in the story of Noddy, realising he had just read his first book.

His breath was full and regular now. A nice stream of warmth was now circulating around in his chest as if he had had a nice little drink. He managed to slightly double expose this picture with his own analytic thoughts: He suspected that the waves did not carry his past per se but that they were just bringing him into the state of auto-generated hypnosis.

He felt a lot better; he was back to the village of happiness. In life there were just two important villages and they were not on the maps. You could not get there with GPS. One was happiness and the other one was sadness, and there was a road between them. You walked this path up and down all your life and you met all sorts of people like you on the road. He remembered that when his father shouted, the wind that came out of his ogre mouth would blow him damned close to the village of sadness.

But he'd come back slowly, following his kite or bringing a sea star to his mother. Then he remembered how he had blown his mother down to it: He had hidden behind an armchair and had made that dried-out sea star climb the back of the armchair by pulling the string. His mother, who had kept this sea star for so long, knew it was dead and seeing it climb up the back of the armchair terrified her. Little Tenace did not giggle any more behind the armchair and started to feel the cold of the grey marble he was sitting on.

Tenace decided to relax again and he saw a hospital room and his mother again. She lay in a big bed and he lay in a little bed. He was tiny. He remembered his first night on earth and what he remembered the most is that he already knew it all. He had brought it with him from the great void of unbornness and nothing had changed since. Then the tape was over and you could hear it slacking as full reels do when they're over.

Slack... Slack... Slack...

Chapter 26: Reflecting on Waves

Perhaps it was the ripples in the pond, or perhaps those years studying physics, or both, that gave him the idea.

Tenace threw a stone in the pond and looked at the ripples it made, and it looked goddamn easy to run to the other side of the pond and wait for the waves to arrive. This was going back in the past.

What seemed like a piece of cake on water was a technical nightmare with electromagnetic waves, and that was Einstein's fault because Einstein had postulated that it was impossible to travel at a speed higher than the speed of light.

The moon grinning at Tenace through the ripples on the water seemed to share his opinion. It was just not possible to catch up with electromagnetic waves. They were too fast. This was not the way to catch up with the past.

The ripples transformed into a grid, and Tenace was surely physicist enough to know it was the interferences caused by the reflections of the waves on the vertical shore of the pond, on that big rock over there.

There were no rocks big enough in space to reflect any of our waves. Plasma walls would reflect waves. They were several light years bright and high.

But the prospect of having to identify in a gigantic chaotic mass of waves the extremely weak signals of a single individual wave was not realistic, and he resolved to dump the project aside in his "probably doesn't work" cupboard. As tenacious as he was, he knew it was jolly difficult to detect such weak reflections so many light years away.

As Tenace walked back from the pond, he could not help wondering about the question whether humans were only wave emitters or also wave receivers. He knew that the mere fact of receiving waves turned any receiver into a small emitter, since the receiving antenna behaved like a small emitter itself. It was so with radio or TV. Why would it not be so with humans?

Were we receiving our consciousness from the Universe? If so, were we all receiving the same waves from the Universe? Just tuning to different spectra to make us different? Each one of us had a spectrum. Perhaps that's why spectre is another name for ghost. A spectrum is the range of sensitivity to particular frequencies. Tenace could conceive that the human body was such a multiple resonator receiving and emitting simultaneously thousands of signals at various frequencies. He could also conceive that our body was the filter, which would only retrieve the waves according to its own spectrum.

Tenace had read the reports on Stammheim, the prison where the RAF terrorists had been incarcerated in the late 1970s. The concrete that was used to build this prison was mixed up with metallic particles so that the prison cells would function as Faraday cages. No electromagnetic waves could reach the prisoners and after eleven months of such isolation they started to get sick, with hair and skin decay.

Tenace hesitated. He was completely in his mind, barely looking at the trees that dangerously approached his head with alarming regularity. He only vaguely saw the light of the puppet room. Who was playing there tonight?

He did not feel his body anymore; his mind was sucking all the energy out of his limbs, breast and stomach. He was just a thinker, an intellectual, and he suddenly hated it. He started to view life as a fight between thoughts and emotions. He was a thought addict.

The idea that our consciousness could come from somewhere else was enticing, inasmuch as it inferred that we could not do anything about our consciousness, that it was all written out there in the big book like in "Jacques the Fatalist" by Diderot. "C'est tout écrit là-haut!" Its second attractive aspect was that wherever it came from, it was given to us. There was an entity that was taking care of us, feeding us, like in our first minutes of life, and that was comforting.

Staggering back to the clinic, Tenace was on the verge of getting one of the weirdest ideas he had ever had. What interested Tenace was whether these waves were deterministic or random? Was life already written or not? He remembered the theory of the great French mathematician and humanist Fourier, who postulated and demonstrated that any signal can be decomposed in a series of elementary sine functions, each of different amplitude and phase. Once you had decomposed the signal in such a series of small mathematical vibrators, if you played them together, you would get the original signal again.

So Tenace thought that each and any of the thousands of signals that constituted consciousness could be decomposed in a Fourier series and if you could manage to get hold of the series, to know the phase, frequency and amplitude of each of these sine function, you could recreate the signal.

In such a banal sentence, lies hidden and dormant a stroke of genius that perhaps escapes the perspicacity of the average reader but certainly not Tenace's. Such an innocent phrase gave Tenace the idea, although it was wrong, that you could look into the past and into the future of the individual human consciousness. Tenace's heart poked faster. He could not withstand the excitement his own thoughts had triggered in him. His legs were trembling and he could barely walk back, even with his stick. He decided to sit down, and fell next to a middle-sized oak tree. Fortunately, it was the north side of the tree, where the hard ground is covered with moss.

Tenace had just realised that he could draw a function between infinity and finity. Life could not be unforecastable and random. If it were decomposable in Fourier sine functions, you could, with the help of a huge computer, calculate the signal at any position in time, be it the present, the future or the past.

Tenace could not believe it; he was jubilating, and

he wanted to cry, to shout, to tumble on his breast like a gorilla, to talk to the trees, the raven watching him, the swallow, the ponds, but he couldn't. He was paralysed, he could hardly breathe, and his shivering hands left his sweaty temples to reach for his forehead, then his eyes, where they met his tears.

It was forbidden to play God, he knew it, and every time he had tried, he had become sick, very sick and Tenace did not want to become sick. His entire body was already shivering, he felt so cold. No! No! I won't do it! he promised silently. I will leave the humans in peace. God, I swear on my life. I will not play the Sorcerer's Apprentice. I won't tell my fellow men what will happen to them. I won't use this to win the lottery. I won't even use it to prevent wars or investigate the traumatic past of patients. No! I swear, I will leave everything as you wanted it, God, as you designed it. I will never compete with you, God, but don't make me sick, not now.

What Tenace did not add to his prayer and died at the tip of his tongue was: *not now, later* - so that I can check on that Fourier stuff right now.

Tenace fainted for a while. When he woke up, it was completely dark, so he must have dozed for half an hour. He stood up and walked straight to the puppet house. It was heated and that felt good. He took a good glass of gin and that warmed him up too. The big question that Tenace was facing was how to get these Fourier coefficients? He could perform the mathematical Fourier transform on signals recorded in the ZEP, but these coefficients would only provide true reconstruction of the signal during the time interval they were recorded. If he performed the Fourier transform in a 2-hour recording session, the coefficients he would get would surely be in a position to reconstruct the signal recorded during those two hours but only within this observation window. He wrote in capital letters with a huge piece of chalk on the blackboard of his hopes: OUTSIDE THE OBSERVATION TIME WINDOW, THE SIGNAL WILL REPEAT ITSELF AGAIN AND AGAIN WITH THE PERIODICITY OF THE TIME WINDOW!

Then he heard Mr Galux, his French math teacher, walk down the row, smacking his ruler on the wooden desks and shouting:

— What's in your brain, Tenace? Do you still have a brain? What is our nation going to become if its alleged elite do not even know the basics of Fourier's analysis?

But the voice faded and the classroom disappeared. Tenace only heard his head throbbing and even this throb was better than those insane memories. He was back to square one. The tip of his toe was on square two though: He was not going to be able to find all the Fourier coefficients but he could look for them somewhere else.

His idea was accompanied by a feeling of guilt. Whatever led to a step further up the tree of knowledge called forth the guilt spirits, as if God was the ogre at the top of the bean stalk, but Jack Tenace's idea was stubborn, like a revelation. He could see the helix of the DNA like a ghost floating two feet above the ground. It was mocking him like a female overwhelmed by her own needs yelling: catch me!

Tenace bit the bait, and chased the DNA helix from one room to the other, in the meanders of his own folly! What had the DNA to do with his idiotic hypothesis on a Fourier decomposition of life?

He believed that since DNA was the signature of human beings, if there were to be a generic signal base for the Fourier synthesis of life signals, it had to be the DNA.

Chapter 27: Dickerdon

As a modern scientist and a lazy or pragmatic scientist, Tenace knew that nowadays it was not necessary to understand the relationships. It was much more important to discover and show them, just like differential and integral calculus was not important anymore, since the most complex differential equations could be easily solved by numerical computation. He just had to establish the relationship between DNA and life signals. This is when he remembered Dickerdon. Oh, Old Dickerdon! Samuel Bill Dickerdon! A friend of his when he was a Physics student. He was actually a mathematician, utterly upset with neural networks and genetic algorithms. Upset in the manner of a lover who can't get enough. He was fascinated by the idea of a great correlator, a great ordering machine, a device that would find correlations between all the instances of chaos! That is what he wanted: a big black box that you could feed with any information, and it would bring order to it! Of course, neural networks were the inspiration source, the hope for such an adventure, but they were so limited, specially the training of these networks, hours of computing power to finally achieve a decision-taking unit that most of the time you could have programmed deterministically with less effort.

Dickerdon had gotten more and more obsessed. He had his own ideas, his own way. Although the Prof liked him at the beginning and was rather interested in his ideas, Dickerdon got on his nerves because he just went too much off the path. At the end, he did not come to the lectures anymore and got sacked. Tenace kept in touch with him and even gave him a shelter when he met him once in the city, muttering more than speaking, and pulling a plastic bag behind him like a bum, full of papers on which he had been scribbling for months. Isn't that what will happen to all of us when we have lost faith in being understood? Dickerdon had not only lost faith, he had forgotten what faith was. But Tenace understood his muttering, full of equations, knots, ponderators, quantic deciders, anti-deciders, parallel propagation, backward number striking, whatever, you name it.

It was just the prospect of having to deal with him that made him refrain from contacting him. However, something was telling him he should. It was indeed strange that he suddenly thought of him after 10 years of total amnesia. Tenace googled his name, and surprise, surprise, there were articles written by him in the IEEE review and Scientific American. He even read that he had founded a company called TGC, The General Correlator. His heart jumped. Tenace rejoiced for him; he was the Steve Jobs of the future. These school drop-outs were the best. He suddenly wished he had dropped out of school, but then he realised it would just have led him to found a dating agency, because that is the only thing he was interested in, after, before and during school.

Tenace rushed to his car. It was a four-hour drive to Rustliberg where Dickerdon had his house, and he intended to be fixed on the question tonight. Dickerdon had been slightly reluctant on the phone, but when Tenace told him briefly about his ZEP, he got all excited and said he'd cancel his bowling appointment.

Tenace hated bowling and he was suddenly so glad to be Tenace and not Dickerdon. He had this mad look on his face, at least this is what he, his very self, thought, while dropping his behind on the driver's seat and catching a glimpse of his glimpses in the rear view mirror.

Apparently satisfied with his looks, he started the engine. He looked at the ham sandwich and Coke he had placed on the passenger seat. That would help him stand the weather. He hated to drive when it was raining, probably because it increased his dependency to this machinery called a car. On the other hand, he loved driving because this is when he did most of his thinking. He was now thinking of Dickerdon.

He realised that he was at least as much interested in seeing Dickerdon again as in getting the answer to whether Dickerdon's Great Correlator for Everything could establish a unique relationship between DNA and his ZEP-recorded multi-signals.

After the first hour, he had actually forgotten about the original purpose of his trip. He was just fascinated by a guy like Dickerdon, who had followed his way against everybody else's advice. He deserved Tenace's respect, independently of whether or not Dickerdon's machine produced rubbish or not, and that was worth the trip.

It was 10 pm by the time Tenace arrived at Brunngasse 8. He drove up the muddy path that led to the house but decided to stop halfway because the path was full of pit holes.

One window was lit. It was a small window and behind that small window Dickerdon's piggy face showed. Tenace was not sure he was not pressing his nostrils on the glass to enhance the portrait he was showing. Whether it was because it was late or because Dickerdon was just an eccentric person is not clear; the fact is Dickerdon was already in his pyjamas, and his pyjamas were made of the same cloth as the one used to make mattresses and pillows in the old days: grey with white stripes. It made Dickerdon look like a huge pillow himself. Tenace thought of hitting him in the belly instead of shaking hands with him, to see if down feathers would fluff out with his breath but he didn't, partly because Dickerdon was huge and strong, even if some of his natural blanketing was definitely more on the adipose side.

— Wow! You haven't changed a bit, James! Except you look ten times more like a shrunken apple than before! Hope you still have your tail, or has it fallen off?

And the most inappropriate burst of laughter followed this odd but certainly affectionate greeting.

— Pillow-man, I hope you don't have goose feathers in your head as well, 'cause I intend to drain your brain! was Tenace's greeting.

There was a huge chunk of Bündnerfleisch on the

table. Next to it were two bottles of French Haut-Médoc and a loaf of bread about the size of Dinkerdon's butt.

The handful of red tongues muttering in the stove managed to heat the place decently. Tenace always wondered if fat people felt less lonely than lean people. If they felt their body more than lean people. They definitely had more to feel, judging by the way Dickerdon pulled up the straw-stuffed chair and crumpled into it to put his naked feet on the one next to it. Tenace realised he had not answered the questions yet. His eyes could not stop watching his brownish toenails, which obviously had plenty of freedom to grow in the last four months.

Dickerdon was picking his teeth, and his massive ox brain was controlling his bull eyes to watch Tenace out of their corners. He must have loved it, because he looked really organic or orgasmic. Perhaps he had ingested too many prions.

Dickerdon, started to mutter; he did not want to listen to what Tenace had to say, but just mumbled between bread, Bündnerfleisch, burps and red wine. Occasionally there were long farts, not that Tenace heard them, but they attacked him another way a few seconds later, depending on the other winds, the ones that came from under the door. There was no point in interrupting him – that was the price to pay for the consultation in advance. It was totally bearable if you did not keep up a pretence at understanding what he was saying. He reminded Tenace of his father, the only difference being that with his father, Tenace did not want to understand but with Dickerdon he simply could not understand.

The Haut-Médoc was certainly doing its best to help him collect the intuitive and poetical cement to make sense of the mathematical concepts Dickerdon was uttering in a very random way. He gathered he had a girlfriend who had refused to say the yes-word on the wedding day, and that he got so sad that he wept in front of everybody. Tenace gathered that his Great Correlator of Everything was slowly making him rich. He was correlating stocks to all the economic, social and political events he could. He was correctly embedding astrological data in his correlator. This is when Tenace dared to intervene, because he was saying something he could understand:

— Astrology is nothing but a correlation of human events and tendencies with astral positions in space. A correlation that has been established by human observation over centuries.

This is when Dickerdon started to talk about the Fire Horse of Chinese and Japanese astrology. People born in 1846, 1906 and 1966 were of that sign and they were bad; especially the women of those years. They were rebellious, untameable and brought bad luck to the family they came from and the family they grounded, especially health and financial problems. Their fathers and their husbands would die young. This is why the Chinese even killed female babies of these years. And Judith was born in 1966! he screamed.

This is when Tenace said to him that he should feel lucky that she had said "No" on his wedding day.

He looked at Tenace with extremely sad eyes, so sad that Tenace wished he would orgiastically pick his teeth again. He said:

— Luckier than me! I wish she had said "No" on my wedding day!

This is when Dickerdon finally showed interest in someone other than himself, namely in Tenace! He hit his huge fist on the table and shouted:

— James, you're goddamn right!

And the red wine in his glass spilled over and the chunk of bread he had just broken off turned red. Again his eyes made this slow circular movement that showed a lot of white and it made Tenace think of the prions again.

— James, your stuff is easy! You told me on the phone!

Tenace's oesophagus suddenly made a knot like the snake in *The Jungle Book*. How could he, Dr Tenace, who had been accepted as one of the candidates to solve the question of Life and Death at the World Health Organisation, how could his ideas be bullshit? How could this thick bovid-like alcoholic pillow-man with the toenails of an eremite insult him so directly? He should throw the glass of water at his face like he had done twenty-five years ago when they were both students and he had insulted Tenace in front of all their peers at the cafeteria. But then, maybe it was the fire or the so-simple decoration of the room that made him calm down. There was no public here, it was just him and

Tenace, he did not need to show off, if he had said something like that, he meant it, and if it was the truth, at least his truth, so perhaps Tenace needed to accept it. Buddhist waves came back to his memory from all the books he had read, not least the one of the Dalai Lama, so he tried to love him, to love the sentence he had just said to him: The way you want to solve the problem you have is bullshit.

This bum whom Tenace had rescued ten years ago from the streets dared to tell him his stuff was bullshit! He accepted it, humbly. He was, for once in his life, possibly the first time in his life, humble, and it was not masochism, this was also a premiere. He was suddenly overwhelmed by a feeling of gratitude, of calm, of bliss. He was listening and Dickerdon talked:

— Man! You don't need Fourier coefficients. This is too complicated, it might be all linked, it might be a way, God knows. But from what I gather, Dr James Tenace, I, Dickerdon, who only has a French Baccalaureate with mediocre grades, and no doctorate title in Mathematics or Medicine, I tell you the only thing you need to look into is fractal signals!

It was like a slap in the face how the word fractal immediately opened a corridor of light in Tenace's mind. Yes, of course! Fractals described so many natural phenomena, from the shape of snowflakes to the nature of terrain, from EEG signals to organic textures. That was one of the main laws of nature, that information repeated itself at different scales and as you zoomed to smaller scales you would see the same pattern again and again.

Tenace should fractally extrapolate the signals he had recorded and get the signal forecast over the life span. These words were the product of his own thoughts, but then he heard them in his brain spoken in another voice, a much harsher voice than his own, and he realised that this voice was Dickerdon's voice itself.

It was pouring rain on the way home. Tenace took the other way back, the one that went through Marrow Forest. He was afraid of the spirits he'd encounter in the woods, and of facing the coachman again. On the way home, Tenace did not care, either it was the Haut-Médoc, part of which was speeding through his veins, or it was the disk he had in his jacket's inner pocket that made him ignore his fears.

Tenace knew that when Dickerdon designed software, it did what it was supposed to do. And when Dickerdon's program was called "Fract All, it would fractalize everything, that is, it would find the highest fractal similarity to anything! This meant, for the novice in this language, that if a signal was fractal, the software would get it, and so would Tenace, 'cause the software was in his pocket!

He could finally prolong the signals beyond the observation window up to the entire lifetime of the individual he had recorded the signals of.

Tenace was as excited as a little kid who had just got his new toy. It was most definitely that excitation that was responsible for the fact that all of a sudden the gas pedal could not be pressed further down. The headlights showed the trees of the forest right and left, like a crowd acclaiming the presidential car on its way to the Elysium of his dreams.

He already saw himself travelling into the past and future of his patients, of himself, of anyone. It seems that as far as he was concerned, driving at 140 km/h on Marrow Road, he did not need any software or ZEP to see into his future; he created it in his mind and his lab was at the moment reduced to the dashboard of his car.

Chapter 28: Gunter

It was late when Tenace arrived. He didn't even want to look at the clock, just as you don't want to open letters from your lawyer or bills from the dentist, or even to open the mailbox. Tenace's mailbox was often jam-packed.

He drove to the main entrance and that Cerberus wanted to see his badge. It was not because he did not recognise him. It was just because he wanted to feel important. The only thing that calmed Tenace's rising bad temper was that he knew the only power these guys had was to say "No!" What they did not know is that they would be much happier if they said "Yes" instead. They'd get smiles, friendly chats, and feel in unison with the folk they served. Yet again, that was not a good idea when you worked for a security company. This guy was no yes-man. He was short, and spent most of his free time lifting weights in the Clinic's antiquated muscle saloon that the Union had imposed on the management twenty years ago. The rest of the time he just sat in his hut at the main entrance pressing the button to open the gate to visitors after having scrutinised them through their windshields. That was his only game besides the one of stroking his blond moustache before deigning to press his one and only button.

Tenace was boiling. He intended to ask him if he thought he was the boss of the clinic soul-transferred to a security officer, but in the very last second, just after having lowered the window and stuck his badge against the lower side of it, he reconsidered:

- Jolly good Gunter! I wish all my subordinates were as professional as you are.

That triggered a bright smile on Gunter's porcine face, which he managed to quickly repress long before the barrier was up. From then on, Gunter never asked Tenace for his badge.

Tenace drove directly to the ZEP. His heart was pounding, not because of the security officer but because of his expectations. Pressing his satchel against his breast, he got out of the car without watching where his boots landed. Freezing water leaked into a slit in the leather, and that came from not being regularly greased. The corridor leading to the computer room was cold. This was because the board had decided to stop heating this part of the building at night. He rushed to the desk and turned ZOE3 on.

ZOE3 was his baby, a matrix of 400 cheap computers that he had bought at 28 Euros apiece at the local hardware shop. With the latest technology of computer networking, he had managed to raise its power up to the equivalent of a Cray 5. While the machine was powering up in the semi-darkness, triggering a fireworks display of LED lights all over the array, Tenace walked up to the safe.

The third attempt was the right one. Tenace had always been prone to forgetting codes, like most of us when we are excited.

All the recordings stood chronologically ordered, starting from the poor cat who inaugurated the ZEP, followed by Randy's agony recordings. Then came the patients' recordings, the three UV disks of Mrs Van Brandstaetten. The last shelf was for his colleagues who had accepted to lie on the new psychoanalytic sofa reincarnated in the shape of the table bed at Focus One of the ZEP. There were Ralf, Julie, Miss Margot. Tenace did not know who to choose. His eyes fell on the bottom shelf. Three discs stood there. These were Tenace's own recordings.

The prospect of being reducible to a fractal saddened Tenace. He looked down on the three miserable UV Ray discs that were supposed to encapsulate his life. The Fract All software would reduce him, Dr Tenace, to a few zillions of bits and bytes on 200 cm3 of recording hardware. That was appalling! Tenace realised how gross his attempt was. Reduce life to octets! Reduce! Reign! Annihilate the complexity of feelings to a bunch of bumps and pits on a plastic dish. It reminded him of a long-forgotten conversation with his first girlfriend Christa. Tenace was a 17-year-old horny youngster who had just read one of these clever books stating that emotions could be broken down to chemical reactions. She had slapped him in the face on Main Street. Now, thirty years later, Tenace understood her mood but still wanted to slap her back.

The remorse faded, and his eyes glittered. Like a lustful predator, he seized the middle disk, as he remembered that the first recording was lousy because his head had not been properly centred on the focus of the ZEP. He shifted the UVD into the reader, and first had a look at the signals. He browsed the thousand coloured lines, trying to recognise a pattern, but he was just playing. He loaded the FRACTALL software. He turned around towards the nose of the ZEP, wondering if it would work. Tenace secretly thought that machines lived. When they broke or stopped, you had been thinking bad thoughts about them. With its nose painted black at its tip, the ZEP looked like a dog.

He pressed the start icon and closed his eyes. When he reopened them a minute later, the screen displayed: Data analysis, please wait! Tenace closed his eyes again, feeling impatient. He shoved his hands in his coat pockets and sensed a change in the light intensity of the screen through his closed eyelids. He opened his eyes and read: "No fractal signature found! Would you like to try the Kalmann filtered analysis?"

Tenace's brain made a few revs. Kalmann? That rang a bell. Of course, when signals were noisy, this was one of the best filters to get rid of the noise and locate the pattern. He remembered, as a physics student, having applied the filter to the re-entry phase of a spatial vehicle during the blackout of atmospheric re-entry, created by the plasma around the vehicle. He also remembered not having understood anything and having faked his way through. He remembered using all those fancy words such as covariance matrix, state estimate, etc. without really mastering the essence of any of them. Later, secretly ashamed, he had caught up with his ignorance and studied two books on the sacred matter. That was a long time ago and tonight Tenace did not give a damn whether he understood the crazy filter or not, he just answered YES. The electronics trotted and Tenace decided to wait on the table bed inside the ZEP.

He woke up because someone was knocking at the window. A torch light was sweeping the floor and the walls. In a split second, Tenace was at the window. He recognised Gunter:

- Just checking, Mr Tenace, just checking!

Tenace knew very well that what had brought Gunter here was his uncontrollable curiosity. He could read it instantly from his suspicious face. Tenace hated not to be called Doctor, especially by a security employee. He had the definite feeling that this guy was jealous and nosy, that if he could have some kind of rule in his book to prevent him from working here at this time of the night, he would have it. Gunter would have loved to prevent him from working at all. He needed a reminder to respect Tenace, and Tenace was just about to give him that reminder:

- And who is watching the main entrance, Mr Hass, while you're having your walk? And he would look him straight in the eyes.

Gunter's face approached the window, squeezing his nasty nose against it and with a threatening look he said:

— I know you're doing something that's not kosher here, Mr Tenace! We all know it here! You're doing evil things, Mr Tenace, I can feel it.

This is when the dog snarled. Tenace felt like

grabbing Gunter's throat through the window and dragging him onto the ZEP's table to flatten his fractal, if he had one, down to the level of the grass he was standing on. But Tenace had neither the physical strength to do so nor the foolishness it would take. Instead, he said:

— I'm sure you're an expert on hell, Mr Hass, as if you'd served there before. Why don't you stick to the main entrance before I report your little escapade and desertion to your superiors?

The speaker of the computer beeped three long times, resembling an alarm tone. Gunter backed away, staring at Tenace through the slightly frozen window, muttering words Tenace could not grasp. Tenace watched him walk backwards while he himself approached the screen. "Fractal detected, noise to signal ratio 0.1" was displayed on the screen. Tenace could not control himself; he screamed, and the dog barked.

If there was a fractal, it could be bred beyond the observation window. Tenace decided to let the ZOE3 pursue its calculations on the remaining signals. He waited though for the next two signals to be processed. Three was his number.

That night, Tenace had a nightmare: the clinic was on fire and his ZEP was melting. He was at the wheel of a fire brigade truck but Gunter would not let him in!

Chapter 29: Russian Jumps

It was already 10 am when Tenace finally gathered enough willpower to get out of bed. He had not been drinking any nightcaps, but he felt drowsy. He'd be late, but then he was the boss. He stepped inside his muddy Mehari unshaved, unwashed, his shirt barely tucked in, and ignited the engine.

Obsessed by what ZOE3 had spat out, he ignored the pile of letters Miss Margot had just dumped into his basket.

— Someone named Dickerdon called, Dr Tenace! said Miss Margot.

Tenace did not bother to answer, but headed to the ZEP. The light was on. Who was in the ZEP? This is something he really hated. He was always afraid that cleaning ladies would unplug some device. The paper basket was empty. He rushed to the screen. It was off. That stupid Cindy had turned it off to save electricity, as was recommended by the new regulations. He hated new regulations, made by administrative managers who had nothing else to do than count pins and pencils. She should have turned the light off before leaving. He touched the spacebar of the keyboard and the screen went on.

Relief! ZOE3 had a screen saver mode. Tenace's face radiated: 3765 signals were fractalized! 213 were not! This was just gigantic! His face displayed a large smile and it didn't go into screen saver mode. His eyes kept on sweeping the screen up and down, left and right, enjoying each line of the cybernetic nectar:

Signal 2322: Fractalized! Noise to signal ratio: 0.08!

Signal 2323: Fractalized! Noise to signal ratio: 0.13!

He felt twice as big, twice as bright, he felt light, he wanted to scream and dance. His hands started to rub his chest, his belly, his knees and his cheeks. He got closer to the screen and started to kiss the numbers. He licked line 2324 and smelled the glass. He embraced the monitor. How much he loved numbers! How much he loved mathematics and technology! He then closed his eyes and sung that stupid verse which made no sense to anyone except for a little kid named Tenace:

— If bits and bytes were pots and pans, they'd be no room for thinkers!

Tears ran down from his eyes as he started to weep. He sneezed and wiped them off with his coat sleeve. He stayed there a few minutes, lost in his digital dream of eternity, convinced he was on something, on the track of consciousness.

He could finally find the knots in people's soul. Just walk back the trail of their life along the meanders of the silicon micro-trenches in ZOE3. Get things right again in their brains. Find the spot in his own life where it had all begun. Where everything had gone wrong! Erase it and start again on a new path void of knots impossible to untangle.

He would become free and stronger. He dreamt of bringing back consciousness to his patients, of being the great Dr Tenace who had brought them all back from coma. He sobbed one more time and then he heard someone walk behind him. He stopped breathing. He stopped sneezing. He was afraid to turn around. Who on earth had dared to spy on him at such a sacred moment?

His eyes focused on the screen again, not on the digits, but on the reflections, to try and guess who was walking behind him. He thought it was Gunter, but the stride was too long for his height.

Overcoming his fear, Tenace jumped up in a whirl and faced the intruder. He did not recognise him. The man looked like a Christmas tree. LED garlands were wrapped over his arms and shoulders. They were flashing, and the light they emitted ran up and around. Tenace recognised Dickerdon.

— What the hell are you doing here? Who let you in? You jolly well scared me!

— Why is she called Cindy? She has such a strong Russian accent, she should have been called Daria or Olga!

— And how come you got through the main entrance?

— The guy was asleep, so I crept under the barrier.

— What do you want?

— 100,000 Euros!

— You've got to be kidding! I thought you were lending it to me!

— Lending it? You're the one who's kidding! What do you think? That I work for years and decades on this and you get it for free? Just because you helped me out when I dropped out of University?

— I thought it was the General Correlator that took you ten years, not the Fractalizer!

Dickerdon's eyes swayed. Tenace, who had a good knowledge of humans and the way they lied, was convinced Dickerdon was bluffing. In the end, you could buy such software from the shelf for a couple of thousands. Dickerdon was haggling. Tenace definitely needed the Correlator as well. He walked up to Dickerdon, looked him straight into the eyes, stepped back, circled around him, secretly mocking his suit, which was too big and had long not seen the launderer: a grey suit with grey and white stripes. He looked like a pimp.

— I already got a copy of your software. I made it yesterday.

— So what? That copy won't help you very long. You can only run the software three times, then it's dead!

Tenace raised his eyebrows; three was his number.

— Do you think that I can't find the counter in

your assembler?

— I'm pretty sure of that, man! You can't disassemble my software.

— All software can be disassembled!

Tenace did not really believe what he was saying. Not that it was not generally true, but when it came to Dickerdon, anything was possible. The guy was such a genius that Tenace was ready to believe that he had designed some kind of programming technique that rendered the code impossible to disassemble.

— Ever heard of random jumps? Russian random jumps?

Dickerdon started to jump back and forth, right and left. His LED garland doing the same around his neck. He started to sing "Kalin kakalinka gamaia" and to dance the Kasatchok.

Tenace had heard of the Russian technique. It consisted in embedding a bunch of unconditional jumps to random addresses in the code. This kind of programming was very difficult to disassemble.

— Listen Dickerdon! I can buy this kind of fractal software from someone else for a lot cheaper. I'll buy both, the Fract All and the General Correlator for thirty thousand!

— No way! Give me that disk back!

— Thought you could only use it three times! Tenace moved to the computer and put his hand on the reader.

— You can, but the two remaining times are still too much for you!

Dickerdon was getting aggressive and Tenace had no intention to solve the conflict with his hands.

— I'll offer you fifty thousand for both programs and your assistance!

There was silence in the room. Dickerdon touched his beard and sneezed. Tenace waited. In this kind of game, it is the one who talks first who loses. They looked at each other, then Dickerdon looked at his feet. He was embarrassed and had lost all his self-confidence, as if his internal spring had given all the revs it could.

As Tenace wrote the check, he noticed that Dickerdon's hand was shaking.

Dickerdon took the check and there was no handshake. They parted, without a word. Dickerdon walked backwards. It was over. As he reached the door, he stopped and said:

— At the fourth attempt, it will ask you for a code, so type: "chuchichachlicheibelolly", in one word, comme ça se prononce, and lowercase letters! I'll send you the General Correlator software by mail. Tenace trusted Dickerdon.

Chapter 30: Leaning out the window

He watched him walk away, swaying slightly. Dickerdon had reached the end of the court and should have turned right towards the main exit. He didn't; he continued straight on and bent slightly to the left, because it was going downwards. He intended to explore the clinic.

Tenace felt like telling him off. It was no funfair here! He opened the window to yell at him. The icy metal bar across the window on which he rested his hands stopped him. The cold reminded him of his own body, which he kept on forgetting. An empathic disposition made him consider that Dickerdon just wanted to have a walk to the ponds or into the forest of the clinic's park.

Dickerdon turned left towards the little cemetery and Tenace remembered that there was a gate to it. This gate was never locked.

Tenace recalled that Dickerdon's mother was buried there. He leaned out the window to see more of him, just in time to see him disappear behind the huge oak which hid the gate to the cemetery. He pulled his head back in, rubbed his stretched neck muscles and sighed. He needed to urinate. Too lazy to turn the light on, he trusted his judgment. That was a mistake. He ended with his shoes and trousers soaked.

He walked to the computer and listed the directory

of the UV disk and there it was, this tiny word on the penultimate line: Generator!

He grinned. Dickerdon had packed the Generator, the Fractal Breeder with it. He was a mate! He clicked on the Generator icon and the computer asked: Generate all signals: Yes/No? Tenace answered "Yes". How many folds? Tenace had no idea what the time span of a fold was. He just typed 3, his favourite number. ZOE3 trotted on. The progress bar at the bottom of the screen hardly progressed.

He looked at it for a while and guessed it would not be finished until after lunch. He left, locking all the doors. This was highly confidential. His life was being extrapolated outside the observation window. ZOE3 was leaning its Hydra heads outside this window.

Having seen Dickerdon walk down to the cemetery reminded him of something he had so brilliantly forgotten for so many years: his own mother was buried there too, and though he literally drove past her grave every day to work, he had not paid it a single visit in twenty years.

He did not feel guilty. He had a good excuse ready in his mind. It sealed the way to her grave like a fortress: No one worked as close to his mother's grave as he did. He even went to the mathematical side of it: The barycentre of his position over time in the last twenty years was the closest ever to one's mother's tomb anyone alive on this earth could occupy. That was a good excuse. But today, this excuse did not work. Was it the fear of this impending digital introspection or was it the sight of Dickerdon trotting to his mother like a mourning dog?

Tears were ready to drop, dry and silent tears, tears only Tenace would know of. He controlled himself like he had been told to, never to cry, like most men.

Tenace walked down the alley, letting gravity do the job, like when you climb down a mountain. He climbed down the mountain of his pride and scars. He walked down to his mother's tomb, something he had not done for 20 years. When he got there, he felt like vomiting and his intestines were on the same track.

Not that he hated his mother; on the contrary, he just hated that she had left him so early in his life, when he had been a boyish twelve years old.

Before her death, he had been in paradise, and then all of a sudden, in hell, alone, no shoulder to cry on.

— There you are, you little prick! Have you enjoyed mummy's love long enough? She left you because you did not hold on to her! God avenged us. He killed her just to see your rotten soul suffer its well-deserved punishment your whole life long! One says goodnight to the dying!

Tenace heard these voices and could not mute them. He pressed his ears with his thumbs but it did not help.

As he arrived at the tomb, he fell down. The energy in his body had just sufficed to carry him there. His forehead dropped on the grave. He started to sob silently, over his youth, his life and future. In between the sobs, he wondered what the hell he wanted to explore. His past? Scan his future with fractals in the ZEP? Wasn't everything already written as inerasable remembrances in his mind?

Technology was superfluous. It was an attempt at denial, a way to escape feelings. Looking at numbers and graphs was easier than looking at the crying faces behind the digits. From doctors to restructurators, they were all hatchet men hiding behind their Excel pages as if humans were the failures, and machines the invulnerable Gods. Could fractals repair the fractures?

This is when he started to hear thumps. He raised his head in their direction and saw Dickerdon. It was windy and the air was cold. Dickerdon was hitting his mother's stone with his forehead.

Bump! Bump! Bump! In series of threes. But there was no rhythm. Tenace counted, because it was unbearable. His eyes fell back on his own mother's gravestone and he read:

"Let fame, that all hunt after in their lives, Live register'd upon our brazen tombs!"

It was not signed. Surely Shakespeare had never meant to have it written on a real tomb, brazen or not. His mother had succeeded at biting him twenty years later.

His attention went back to Dickerdon. He heard him cry and yell and the wind brought these words to him:

— You wretched whore! Why did you let my

brother rape me? Why didn't you punch him in the face for that, like you did to me so often? And Dickerdon punched himself in the face and hit the stone with his forehead.

— Why did you force me to eat my poo-pooh when I was five years old! I will never forgive you! I wish I could resuscitate you and make you suffer the way I have. I would smash your face with my own face and break your nose 'til you eat it! Tastes better than shit.

The wind stopped or changed direction. Tenace could not hear anything more. He could still see Dickerdon hitting his forehead on the gravestone. He wanted to run up to him and stop him. The wind changed direction again and brought him these words:

— Mother! I'll sodomize you just like my brother did to me! Dickerdon stood up, pulled his pants down and masturbated on the grave.

When Dickerdon was done, he fell on his knees and cried:

— Nothing will repair what you've done to me. Why do parents abuse their children? Why do they take advantage of such loveable creatures, who have no means of defence? Children are Gods!

Dickerdon started to hit the grave with a massive, long hammer this time. He had found it in the cemetery staff's hut. He was trying to break the tomb! Bump! Bump! Bump!

— I'm going to crash and burn your bones! Dead

witch! And Dickerdon squatted on his mother's tomb.

The monologue faded again. Tenace felt the cold wind on his lips. They froze as they had done when he had last kissed his own mother. That was forty years ago, as she lay in her coffin.

The bells of the little chapel rang. His sight was blurred; he tried to focus again but he couldn't. He gave up trying and suddenly he could see again and it was all crystal clear:

Sons and daughters of all ages were kneeling on their parents' tombs. They were all singing the same song, the song of revenge and vindictiveness, the song of abandon, abuse and humiliation. One by one, they turned around. The boys pulled their pants down and the girl just heaved up their skirts and squatted. All urinated on their parents' tombs as an ultimate liberation.

Tenace squinted but the image would not disappear. The cemetery was full of them trying to fix their past, in an ultimate act of profanation. The vision persisted in slow motion. It slowed down until it became still photography. Tenace heard a metallic squeaking. He finally opened his eyes. Dickerdon had left on his bicycle. The front wheel was bent, as if the bike had been squashed by a car or padlocked too long to a lamp post.

It did not bother Dickerdon. He swayed right to left on his camel back home. This is what happens when you lean out the window.

Chapter 31: Falling Out of the Window

Tenace ate his bean soup at the canteen morosely. He had hardly acknowledged the greetings of the other doctors or of Miss Margot, who were all surprised to see him there, because Tenace never had lunch at the clinic's canteen. He was just happy about the warmth of this liquid that the Mexican cooks dared to call soup. Crunching beans every now and then was an occupation that suited his absent mind.

It is not clear what made him morose: his visions at the cemetery or the imminent prospect of immersing himself in the fractally extrapolated signal of his own life in the ZEP. He felt like a patient just before going into a magnetic resonance tomograph, awaiting the verdict of the doctor, except he was his own doctor and his only disease was his own life.

Between two crunches, he would raise his head and look at the faces of the clinic's staff obediently bringing their tray to the kitchen before going back to work. He dreaded that moment when the bowl would be empty and he would also have to stand up and go back to his work. He was apprehensive, as everything had worked so well, but the game would be soon over, and he wanted to dream a little more, to hope, to play in his fantasy world. Now that he had nearly reached the end and could collect the fruits of months of hard work, he was not interested. He was ready to drop the whole thing. He knew it was a recurrent pattern of his, just to stop one step before it was finished, a sophisticated self-sabotage he was accustomed to and which had already jeopardised a lot of opportunities.

He was the kind of guy who would, if he had been a writer, burn his play when it was finished. Excuse himself for having written it and not have remained a humble unknown and insignificant person. He was the kind of guy who would even swear that he would not do it again, who would apologise for having dared to try, to have even thought about trying. He was constantly attracted to a dark planet in which he should collapse, the planet of self-destruction.

Just now, he wished to creep into his empty bowl of soup, like he had been to told to. Never grow, remain a nothing, go back to your closet behind the stairs of fame and stay there. For some unknown reason he felt attracted to such a posture, like someone finally paying all his debts, eager to ask: Is it alright now? All right? I don't owe you anything anymore. Can I leave now for ever? It was a recurrent obsession, of being buried by a mountain of guilt. Who was it that was secretly but so intensively pushing him back into this closet? Whose were these dark eyes that he saw floating below the ceiling of the canteen? Who did these low and nasty voices belong to?

Then, another Tenace spoke inside of him with the timid voice of a 10-year-old:

— Jamy, this is what you are going to find out! Soon, very soon, just walk in there, set up the time cursor to forty-five years ago, feed in those signals from your pineal gland! Jamy, you're nearly there, go for it, and don't listen to them!

And the tiny voice shrunk and big Tenace looked around, fearing his neighbours had also heard it! He watched the nurses from the reanimation team walk by, closing their lips contemptuously between their fat cheeks. Everything in them perspired of self-righteousness:

— We're on the right side. We do our job and we will be thanked for that. We're not like you, trying to be special, always apart, never a simple human like us! We don't ask ourselves so many questions, we are simple. We go to the movies with our friends and have a few drinks. We cry and hug and fight over nothing and don't know much, but we are happy, we are together! You chose this way, that's why you're alone in your bloody thoughts! Alone! Alone!

The third nurse, who was smaller, giggled and added:

— And miserable!

Tenace looked the other way, but the other way was full of clones of these nurses, but with other masks, and even the painters renovating the north wing looked the same way. His eyes fled to the surface of the wooden table and he started to follow the meanders of the wood, wondering about the fractality of its patterns. He wanted to take a deep breath, stand up to his own self and shout:

— Yes I am a scientist! Yes I will find out what tortures mankind since it's been on earth! Yes! I am what I am and am ready to die for it. His sight was blurred again. The deep breath did not go down; it stopped half way, so he took another deep breath.

Something was locked in his thorax, just beneath the sternum. The heart chakra was messed up. He felt the wood this time, his only friend, scraping the natural grooves of it with his nails, as if he were falling and would desperately try to get a grip and remain with the guests.

Then, with a superhuman effort, he stood up. He forgot the bowl. By the time he had left the table, he had regained all his dignity and conviction. His aura was powerful again, so that even Laura, the insolent kitchen cop, did not dare to remind him to bring his bowl back.

Tenace heard only the blood in his ears. He walked like a sleepwalker out of the canteen, except he did not have his arms stretched out in front of him. He was determined to complete the experiment. What counted was not the result but the fact of trying. He knew this. His hands were shaking as he impatiently unlocked the first door of the ZEP, hardly managing to push the key in the hole, like a drunk going home. He locked the door behind him and went to the phone to unplug it. As he closed the shutters of the windows, he heard the distinctive mewing of a cat as it landed on the grass. The cat stopped, looked at him and mewed again.

Tenace had randomly chosen the date of 4th of April 1966. The fractal generator would calculate all the signals from that date onwards. He had just pressed the start button, where a timer was included, just like on cameras, and had set it to "3 min." He had three minutes to get installed in the ZEP and place his skull properly at Focus One.

Tenace had turned all the lights off, and the remaining light, beside what came through the shutters, was from all the LEDs of the ZOE3 computer array, but much more light came from the emitter head at Focus 2, on the other side of the ZEP. This did not disturb Tenace, though, because he had brought his sleeping mask, the one he even wore in public transports.

He tried to calm himself, but it was impossible. Not only was he excited to see if his experiment would work but he was much more excited about what he would discover about his life. It was science fiction. Travelling in one's own past! Suddenly he felt like a small boy again, playing with Dinky Toys model cars, humming like an engine while pushing the cars around the chair's legs, knowing perfectly well they were not real cars and that he was driving none of them. But he had no time to pursue this thought. The last beep of the three-beep warning of the signal emission start had just faded.

Tenace closed his eyes and tried to relax. It was like starting meditation. He compelled himself to breathe regularly and deeply, although he kept on holding his breath, like pearl divers in apnea. He always did so when apprehensive. Then a feeling of peace overwhelmed him. He could still hear the humming of the head at the other Focus and the rattling of the UV-Disk reader biting the bytes on the record.

He expected other sounds, other visions, scenes of his childhood, but nothing came. His mind did not come to rest, but was shaken back and forth by incessant thoughts, including the one of trying to stop thinking.

Monkey-talk as the Buddhists say. Then suddenly he felt the urge to kiss his teddy bear, but he had no teddy bear anymore. He wondered what he was doing there. Why had daddy put him there? He was not sick was he? He yelled Mummy! and wanted to get away, and play with his Scalextric cars. He'd had enough of playing with the Lotus and the Jaguar Le Mans, but there were no cars either. It was like a movie but there were no pictures. His attention focused on the ZEP head again. It looked like the ugly head of a luminous octopus.

— When I get older, I want to be a doctor, he said to himself. He giggled, and his voice had a higher pitch. He started to move his legs and arms; they were responding much faster, as if they were shorter. He felt like he had another body inside his body, a much lighter and faster one. He smelled differently, much sweeter.

He wanted to hug this little body in his with his long arms, but this is when realised he had smaller arms and could not hug himself. He decided that he would kiss him. He tried to turn around on his stomach but he couldn't, because something was holding him on his back. He realised he could not move his head. A voice was telling him not to move...who was it? The doctor? But he wasn't sick. He looked up. And there was this man with a helmet on looking at him. He was familiar, and he was giving him kisses with his lips. But it was not his father and doctors don't give kisses.

The man who was familiar could have been an elder brother but he had none. Then he realised something and started to scream. The man was him, just much older. This is how he would look in forty years!

He was terrified! That was a real nightmare. He'd tell mommy tomorrow and maybe daddy would be there at breakfast. Wow! What a dream!

The idea that it was only a dream reassured him, so he started to watch his 40-year-older face attentively, those long eyebrow hairs, grey and black, the ones coming out of his nostrils. He liked himself; he was pleased with the way he would look in forty years' time and he smiled. And that smile quickly disappeared because it had unveiled ugly crooked teeth on the upper gum. He did not like them but the eyes were so nice, so benevolent, that he reached for the face with his small hands to stroke the cheeks, but they were no cheeks. It was hard and cold; it was glass, and his own hands were about as old as the face and they were hairy. He screamed again, and this time it was a long scream. Oh! How horrible! He didn't want to be old. He was not old. What kind of joke was this? His little body wiggled right and left to stop the nightmare. His breath had accelerated. He wanted to stop it, and concentrated on how to wake up and stop the nightmare. Thank God! The alarm clock went on: Beep! Beep! Beep!

It wasn't his alarm clock, though. His alarm clock rang like a hammer vibrating between two bells. Then something changed, and the slight heat he had kept feeling under his skull and had thought was fever disappeared. A wave of coolness swayed through his body. He felt heavier, slower. All his flesh was slowly hardening, his muscles tetanized, as if he were ageing forty years in just three seconds. It was atrocious. He fainted.

When Tenace came back to consciousness, all he could hear was this powerful Beep! Beep! Beep! emanating from ZOE3 and indicating the end of the session. The octopus had shut its lights off. Dr James Tenace realised that his first fractal voyage was over!

Chapter 32: Wild Dogs

He was drowsy, and it took him a few minutes to come back to our time. He walked to the control screen of the ZOE3, overhearing the steps on the gravel at the front door. He was busy with the question as to why he had not gotten pulled fully back in time. Why had he not been completely immersed in the day of April the 4th 1966? In his folly, he had expected to be thrown into the movie of his past, entirely re-living the day.

He remembered having felt like a little boy, but nothing had been happening really. It was as if something had been missing, cut off. Only when he allowed himself to remember his childhood he had thought it was resisting the signals images and feelings appeared. They were not remembrances, but vivid and organic feelings, perhaps since they were experienced through the consciousness of a child this time.

That actually corroborated his idea that life was a synergetic cocktail of consciousness interacting with external triggers. The ZEP would be able to fractally recreate the state or the consciousness anywhere on the timeline. However, the signals it generated would not contain any events. They were gone, except some times when they were in one's own memory, when one still had one, and that was all. It might have seemed disappointing at first, but not for Tenace, who was always looking for challenges. He grinned and thought:

— We are not there yet! The game would go on.

He heard someone knocking at the door. He waited, considering not giving any sign of life. No one knew he was there and the lights were off. Then the knocking started again and he heard a voice:

— Dr Tenace! Are you there? Dr Tenace?

Tenace turned the light on and by the time he had reached the door, he had recognised the voice: Gunter. Without a word, he opened the door. Two policemen stood behind Gunter. He recognised one of them: it was Frangier, an inspector he had already dealt with. Frangier had been enquiring about a ring of organ traffickers. They had been trying to corrupt doctors in the various clinics of the country. None of this company was really good news to Tenace. They all had this funny look on their faces, as if they had come to arrest a lunatic and this lunatic was Tenace. Tenace ignored Gunter and spoke directly to Frangier:

— In which affair will I have the pleasure to help you this time, Inspector?

His face did not look like he was feeling any pleasure, though.

— Dr Tenace, we have had a phone call from the cemetery-keeper, Mr Prat. He reported that someone had been trying to profane a tomb earlier this afternoon. A long hammer has been found near it. He said that he had seen you leave the cemetery through the north gate shortly afterwards. We thought you might know something.

The look on Frangier's face was actually saying something else. If it could have talked it would have said:

— You've been caught hammering on a tomb you weirdo! But his professionalism managed to silence his face. Gunter's mouth went on:

— What can you tell us about it, Doctor?

Tenace looked at him. Gunter could not dissimulate his satisfaction in thinking he had finally caught the doctor in some devilish activity. He looked with full contempt at Tenace and was on the verge of uttering some complement to Frangier's overture but Tenace hindered that:

— Who is "us"? I don't think Mr Hass has anything to do with this.

— I am responsible for security here, Dr Tenace!

— "Here" is not the cemetery. Whatever happened there is none of your business. Could you please return to your post? Frangier gave Gunter a nod.

— I didn't know you'd changed jobs and bosses, Mr Hass! Next time, would you be so kind to give the clinic's management the obligatory three months' notice? Unless you want me to do it for you?

Gunter rearranged his stick and left, noticeably frustrated, then Tenace spoke:

— Inspector! I'm sorry to hear that, but I fear I cannot be of any help. I was indeed in the cemetery, paying a visit to my dear mother's tomb. I also heard some thumping nearby. I did not pay too much attention, you will easily gather why. I thought it was Mr Prat doing some 'gardening' there, as he's paid for. But I did see a man leave on a bicycle soon after.

— What did this man look like, Mr Tenace?

Tenace answered:

— Can't really tell you, saw him from behind, a trench-coat and hat. Surely there must be a name on the tomb he opened!

— No tomb was opened Mr Tenace.

Tenace grinned inside, as this was precisely what he wanted to hear.

— Well...damaged, then. You could surely trace the relatives and start your enquiry there.

— I start the enquiry where it suits me, Mr Tenace.

— Dr Tenace, if you please! I'm sorry I can't help you more, Inspector.

The other policeman was staring at Dr Tenace's forehead, where the sleeping mask was still affixed. Tenace grabbed it and stuffed it into his pocket.

— We have intense light in this lab, which is for translumination takes.

The second policeman did not seem to understand, but Frangier did:

— Our jobs are quite similar then, Doctor! We

both examine matter with a lot of attention! Another question Dr Tenace. Did you see this man in any strange position by the tomb?

Frangier was embarrassed, and looked at his colleague, who added:

— Squatting or something?

Tenace's mind made a rev.

— Squatting? I don't know. I didn't pay attention. What's the matter? Is it against the law? Some people kneel down, some squat, some stand!

— You're right, Dr Tenace. Sorry about all this. Have a nice day!

And both policemen saluted and turned around on their heels like soldiers. When they had nearly reached the end of the courtyard, Frangier turned around and came back a few steps, embarrassed:

— You know, there was a turd on the grave.

Tenace burst out laughing.

— A turd! So what? Have you got nothing else to enquire about?

He could not stop laughing. Someone who would have known Tenace well enough could have told that his laughter wasn't genuine.

— There are a lot of wild dogs around, Mr Frangier!

— You don't say! It's my job to get them, Dr

Tenace! Frangier looked Tenace straight in the eyes, a couple of seconds too long.

— Wow! You can tell the difference between a dog's turd and a human turd!

— Have you ever seen a dog use toilet paper?

Chapter 33: Snap

Feeling like a criminal when you have not done anything wrong is something that was not quite unknown to Tenace, but he had to move on, and he could not spend his time in any kind of introspection, although this is what his dark side would have loved to do. He had work to do. He wanted to scan some of his patients to see if there was any fractality in the weak signals their comatose brains emitted. He had decided to start with Mrs Van Brandstaetten. Since the death of the black Vietnam War veteran, he wanted to be extremely cautious and discreet. He did not want anyone to know. The only one who was in with it was Ralf. Ralf did not follow all of it scientifically, but he trusted Tenace. The whole thing had a taste of illegality and a drop of Frankenstein, but it was for the good cause, to wake comatose patients.

At 8.10 pm, Ralf dialled 801 on his desk phone and whispered:

— Maria just went to the television room.

Maria was a young nurse and since she had gotten the job at the clinic, she had managed very well. She had only one vice, and that was television. She'd start watching TV at around 8.00 pm after having brought the last patient to bed, and if no emergency disturbed her, which was the rule, you could find her still snoring in front of the TV at 1.00 am the next day.

Tenace would have wished a more entertaining and nicer-looking nurse. Such a nurse would have been willing to do what young doctors and nurses usually do during the long nights of watch duty. Tenace had no say in this matter, unfortunately, and Maria was just the ideal nurse for tonight.

— I'll be right there. No! A wheelchair will do! was his only answer.

Mrs Van Brandstaetten was a very peaceful patient. Her face did not look tormented. She was just a bit heavy, like they all are, not specifically because of their weight, but more because of the total absence of tonus in their muscles. A corpse feels much heavier than its corresponding living body and it is not due to the 21g that the soul allegedly weighs, rather it follows the "felt weight" or "dead weight" law; just like the "wind chill factor" is different, being the "felt temperature", though the chill involved is different. They pushed her in the wheelchair along the bumpy path to the ZEP. Her head, hardly maintained upright by the flabby neck, jerked back and forth. It was not sure whether the vertebrae would take it.

Ralf had not seen the ZEP after it was finished and fully equipped. He remembered as when it was still empty and how Tenace had lit the match at Focus One, nearly burning his head as he stood at the other Focus. It now looked impressive. Everything except the mirror surface of the ellipsoid was painted white. What impressed Ralf the most was the array of mini computers with their coloured LEDs shining around, decorating the array like Christmas tree.

Ralf suddenly heard a strange series of beeps at three frequencies. They slowly converged to a continuous C major chord. Mrs Van Brandstaetten was now lying on the table bed wearing a helmet he had never seen before. Tenace was watching waves on the screen. There were thousands of waves of various colours, on various vertical planes. Ralf said:

— Looks very flat to me.

— Of course it's very flat! Who do you think we have here? Kasparov in the middle of the world championship, or Einstein drafting his theory of restricted relativity? It's coma land here!

Flat as it was, Tenace had instructed ZOE3 to record and fractalize. He had planned a good hour of recording.

— You can come back in an hour Ralf, I'll stay with her.

The signals had been flat all the way through. Tenace, who had been close to dozing in front of the screen, was suddenly attracted by some change. The curves were getting lively, and at the same time he heard Mrs Van Brandstaetten move violently.

He rushed to her and watched her rocking right and left on the table. Instead of fastening her with the belt, a precaution he should have taken in the first place, he shouted at her:

— This is not how it's supposed to work!

Goddamn it! We are here in the recording session Mrs Van Brandstaetten! Not in the playback or animation session. You're messing everything up. Stop this!

But what was happening was too late to stop. Swaying her legs right and left with such violence, her body, which was already making huge jumps on the table bed as if it were being tortured by massive electrodes, rocked a little too much and fell on the floor. That is, what could fall of it. The rest, and that rest was basically her skull, was attached to the positioning helmet of Focus One. When the legs and the lower trunk left the table bed, her bare heels hit the floor with a big thump, followed by another sound, dampened by the flesh around her neck. It was the sound of the cervical vertebra cracking. She died immediately.

Shit! was the only word that came to Tenace's mind. He had no emotions. She died, it was a bugger, but she had been brain dead already. What did it really matter? In a little corner of his mind, he even rejoiced: another recording of death! Perhaps he would find something! But for now he was in deep trouble. How was he going to conceal how Mrs Van Brandstaetten had died? She had to die tomorrow or the day after tomorrow, or at the weekend, when he was not on duty!

He picked up the phone, dialled 808 and said:

— Ralf, we have a problem!

Chapter 34: Retouche

They were all ready. The ritual was well established. Everyone in their wheelchairs, like every Monday, for the big picture, attached with strings from the old puppet automaton. Except this Monday, there was no newcomer; on the contrary, there was someone going, more precisely someone who had just gone, one day ago, and the one who had just gone was just about to be brought back.

Mrs Van Brandstaetten might have been the one who needed the least threads to sustain her in her wheelchair, most probably due to the coldness of the night she had spent and of its following day.

It is known that cold people are stiff, showing no empathy, no flexibility, no understanding, and this is true not only in bed, where it yields probably the most regrettable consequence for their partner. It is also true of the corpse, which likewise remains stiffened in its position until some kind of fire warms them up again, if ever.

It occurred to Tenace that by the look of Mrs van Brandstaetten, she must have been stiff long before her stroke. While Tenace was painting Mrs Van Brandstaetten's lips with Chanel Rouge, Ralf slid the colour plate in the camera and took a look at the Gossen light-meter: 60 seconds at F1.8: that was too long, because many of the patients were randomly moving. It must have had something to do with supper. The digestion probably triggered the autonomous nervous system to go a little wilder than in the afternoon, which was the usual time for taking the picture.

An aggravating circumstance was that it was already dark outside and the meagre lightning of the theatre did not suffice.

— Magnesium flash! muttered Tenace.

Ralf did not understand why Tenace did not purchase one of those electronic flashes and insisted on this old fashion technique instead! But then again he could have asked the same question about the plate camera, which could have easily been replaced by a modern high-resolution digital camera. He didn't ask. Even his tired brain managed to find the answer between the reminiscence of the pornographic shadows imprinted on it: Tenace wanted no electromagnetic interference with the auras which gave such vivid expressions to the portraits.

Woof! it went, like a firework, as he squeezed the rubber pear that triggered both the obturator and the ignition of the magnesium. A magnificent bubble of white light exploded from the metallic dragon, accompanied by the white smoke that we are all acquainted with from this technique.

This did not wake any of the subjects from their perpetual coma. They stared so unshaken in front of both of them that Tenace thought they would stare the same deadpan way if the white ghost had been death itself.

Tenace then rushed to the camera and pulled the plate out of it in such a hurry that the sturdy three-legged Cyclops vacillated. He ran with it to the photo lab, though that was usually Ralf's job. Ralf waited for the plate to be developed and fixed. He walked to Haridana and started to make faces at her, but the faces didn't trouble her. Montgolfier puffed as if he was going to deflate. That scared Ralf and he stopped. He decided to inspect each one of them like an officer his troops. He started to gesticulate in front of them in a frenzy, probably ill at ease with this long, incomprehensible contradiction they represented: alive, but yet dead in the brain.

— What do you think of that? finally shouted Tenace from behind. The paper print still dripping on the line was impressive. Mrs Van Brandstaetten in the middle was more alive than she had ever been.

It looked as if she wanted to say something. There was a mixture of indignation and fear on her lips. Something that had not been there in reality, as he was making faces at her. Ralf was so impressed that he did not even notice that the print was black and white, instead of colour as usual. Tenace had never printed on black and white paper and why he did it this time was another question Ralf could have asked, but he forgot.

— Fantastic, isn't it? said Tenace, adjusting the photograph in the dryer.

After the dryer had beeped, Tenace lifted the framed cloth that pressed the paper against the heating plate, and checked that the gelatine hardened by the heat was impeccably glossy.

— That's my best! he shouted, triumphal.

Then they heard steps in the corridor. Ralf shivered, and was about to go and stop the nosy visitor, but Tenace held his arm:

— Let her in!

Sister Ruth, who knew about this strange ritual at Falkennest's clinic, could not help uttering a slight sound, which most definitely expressed the horror she felt.

— Sister Ruth, could you help us bring the patients back to bed? Start with Montgolfier, please! said Tenace.

That was a smart move, as Montgolfier had his room at the other end of the building, in the east wing. It would take her at least five minutes to come back, and that was enough to finally bring Mrs Van Brandstaetten back to her bed. Sister Ruth obeyed, but not without staring at Mrs Van Brandstaetten.

This time it was Tenace's turn to shiver. Did she know Mrs Van Brandstaetten had not been in her room the whole day and the whole night before? She couldn't know. She had come on duty ten minutes ago, at most, and the night team does not usually communicate with the day team except through the written reports that hung at the foot of each patient's bed. Tenace had taken good care of Mrs Van Brandstaetten's report that was for sure.

Tenace calmed down; actually it was a blessing that Sister Ruth had seen her, as she would be a witness.

As soon as she disappeared around the corner, rolling Montgolfier back to his Penates, they both rushed to Mrs Van Brandstaetten and off she went, back to bed for one more night, one extra night after her last!

When they were all gone, Tenace looked at his work, focussing on Mrs Van Brandstaetten's face, definitely pleased she looked so alive. He approached his cheek towards the paper and caressed it. He raised his head again and in a final dive he kissed Mrs Van Brandstaetten on her grey lips. The red lipstick did not show.

Chapter 35: Smoke to Heaven

Mrs Van Brandstaetten's visit at the ZEP was more than upsetting, as not only had her spinal cord snapped, which was the cause of her premature death, but Tenace's hope of ever bringing back consciousness to brain-dead people had snapped as well.

— If the Zepograph of comatose patients is flat, what signals do you expect me to use to revive your consciousness?

Tenace was asking this question to Mrs Van Brandstaetten while she was looking at him straight in the face, sitting in the middle of this black and white photograph he had come back to look at.

Tenace was not only upset, he was abashed. His body curved inwards like a shrimp. What now? Suddenly, a grin appeared on his face, a rather dirty grin, which he repressed immediately. The thought triggering that grin came back like a recurrent dream. How about feeding signals from someone else? Tenace walked to the fridge and poured himself another glass of champagne. Champagne was not the right drink for such a blatant tragedy. Thereby he mainly meant the scientific tragedy, and though he had quit smoking for the last 25 years, he decided to light another cigarette from the packet he had bought that evening when Mrs Van Brandstaetten decided to break her neck. Puffing the smoke into her eyes so that they would go red, if they had been real instead of grey silver-halide grains, he asked her:

— How would you like to be me?

As if she had answered, he added:

— No! Don't worry, not me, just my twin sister, in spirit?

Then he waved the smoke away so as to chase this devilish idea from his mind, suddenly invigorated by the bubbles of his champagne.

— Why not? We're all the same, aren't we? We're all one, all the same unitary human and we just cultivate our differences to entertain ourselves to the point of starting wars.

But this sounded more like he was talking to himself.

He let his head fall on the photograph and remained there awhile, his arm stretched towards the ashtray where the smoke rising from the cigarette might be sending his question to God. Lifting his right eyebrow to contemplate the smoke, he remembered when he was a child in that Swiss home in Villars where Tante Betty, who ran the home, fancied putting a kettle on during the prayers.

— The vapour will help the prayers reach heaven! She kept on saying.

Maybe it was the smoke, maybe it was the contact of his forehead with the photograph, who knows? But suddenly Tenace had an answer. He raised his head and straightened himself back on the chair, remembering what Dickerdon had said:

— DNA! Organics! Carbon! Your fractal must be correlated to the flesh and bones!

At that time, he had not paid any particular attention to these words, so confident in his own ideas and particularly suspicious about Dickerdon's regular delirium dabbling-on about the fringes in the wood, which he reckoned as typical correlates of the tree's own life. He smiled. No! That was too far-fetched, cheap science fiction, he thought. But the thought did not go away; it stayed, blinding his eyes like the headlamps of a car driving towards him on the main road shortly before a collision. That was more than a delirium; that was a scientific hypothesis, and as such:

— It has to be checked, he caught himself saying, hitting the table with his fist.

If that was true, then he could recreate the Eigenfractal, the fractal specific to each human being from his very body.

— Even from corpses if you have to! added another voice inside of him.

That second thought froze him. His icy face then melted into a demoniac smirk and he jumped to his feet while the chair fell over behind him. He was suddenly overwhelmed by an unbearable feeling of impatience. It had to be checked quickly. He sensed an invisible claw pressing his throat, visions of an army of Frangiers intermeshed by an army of Gunters coming to arrest him.

Then he realised. This is why Dickerdon had given him the General Correlator software. He must have known, or was he just a correlation fetishist? Correlation as a general problem solver, a trump, the scientist's magic wand? And the concept of wand made Tenace think about Gunter's Billy stick and he rushed out, in need of immediate action. But the immediate action he was fancying could by no means be immediately perpetrated. It was a Sisyphus task! He'd not only have to ZEP scan at least a thousand conscious humans but also get hold of their DNA. You don't complete that in one night, even if your name is Tenace. Once you had this data, you'd have to launch Dickerdon's General Correlator on it, in the hope that this digital *chasse à courre* would bring back the mathematical function in the teeth of the hunting beast, the function that generates the Eigenfractal from the DNA.

How long would it take to crunch the zillions of digits? The amplitude of the job hit him like the car on the main road, and all his hopes went up into smokes again, smoke to heaven or ashes to hell?

Chapter 36: Sequencing

Jeannette did not quite understand why she suddenly had to cut the nails of some hundred patients, all spread around the entire clinic. Thank God, there were none from Block 13, the coma department, as she dreaded going there. It was a weird order, but what was even weirder is that she had to collect the nails and put them in little plastic bags tagged with the name of each patient. What she did not know is that all these patients had been volunteers in the antidepressant program initiated two months ago by Dr Tenace. He had called it Selective Psycho-reflection. All these patients were more or less cyclothymic, and Tenace had recorded their signals in the ZEP when they were in a good mood, and fed them back to them when they were in a low part of their cycle. The results were impressive. They felt jolly good afterwards. However, the relief only lasted a few hours. All in all, it was a rather cumbersome and expensive antidepressant therapy. It was actually no therapy because it did not deal with the cause, the patients just showed more signs of addiction to the ZEP signals after the therapy than their condition showed signs of improvement. So Tenace dropped the study. What remained of it was an interesting article for the Lancet, but Tenace did not submit it, being afraid of premature publicity that could mean more trouble than help.

Actually, what also remained of it was a collection

of recordings of the ZEP multi-signals of a hundred different patients! When Tenace woke up, the morning Mrs Van Brandstaetten was found dead in her bed, he recalled this collection of recordings and suddenly the huge task of collecting data for establishing a correlation between DNA and the Eigenfractal seemed much easier. He only needed the DNA of these patients. He jumped out of bed like a kangaroo, secretly congratulating himself for his own creative detours on the way to his goal.

He literally thanked himself with great humility for his apparent lack of focus in his research, for his escapades and lack of discipline. His humility matched in intensity the smugness and delusions of grandeur of the man he was worshiping, who knelt down in the mirror, namely himself!

It was as if all his moves and blunders had a hidden sense, which would ineluctably reveal itself at a later instant.

This was such an instant. He did not even have breakfast, but rushed to the clinic, put on a face of deep mourning when sister Ruth announced to him the death of Mrs Van Brandstaetten, nearly forgetting not to say: "I know", and headed to Mrs Jeannette to tell her to cut some nails.

Edmund was as grumpy as ever but when he saw Tenace, his face displayed a genuine smile. He trusted Dr Tenace, especially after he had treated his wife with the Selective Psycho-reflection, even though, as for the other patients, she was not really healed. Edmund saw its potential. Edmund was the lab technician of the Sequencing Lab of the clinic. He had been more than delighted to have been asked to participate in a project led by Dr Tenace, and when the latter gave him the bag full of 100 other small bags full of nails, his eyes widened and he accepted it like a Christmas present.

— Shall I cut my wife's nails as well, Mr Tenace?

Tenace looked at him with two huge interrogation marks printed in his eyes. They were saying something like: "Well, it's up to you if she needs it!" He recalled the context just in time and said:

— Yes! Great! We'll have a hundred and one sets then.

— I can only do thirty a day if nothing comes across, sir.

Tenace, who had expected a much longer delay, was grateful. He walked to the sequencer, remembering that the last time he had sequenced DNA, years ago, it had taken ages.

— Oh! A Siemens 610, when did they get that?

And without waiting for the answer he shook Edmund's hand:

— I'll come back Wednesday evening then, and remember, this is highly confidential!

Tenace spend the rest of the day studying Dickerdon's Great Correlator program. It was not only written and structured well; it was perfectly documented and commented-on, a masterpiece of precision. That was good, because Tenace had to make some slight modifications to match his own needs. Basically, the General Correlator was a neural network with a backpropagation subprogram. You gave it pairs of data sets and it would find the mathematical operation to transform one data set of the pair into the other one. This definitely makes little sense for a novice in the art, since frankly, what is the point of recalculating the second data set with the first one of the pair when you already have it?

The point is that once you have this mathematical operation, you feed the beast with a data set from which you do not have its counterpart. That was exactly the purpose of the machine. In this case you'd feed it with the DNA of someone you don't have the Eigenfractal for, and it would calculate it for you. That was the theory on which Tenace was betting. If it worked, he could calculate the Eigenfractal of the patients of Bloc 13 who had a flat Zepograph and verify that by irradiating them with multi-signals generated by this Eigenfractal, consciousness would come back to them.

It is probably quite unnecessary to mention that Tenace was excited again. That was good, because it gave him the energy and concentration to adapt the program in a few hours. The General Correlator which Dickerdon had originally named the "General Backpropagated Neural Network" - and he knew that because this original name was still in some of the comments of the program - the General Correlator was ready to accept the format of the Siemens 610, which Edmund had handed him that morning.

When Miss Margot told Tenace that Inspector Frangier had been at Bloc 13 in the afternoon, he shivered. He had the feeling that Miss Margot had noticed it, but he ignored it. With his eyes squared by the incessant looking at the monitor, he walked to Bloc 20 where the Sequencer Lab was. He had decided to use the underground corridors that united all the blocks of the buildings of the clinic. It was less conspicuous. What was going on his head that he felt so guilty of his research?

The lights went on and off, area after area: on when he came, off when he left, following him like a star on stage on his way to greet the public, except that in the fan crowd, there was only Edmund. But he was a great fan.

— Done them all Doctor! said Edmund with the expression of a good dog waiting for his pat on the back, which he got.

— I can cut my nails too! He added with a large grin that showed such impeccable teeth that they could only belong to a prosthesis. Tenace, who had to force his mood into joking, looked ostentatiously down at his hands and said:

— Maybe you should!

Edmund handed him a large hard disk marked "Babel", under which a list of pending patent numbers was printed, and he said:

— I want to have it back, James, as it's the only one which did not crash yet.

Tenace's still-squared eyes warped into two interrogation marks again. He wondered what kind of patents were pending if that darned thing turned so unreliable. His eyes then faded into exclamation marks as he commanded, like the clinic's boss he was:

— Give me the nails back, will you! And he added with a grin:

— For my personal collection!

Edmund delicately pulled the two banana skins and the cardboard coffee mug from the top of the bag in the wastepaper basket, and wiping off the coffee droplets from it with the hairy back of his left hand, he grabbed the knot he had tied at the top of the bag and handed it over to Tenace.

— Glad you don't collect bones, James!

That word made Tenace's spine backlash, and stopped his breath. He looked deep into Edmund's eyes and what he really wanted to say was: How come you know? But what came out was: What makes you think of that! And even that was a mistake. What was much more of a mistake was the strange grin that had covertly invaded his face. For a split second, Edmund got frightened, but Tenace, by that strange habit of duplicating himself, a habit he had been bred into as a child, managed to send the grinning Tenace down to the bottom of his shoes and shake awake all the empathic neurones of his system: The neurolinguistic programmer Tenace jumped to his feet and burst into laughter:

— Spooky eh! he said.

This all happened really fast, but Edmund got scared one last time before he managed to leave Scaryland. Now he was laughing, laughing all the more that he had been scared, wiping the fear off, like the coffee from the bag. What fear actually? He didn't, want to know, not anymore. Tenace should have been glad that he had won so easily. He wasn't; he nearly despised Edmund for being so gullible. To soothe his need for challenges and raise the wits of people he liked, he added, like a criminal prospecting the location of his crime:

— You always know where you start, but never where you end!

With that he left, overhearing Edmund muttering with a sad voice:

— Oh yes you do!

Chapter 37: Supper for Tea

He walked back the same way he'd come, the lights tracking him like the artist he was, back to his loge where he'd tune the last colours of his make-up and rehearse the last lines of his show for the next Act. Except there was no applause yet; surely at the end of the next one though. One could only hear the regular beat of his ray-skin shoes Ralf had gotten for him at half price, on the concrete floor of the underground corridor. He emerged in his own house, his own clinic house that is. He did not waste time walking up to his office but stepped straight outside. The cold air reminded him he had a body too, and this one was complaining. He pressed with his elbow the brown leather satchel in which he had slid the cybernetic gold, feeling like a smuggler in the no man's land between Customs and his gate, walking hastily on the timid skin of snow that covered the landscape, partly because he was freezing, but mostly because he was unbearably impatient.

The satchel nearly fell to his fish feet when he unlocked the door. As he closed it behind him, he stopped, slightly panting, squeezing his treasure against his heart now, slightly bent forward as if he'd been brooding it. Maybe he was, feeding the digital eggs through the leather with his unbreakable will, each time his heart beat, so that they would hatch. The ZOE3 would back-propagate the numerical alevins into his guts to tune his neurones and finally spit out the coveted

Eigenfractals out of any DNA sequence. Well, that is what he prayed for.

He lit a candle, and another one, as he cherished that when he was doing something special, like writing in his diary. That was healthier than lighting cigarettes. He slid the Babel ingot into ZOE3's rough, which greeted him with a mechanical grunt of pleasure. He first checked the files, the 101 files, and read the names of the patients:

Siroco, Penin, Zakrit, Müller of course, there is always a Müller. His heart missed a beat when he read his own name, wondering what on earth it was doing there. Then he remembered, it was his ex-wife. She had never wanted to take his name when they were married but had added it to her own when they had divorced. Well, added it before her own name. At first, it had flattered his insatiable ego, but soon enough he had realised she was just betting on his fame. She'd call herself Frau Dr Tenace-Schein if she was allowed. It helps when you check in at hotel desks. He'd have to correct this file name; you never know, in particular since Edmund had simply omitted the second name. But that darned Babel patent-pending ingot was write-protected and Edmund was driving on Road 109 right now, the 109 that runs in front of the clinic towards Zinkow, where Edmund lives, and where his ex-wife also lives. He gave ZOE3 a knife and fork by dragging the General Correlator icon onto the Babel's. ZOE3 started crunching avidly and did not ask for a napkin. Tenace was convinced that machines lived, thought, desired, and got angry like human beings. If you insulted them, they'd get back at you. But ZOE3 was hungry and pleased to finally get for tea something that tasted like supper.

Tenace, who knew how the program worked, was well aware that there'd be no result until sunset, but then it would come out at once, like a big plump out the arse of the monster. Digestion is a long process.

He thought of lying down on the ZEP bed and feeding himself with some of his own multi-signals, recorded when he was at the top of his mood, to cheer up and calm down, just like when you put on a good movie and have a nice drink. He reconsidered, since it would slow down ZOE3. Exhausted by the tension of the day, Tenace saw the big black curtain fall down on his eyes. *Entr'acte* it was. His head went heavy and dropped. It is not clear if he was still awake when it gently hit the table, but he slept with his pet, head to head, leaving the candles burning, right till the morning.

Chapter 38: Standard Deviation

The standard deviation was 0.86. Tenace liked the name, possibly because it was an acknowledgment by the scientific world of what he regarded as the utter essence of creativity. What he liked the most was the figure next to it. That was a great result, one you only got in textbooks. Tenace rejoiced, he had expected at most something like one sigma: 0.67 for the novice, a figure that would confirm the theory but not necessarily yield usable Eigenfractals. It was not quite two sigma, which started at 0.864, but it was jolly close to it. What this meant is that the Eigenfractals reconstructed by the General Correlator, using the meagre 101 samples Tenace had fed him, were very close to the real Eigenfractals of these 101 patients to which they were compared. That was excellent, and Tenace could hardly believe it. That was good enough to try the General Correlator on his comatose patients; that is, to calculate their Eigenfractals from their DNA.

By 9 o'clock, Tenace had made two phone calls, one to Jeannette and one to Edmund. In both case, he had made the call with the same opening: "Same procedure as last time", imitating the voice of the bottler from that movie the Germans love watching on New Year's Eve. Only the first name changed in each instance and poor Jeanette had to cut nails again, but now in Block 13, from the patients she dreaded, the ones who reminded her of her own mother.

Just after lunch, but Tenace hadn't had any, so obsessed was he by his project, he had their DNA sequences on the big Babel hard disk and by teatime, ZOE3 had spat out all synthetic Eigenfractals of the comatose patients of Block 13.

Tenace couldn't wait to try them, but he had to wait. Such a devilish enterprise could not be done during the day, should not be done at night and should not be done at all. It was if it worked, nothing less than digital black magic, sorcery going against the laws of God, resuscitation it was! No more nor less.

Tenace did not care. Well, he had cared too much. It was his toy and he could not wait to unpack it. He looked at the pictures of all the patients one by one, and stopped at Rosita Almeida de Barros. She had not been a cleaning lady but a dentist in Zinkow, where his ex-wife lives. On a Friday night just after midnight, she and her husband had been driving on that very road 109. Her husband had been driving; he was a dentist as well, and still is. Just after that bridge that spans the ponds, they had crashed into a tree, after having overtaken a car. The lorry that they had seen at the last second had no lights on and he had decided to head for the tree, especially since he did not know about it then. That didn't help much, or maybe it saved her husband's life, but Rosita lost consciousness, among other things, and never recovered. That was two years ago. Her husband, a Portuguese named Juan, who had been drinking on that night, fled into the woods. When they caught him, hours later, the alcohol in his blood was below the limit, and he got away with it. Except now, it is over the limit every single day of the week.

Tenace chose Rosita, not only because she was cute, but because he had the strange feeling that she was not that far behind the moron curtain. When he was close to her and talked to her, he always had this insight that she understood him but just couldn't answer. He somehow sensed that she did not really belong to No-lobe Land.

Someone had made a snowman in front of the former puppet theatre where Tenace takes the plate photographs every week. You could see it from his office as well. What was particular about it, is that it was sitting on one of the chairs left out there. Its shoulders were covered by a blanket. Tenace wondered who had made it and what meaning it had. It intrigued him because it was facing the windows and wherever you stood, it seemed to look at you like a witness of whatever would happen.

Perhaps it was just Tenace's paranoia, but he didn't like that snowman or snowwoman sitting outside and covered with a clinic's blanket. He had asked Gunter to destroy it, but Gunter had refused, saying he was not his boss. That had annoyed Tenace so much that shortly after the phone call, there was not much left of the snow-being apart from the blanket.

Tenace had decided to invite Ralf to the upcoming scientific party. That's how he named it. In the back of his mind he required him. If Ralf had declined the invitation, he would have pulled what was in the back of his mind forward, in one of his terrible fashions that made people feel they'd rather accept the invitation. But none of this was required for Ralf; he was just too eager to be on such a spooky boat.

Tenace had decided to start late, after midnight, just after Gunter's checking round. He took two pairs of infrared goggles that he had bought on the Internet. These goggles have a pair of integrated cameras and collimated displays in front of each eye, where the IR filter you usually find on cameras had not been installed. On top, a huge infrared torch on the forehead made them both look like miners, except they needed no pickaxe for what they intended to mine. The nurse had fallen asleep in front of the TV, as the subtitled Russian original version of Bulgakov's novel "A Dog's Heart", kept on irradiating her sleep. What a pity for her, thought Tenace, who loved the movie. In a split second, Tenace's face turned even darker than it was without the infrared. Wasn't he himself a Professor Preobrazhensky on the verge of implanting alien life into Rosita's brain? Alright, he wasn't implanting the pituitary gland and testicles of a drunken bum called Chugunkin into Rosita's crotch and head, but what guaranteed that this synthetic Eigenfractal he was about to beam on her while she lay flat on the ZEP bench, in the hope of making her regain consciousness, was not somehow alien, digitally alien?

He stopped, four strides away from the TV room. They had just caught Sharik the dog, just as he had caught Rosita. Tenace refused to view that synchronicity as an omen, but if it was an omen, why should it not be a good omen? An omen saying:

— Go ahead Jimmy, we're all waiting for you!

This is what Tenace preferred to think, specially as he heard some Russian voice say: *ochen horosho*! That was it, very good, *ochen horosho*, he agreed, greatly consoled by the fact that he, contrary to Professor Preobrazhensky, was not ripping any testicles from any Chugunkin on the planet.

It was a piece of cake to roll Rosita to the ZEP, although a sled or a sled-chair would have been far better than a wheelchair, given the snow that had fallen. Perhaps they have this in Finland. Tenace loved snow. What he particularly loved was the silence above it. Though snow remembered the footsteps, it caught and forgot the spoken words. It was freezing, and the blanket on Rosita was definitely not as warm as Tenace's fur coat which Ralf was sneaking looks at. A dog howled down below, by the cemetery, one of those running dogs. That's an omen too, thought Tenace with a smile. They hurried; Sharik was not to catch a cold.

They hurried and that seemed very appropriate, because they heard someone grunting. It came from above, near the kitchen. Tenace felt a slight rise in his pulse. He looked in that direction and saw someone approaching. They hurried more and that person was now shouting. It was Gunter. Tenace pushed the wheelchair faster, and as written in the book of mishaps, maybe the stupid wheels blocked, maybe Rosita's foot fell on the ground, but the damned chair stopped and Tenace's pushing only helped to tip it over, so that poor Rosita fell nose first into the snow. The chair came right after her.

By then Gunter was so close that it was not Tenace's priority anymore to pick up Rosita from the snow. Tenace had perceived something strange about Gunter, something that made him stare at him in the dark a few seconds. It was not difficult to guess, Gunter was drunk, and snow would remember the shape of his foot-track longer than it would take him to sober up.

— What the fuck are you doing here, you two? he muttered, barely in a position to counter the sudden fear that invaded him.

By then, Tenace and Ralf had picked up Rosita, who was sitting upright in her chair now, only she was so covered with snow that she looked like a snow-woman, a sitting snow-woman with a clinic's blanket on her shoulders. That similarity struck Tenace like lightning. Watching Günter's red face puffing its damp air like a steamer, he took advantage of it as well as of Gunter's drunkenness, both omens, he thought later on, and shouted right into his face: We're removing the snow- woman, the one you didn't want to clean up, Gunter. We're taking her for a walk, so she doesn't stare at us like you do!

Gunter did not know whether it was real or the effect of his beloved Jenever that he regularly imported from Utrecht, but looking at the sculpture packed on the wheelchair with a blanket on top, he had no doubt that the mad doctor was mad enough to take a snowman for a midnight trip on a wheelchair. Except that when that snowman's head moved and a brief mutter escaped from below, Günter's mind snapped and horrified, he buzzed off the straightest he could.

ZOE3 the dragon was now ready to spit its fire, forty-five minutes of consciousness, carefully bred from Rosita's Eigenfractal and generated by the neurones of the General Correlator, from the DNA of her nails. Mandelbrot was probably turning over in his grave, like the French say, possibly over to his French one.

Rosita was lying on the table-bed. Her lips were slightly swollen from the fall. Her white night dress with the word Falkennest sew on it on the left breast, looked like a frivolous tunic. This is what Ralf thought as he combed her blond hair before centring the helmet.

Tenace, sitting in front of the ZOE3's giant square face, was one click away from beaming small Rosa with 45 minutes of the fractally-generated multi-signal bouquet. It had been the third time that he was one click away. Somehow he couldn't depress that button on the remote control unit. He had been too much of a coward to face her, although that was the whole purpose of the RC unit. He turned around, looked at the nautical clock which showed it was two minutes to one, then peeped at the oval side opening of the ellipsoid. It looked like an egg, due to the dimmed yellow light inside the "fuselage", and he just couldn't start the show.

Something in the back of his mind made him hesitate again, even though he was so close. The red eyes came again, floating in the room and a symphony in NO major rambled up his ear. He shrunk in his own body to become little Jimmy again: He had no right to do that. What kind of monster was he taking the risk of giving birth to?

Perhaps Rosita was perfectly happy where she was. Perhaps she did not want to come back - come back from where, by the way? But something in Tenace made little whiny Jimmy vanish. The muscles of his jaws hardened, and a slight twitch appeared on his lips as his right eyebrow raised. He rubbed the back of his ear, gathering sweat and smelling it; that was good sweat, he thought. Suddenly, he realised the real meaning of his hesitation. He was not really questioning the general line of the task he had been preparing for months and years. There was just something missing. After having checked all the drawers of the medical closet in the attic of his mind, he jumped to his feet and shouted:

— Where is the reanimation kit?

He walked up to the ZEP and the sight of the beautiful Rosita lying there in her white Greek tunic, inviting everyone to kiss her swollen lips, made him blush. His eyes slowly scanned her thighs, whose shape just seemed to show the way and then up to her breasts, whose nipples were - God knows why - so erect that even the dress lining could not hide them. Tenace felt funny and ashamed.

— I'll go and get the defibrillator and the oxygen mask, Ralf!

Then he caught Ralf's eyes and there was something sleazy in them, something lubricious and mean, like he'd been up to something that no one wanted to hear about, because one has heard such things too often.

Tenace knew what Ralf had in mind, because that thing had caressed his mind a second ago, and he shouted, his finger pointed at him:

— Don't you touch her, my boy! Don't you dare touch that girl!

He was so angry at Ralf, angry as one can only get at oneself. Then, seeing that Ralf's sleazy look was still there, since it was always there, only that in such circumstances it was less than welcome, he decided.

— No! You go and fetch them!

When he was alone with her, he took her hand and said, bending over her forehead:

— I'm not sure you want this, little Rosa! Forgive my selfishness and ambition! Forgive me for calling you back, if I do, but I am a doctor and doctors always want to call patients back. It's their job.

Perhaps Rosa could hear him, as he secretly thought. Perhaps not, but reposing on that bed, she looked as calm as ever, as calm as they all are in Block 13.

As Ralf opened the door, loaded with the emergency kits, a bunch of running dogs barked in concert from below, like the ones tied up in front of the supermarket in Zinkow, except those ones had no one to wait for.Tenace was sitting on the stool his mother used to milk the goats on, back when he was a kid. He did not want to sit inside the ZEP, so as to not interfere with the waves. He held the remote control in his hand and was ready for countdown. He slid his finger on the button named "enter", finally depressed it, and wondered what kind of world he would be entering.

The coils of the ZEP at the other focus started to hum. He could smell the characteristic smell of warm copper and heated isolating resin. It smelled just like the transformer of the Scalextric racing car track of his childhood. The hum was catching the mirror panels of the ellipsoid and he did not like that because it could defocus the waves. It was the first time such a thing had happened. He'd have to damp those panels sometime. His throat hurt as if the top of his oesophagus had just caught a stenosis, if that had existed, but that didn't exist. His heart sped up and sweat was dripping again from behind his ears. He wouldn't smell it this time. He kept his eyes riveted to small Rosa's eyes.

He briefly looked at Ralf who was standing in the other oval opening, across him. Ralf was pale, and his eyes were moving right and left. He forced himself to look at Rosita but you could tell he just wanted to turn around and flee, flee out into the woods. He wasn't eager anymore to be on that spooky time vessel. He was just goddammed scared but he did not know what scared him the most, the experiment or that mad doctor milking a TV remote controller on his stool at midnight.

During the first few minutes, nothing happened. Somehow that was reassuring: Nothing happens! Nothing can go wrong! The heart beat was regular, the blood pressure was a bit high but it was alright. Tenace would have loved to glimpse the electroencephalograph, but it was dead, not because there were no signals though, but because it wasn't hooked up. The electrodes would get in the way of the waves and anyway they had close to nothing to pick up, at least so it had been so far for each patient of Block 13.

After the first tide of apprehension had retired, leaving the inert Rosita on the same sad beach of No-lobe land, a second tide followed, a tide of impatience. At the beginning of the sixth minute, Tenace was wagging his knees in front of him like a dog wags its tail.

He stood up and checked the monitor, which showed the thousands of coloured wires dancing like the reflections of blinking advert signs on dark water at night. Sweat was now drooling down his arm pits, and he regretted wearing his silly French undershirts called "Marcel" by the French. The lack of short sleeves did nothing to blot the sweat. He was trying to think. Maybe the emitting power was too low, but he didn't want to fry her. He checked that the coil head was at the right place and had not been dislodged by the zealous Olga wishing to clean under it.

It was one thing to beam multi-signals on a conscious person and observe the results, as he had done until now, but it was an entirely different thing to beam these signals onto someone who had been in coma for two and a half years. It was a bet, and by now, Tenace was not so sure he was going to win it. By the eighth minute, he was pacing the lab up and down like a chicken short of his head. Except that there was no blood gushing out of its neck hole, just blood in his eyes and it made them red. He walked up to Ralf and shouted at him:

— Get the goddamn thing ready. Turn it on and get the lid off the mouthpiece. Are you going to read the manual when she pops off?

Tenace knew it was unfair, he was just letting his temper out, but then again, that was fair, fair to him. He kept on thinking about the hysteresis, the cell hysteresis. And as he always does when he thinks hard, he spoke to himself aloud. But what came out was the cell hysteria and it annoyed him. He hit his left hand with his right one. And he started again, reading from his own manuscript stored in his memory, like a student from his textbook. Except it was his own textbook, and this thought made him justify himself. There is nothing wrong with that! he muttered. Just like there is nothing wrong when an author writes a critique praising a book, except perhaps, if he is the author.

Tenace knew the regaining of consciousness was something that had to be non-linear. Each of the cells was excited by the complex wave bundle that holographically acted on the organic volume. The cells reacted as if they were resonating at their own Eigenfrequency, like a huge bunch of tuned radios. According to his theory, in Theorem 6.6.6:

"The resonance of each cell should grow and grow till it goes over the inflexion point of its hysteresis at which point it reaches the level where it continues to vibrate on its own, that is without the effect of the incoming waves".

Further at Theorem 6.6.7: *"The Eigenvibrations of the zillions cells are then autonomous and that is consciousness".*

Tenace's near catatonic gaze wandered between the lines of his yellowish, highlighted text lines. At the third round around the fuselage, he dared to peep in at Rosa. What he saw stopped him: her eyes where moving right to left in a frantic manner. She was breathing intensively, like an exhausted runner. Exhilarated, he nearly walked into the ZEP to kiss her. Something was happening!

He looked at Ralf, who on his side, looked like he'd need a new pair of pants pretty soon. Then, her arms moved. Tenace stopped to breathe. The coils at Focus One were humming some tune, it seemed. Rosa's face got all red, Ralf squeezed the oxygen supply tube he was holding and then, a cry, a long weird cry came out of her mouth, a baby cry in an adult voice, something Tenace had never heard before.

Tenace started to shiver. Her body was trying to sit but she couldn't because that helmet was sticking her to the table. Her legs wiggled and she cried again. This time it really sounded like a baby, only it was much deeper, maybe like an old woman's voice who had been smoking too long, hoarse and guttural. Tenace's marrow melted. He wanted to stop, and press the exit button on his RC but there was no exit; you just enter, and this is no world you exit.

Then she relaxed. By now it was the forty-third minute. Her eyes turned to Tenace and she stared at him. There was suddenly life in her eyes. Life! Tenace's heart jumped as if someone had suddenly shifted the gear stick down to first gear on the highway.

An incredible heat flew through Tenace's veins and then, still looking at him, Rosita smiled, a genuine smile that only infants can have. Rosita had regained consciousness!

This certainly deviated from the standard!

Chapter 39: The Greylag Goose

Tenace smiled back at Rosita, and his smile was just as genuine as hers. The smile of a kid who had finally managed to plug the wires with the right polarity on his Scalextric racing track and had dried his tears, enjoying the first round of the British Green Jaguar Le Mans whizzing past the tribune of his eyes. But Tenace's smile was not a response to her smile. He had little left in his own consciousness to be touched by such a golden gift only mothers can get. Rosita could not tell the difference, a difference to what anyway? Something she did not even know about or had forgotten?

Tenace's egocentric intellectual orgasm eventually faded to actually give way to an emotion. He looked at little Rosa, still smiling, and a motherly instinct he didn't suspect himself to possess came out through every single pore of his skin, even the pickled ones.

He kneeled down next to her, squeezed her hands, then stroked her forehead. He was overcome by an immense need to kiss her, not on the lips this time, but on the cheek. He released her from the positioning helmet and helped her sit. Rosita cried again and swung her arm around his neck. Tenace felt like a mother having just given birth.

Wasn't it this innate incapacity of giving birth that made men restore old cars from scratch in a cold and muddy garage, and then call them Sweetie? Wasn't it that frustration and jealousy that made them design airplanes, rockets, televisions, write correlating software, books and spooky stories like this one, or create such monstrous machines as the ZEP?

One day, they'll come up with a bio-digital womb designed with the help of the most sophisticated CAD software. They will solve the differential equations of birth in a single horny night. They were actually well on their way, and had even passed the In Vitro central station. All this because the Lord had decided that their only contribution to birth should be those few minutes of fiddling around with the only finger women took seriously, at the furry main gate of Life Park, before snoring.

Indeed, Tenace had never felt that his modest contribution to procreation had entitled him to consider his son Bob, whom he loved so much, even partly as his creation, although big chunks of him were undoubtedly his design, but a design he had had no influence on.

After Tenace had resumed the disruption of the digital umbilical cord, by freeing her from the helmet, he noticed that his own eyes were wet. But that shouldn't be; he was a doctor. He was neither her mother nor her father, nor was he Konrad Lorenz and Rosita the Greylag goose. Pushing himself up, he repressed the emotion while seating little Rosa in her wheelchair. He had to carry on, on his racing track and there was no stand for whining, because this was no Scalextric track. Little Rosa felt that Tenace's soul had turned to steel, and an immense sadness invaded her face. She cried again, but for the first time in her new life it was with tears.

Neither Tenace nor Ralf was ready for all that. It was not in the manuscript. There was no theorem for that. They had just ordered a parcel from the wide web of the universe and it had come. But what they had received did not correspond to the description because there was no description. They wrapped the parcel back into its package, intending to roll it back to the shop, shop 13, with the other parcels, the unwrapped ones, because they were panicking. Only that this parcel was loud now; it was crying and the only thing Tenace thought of was to give it some sedative and let the nurse take care of it until it woke up. But little Rosa wouldn't drink from a glass.

By the time Ralf came back with the baby bottle, Rosita was asleep again. Asleep, or back where she came from? Although the question had slightly tickled Tenace's mind, he did not care. For the moment, he was just happy that the door he had forced open had been closed again by a gasp of cosmic wind, if only temporarily. Well, that's what he hoped for.

It freaked Jeanette out of her mind when she looked down to her feet to check what was grabbing her right calf while she was signing the night report. When she saw the naked back of Rosita on all fours, she jumped back, terrified. The terror warped into panic when Rosita raised her head to her with a begging look. They both stared at each other, still and silent for a minute, until Jeanette had regained some of her spirits.

Boy! She'd have to change this night report. By 9

o'clock, the entire clinic knew that something incredible had happened at Block 13.

Chapter 40: Juan Almeida de Barros

Tenace entered her room hastily, as if paying the obligatory daily visit to his patients in a huge hospital, the way he had done years ago. The routine had been indelibly printed into his mind and muscles, so that he could play it again like an automaton. That was handy. It helped him to hide. He grabbed the report board at the end of the bed, business-like. Sister Rebecca was following him. He pretended to look at the digits and notes on the pad. He was nervous, like an assassin confronted with his deed or his victim. Just that the victim in this case could also be a dead witness. Sister Rebecca had called him at home, early in the morning. He had played the part perfectly, an intelligent cocktail of astonishment, medical explanations and a drop of self-praise. Just a drop, which he had quickly known to mix with a joyful shake of congratulations to the team, as if the team had in some way been involved in Rosita's surprising "recovery".

He had come right away, as fast as his Mehari would allow. He had to. Now he was there, gesticulating like a chipmunk, pretending, lying, frowning, talking, shaking hands, giving pats on the back; the entire collection of bullshit invaded his habitus like the flush filled the basin of a toilet. He played the role he had rehearsed well, better than a politician. Except that the role was not quite written for this play.

Rosita looked at him and froze. Then, her eyes

widened, and her tranquil expression changed into a smile, just like when you meet a good friend, briefly though. The smile stopped half-way through and sadness made its way in. She then turned sideways, avoiding Tenace's look, expressing something that, even looked at sideways, resembled a sulk.

All this had lasted a second, the time it took to turn one's head sideways. Maybe it didn't even happen, only in Tenace's mind, carved by remorse and paranoia. Rebecca did not seem to notice.

— She cannot remember anything, Dr Tenace, she can't even speak! said Rebecca in a slightly trembling voice in which even Tenace could sense the pitch of pity. He folded himself fives time into what was left of him.

What had he done? Rosita's look reminded him of his ex-wife's look as he announced to her that he wanted a divorce. He felt like a mother annoyed by her new-born child, bad mother.

The person who walked into the room just after Tenace was someone who could very well compete with Tenace's bad conscious. This person was now standing by the bed. In his bad conscious tray, it was not clear which folder was on top, the memories of his own responsibility in the accident or the night he had just spent between the thighs of Svetlana. He had been warned by the nurse on the phone that his wife did not yet remember anything, and worse, that she seemed to have the mental age of a - and the nurse had hesitated before saying it- baby. This hesitation had paralysed

Juan. Despite the warning, he had come with expectations. But Rosita did not show any sign of recognising him as he walked in. She just started to turn her head right and left, uttering small guttural grunts. Juan felt tears running down his cheeks.

— Mr de Barros. It's great news! It's only the beginning. Tenace said, walking up to Juan, his right hand stretched for the obligatory shake.

Juan agreed and nodded, trying to show gratefulness and enthusiasm. The beginning of what? Hell? Spoon-feeding Rosita and teaching her how to speak? He never wanted a child and the thought of having his own wife as a child terrorised him. In his own Portuguese bigotry, he was convinced it was God's punishment. He was now looking at Rosita with a mixture of annoyance and pity, whereby the first aspect must have been the foam in the beverage because it was coming right up to the top and there was a lot of it, like in a draught beer from a Bavarian Inn.

— It's the start of a long journey, Mr Barros! added Tenace, who had intentionally forgotten the particle this time. Due to his Anglo-Saxon upbringing, Tenace had never accepted that nobility could be genuine anywhere south of the Alps and even less south of the Pyrenees. This omission annoyed Juan, as expected, but Tenace, who was convinced he knew his congeners better than his own self, soothed him in that hypocritical way he was such an expert in:

— I'm sorry this long journey will remain confined to the walls of this clinic Mr. Barros!

Tenace, perversely tracking through his black-framed glasses any sign of relief in Juan's eyes added:

— I can't promise you much, as we have little experience in this. It might be that the destination of this long journey will remain within the very walls of this clinic.

Juan did not answer and Tenace did not expect him to. He had detected that sign of relief in Juan's mind, and Juan had guessed he had. He just wanted to leave. Wake up from the nightmare. But he kneeled down to Rosita and took her hand. Rosita let him take her hand and she looked at him in the eyes and smiled. It was a smile Juan did not recognise from her and his frozen heart cracked slightly, like when you walk on the ice of a frozen lake and the ice is still thin. He did not want to fall in. He moved back, and then left, his beret in his right hand. He was more a mess than ever.

Chapter 41: One-Way Street

When Tenace left Rosita's bedroom, he had only one thing in mind: Carry on. He couldn't explain why Rosita had decided to start life all over again. His first thought was that the Eigenfractal didn't include memories. But that did not quite fit. He could envisage a loss of memory coexistent with a mature brain. Patients awakening after prolonged coma with a complete loss of memory did exist, but they could talk, eat and think like a grown-up. Tenace had been puzzled the entire day by the unlucky fall-out of Rosita's awakening, and to be complete, of the entire previous night.

Suddenly an awful thought crossed his mind, immediately followed by strong waves of guilt. He began to suspect that he had made a terrible mistake. But then again, that was not sure, well, he hoped he had not made this mistake. His breath shortened and he started to sweat heavily. I am just an amateur, how could I have not checked that? The horrible suspicion was turning into certainty as he walked like a Nordic walker without the sticks to his ZOE3.

He had forgotten to set a date for the fractally-generated multi-signals and the damn program, instead of asking for a date, had taken the default value, which was: zero. Birth, that is! Rosita had been beamed with the consciousness of a new-born baby! Christ! He could have punched himself, plugged his fingers into his eye sockets and broken his fingers afterwards. He hated himself. What a goddamned mistake! He opened the program on the screen to check what date had been taken and he was bloody right, it started at t=0! Then, his self-bullying changed into hope:

- That was great news! he thought. It confirmed the theory, and the next patient was going to wake up with mature consciousness. That was written in stone! He laughed, and shouted with joy and hope. He had completely forgotten Rosita by then and was obsessed with carrying on his project at all cost.

He felt like the kid he used to be. After weeks and months of building a circular-flight model aeroplane and days of trying to crank the 0.5 cubic engine, he was ready to fly it. It had to be now, at the cost of breaking it, like he had broken his plane after half a circle, as it crashed into the ground trying to counteract its too-steep take-off. But this time, he would not counteract the too-steep take-off. He was now picking up the next patient down the lane, from the menu.

It was going to be Ronald. The average facial expression of his life was well-printed on his face. This print was jovial and calm, carried by a still sporty body. It was a wonder that even after six months of inactivity, Ronald's muscles remained in such good shape. Tenace chose him because he made a steady impression on him, and if something went wrong again, Ronald was not the kind of guy to morph into a Greylag goose.

Tenace couldn't afford to wait. He knew he had to pull his patients out of coma in a row. If one case of regaining of consciousness could be put to the account of miracle or chance, the second case would definitely raise suspicion, and the third would seal the conviction that Tenace had his fingers in all this. And then, the establishment or *folie populaire*, which-ever came first, would watch him and stop him. On the other hand, if he woke them up fast enough, by the time they reacted, he'd be through. He'd have to give explanations but he'd be through with Act I and no one would ever stop him. It was a one-way street and he had to take it, the wrong way around.

The second one for the night was Müller. He hated the name, but it was a name anyone could relate to. Anyone could be Müller and that was good PR. It was the same procedure as for Rosita, except it would be a longer night because there were two.

This time, Tenace asked about Ronald's date of birth and set the time cursor of the multi-signal fractal generator to his real age on that night. He had not told Ralf about the mistake with Rosita. He had just assured him twice that Ronald would wake up with his full mind.

It was the thirteenth minute after countdown and nothing had happened. Tenace, who was worried like as if the constables were going to seize his house the next morning, did not show an inch of it. He waited, externally inexpressive, watching the coloured signals dance on the screen, hypnotised. Possibly he dozed away a split second like you sometimes do on the highway, because he woke up at the sound of a deep voice he did not know, saying:

— What the fuck am I doing here? What's this on my head?

Tenace jumped to his feet and literally leapt to Ronald, then removed the positioning helmet and helped him sit up.

— Ronald, my name is Dr Tenace, in charge of you. Everything is under control; you have just regained consciousness after a tragic accident.

Tenace was smiling warmheartedly, at least the most he could, shaking his hands and patting him on the back.

— How is it to be back, Ronald? Call me James! I'm so glad you can talk.

He then asked him to touch each of his fingers with his thumb or the other way around, as you like it. He then asked him to move his legs, his feet, his arms, turn his head right and left, stand up.

Ronald obeyed and was fine and Tenace was incredibly happy and proud.

— Looks like you'll be back to work on Monday, Ronald!

But Ronald, who had been able to understand and execute Tenace's orders, who had been able to talk, would not say a word more. He looked afraid, lost, alone, like someone new and lonely in a group of strangers. He stared at Tenace and asked:

— How did you say you called me?

— Ronald! Ronald Jameson! Isn't that your name, sir?

Ronald took some time to answer.

— I suppose it is, of course it is! What am I thinking of? Yes, Ronald Jefferson.

Tenace realised. It was high time to realise it. But sometimes you don't want to face the truth because it doesn't suit you. Ronald, who had all his intellectual and physical faculties back, missed one feature: his memory, at least chunks of it, so it seemed.

— Ronald, we're going to bring you back to your room now and Sister Ruth is going to take care of you. We have to cross a little park and it's cold outside, but Ralf will cover you up with warm blankets. It won't be long and it's nothing for a sportsman like you.

Ralf stared at Tenace and whispered in his ears:

— How about the 'good-night drops'?

Tenace was fed up with hiding. He wanted the nurse to take care of Ronald immediately. He wanted to take Müller on the way back from the clinic to the Zep, right in front of the nurse. He had enough of playing hide and seek, of beaming the patients at night, like a criminal, just because the medical establishment was scared, conservative and jealous. He had succeeded; he was a great scientist and a great doctor and this had to be known. He looked at Ralf with a very nasty look, as if Ralf were his deadly enemy, and shouted at him:

— You can take them yourself! We'll wake up

Sister Ruth if she's already asleep. She'll have something to do finally! I'm not putting up with this masquerade anymore!

Ralf's body expanded, he stood in front of Tenace like a cock ready to fight, and defiantly replied:

— It's too early, Dr Tenace! They'll stop you! Wait till you got them all back. Let them wonder why they wake up night after night like eggs hatching.

For the first time in his long cooperation with Dr Tenace, Ralf had opposed him. Tenace was furious, and turned red. He was looking for words but couldn't find any. He was dumbstruck by Ralf's audacity. Tenace had just started the engine of his little model airplane, it was roaring and this wimp Ralf was telling him to stop, so he didn't hear when Ralf added:

— Dr Tenace, I'm in for it as much as you are, and I don't want it to flunk because the head of the federal health services tells you to stop, and probably fires you... and me!

Perhaps did Tenace hear the last words but what he saw was his Flying Badger crash into the ground. That's the name he had given to his model airplane. He saw himself pick up the broken wings and the smashed Baby Bee engine. His look focussed again on Ralf, and then on Ronald, who very elegantly asked from his wheelchair:

— Shall I leave you alone?

Tenace burst into laughter, a nervous laughter like the one he had as a child when he was told that his mother had died. He regained some of his spirits, and bending his head forward, he agreed.

— Alright then, you're probably right!

Like after an edit cut in a film, Tenace was metamorphosed. He smiled again, and turning round to Ronald he said:

— Ronald! My assistant is going to give you some medicine, highly appropriate for patients recovering from coma. I'd be very pleased if you would take it right now.

Ronald didn't even see the snow or feel the cold air, as he was away in Morpheus's arms within five minutes, and in his own bed within ten.

They came back with Müller. Müller was small, with grey hair on the sides of his head, tanned, but not by the sun - it was his natural skin colour. You got the feeling this guy had been used to giving orders. He was impatient, egoistic and probably mean. His facial print said so. He had been a foreman in some German car assembly line at the time they were still assembled in Germany. He had slipped on an oily spot while shouting at the guy who was installing a gear box. He fell backwards, hitting his head on the concrete floor, more precisely on a concrete step that separated the mounting platform from the regular floor. He had never shouted afterwards, and that was two months before he was due to retire. Tenace had the feeling that the guy would wake up like just like Louis de Funès in the film *Hibernatus*.

He reminded him of the actor. He expected that

you just needed to press the right button and the coil spring would unwind, activating the puppet with everlasting energy. Tenace had this button. He was actually just pressing it on the RC Unit.

Müller woke up way before the normal time, and it was not a piece of cake to make him drink the sedative. He threatened Tenace with lawyers in that stubborn Bavarian accent Tenace was so allergic to. Tenace nearly regretted choosing him as the third patient, but one thing consoled him: this guy had not lost a drop of his memory.

They did Frau Ines Sauerblut the same night, so eager were they to get the numbers in, and since three was Tenace's magic number. They had not been caught taking the one-way street.

Chapter 42: Madame Lavenue

The call had not woken him up, as he was awake. The call had run through his spine all the way up to his semi-somnolent brain and had woken up that part of the brain which didn't want to be woken up. He felt the call was no good news. In a sort of multidimensional linear prediction based on the recent events, he had expected it.

There was no preliminary politeness, neither in the choice of the words nor in the tone in which they were spoken. The Federal Minister of Health in persona went straight to the point in a firm voice which left no room for questions:

— Dr Tenace, I expect you at 9.30 in my office.

Tenace did not have time to say a word; Madame Lavenue, usually friendly and tactful, had just put the phone down, leaving no other choice to Tenace than to follow for once her example.

The only visible reaction that these words had triggered in Tenace's wakening brain was to press his "Heudebert" rusk against the slightly elevated rim of his plate until it broke. He then faced the difficult choice of patching the bits together again with butter or pursuing his destruction to the point of grainy powder that anyone would hate to find between his sheets.

The dilemma was probably an unconscious

metaphor for the puzzle he was soon going to have to solve. He opted for the first approach: Fix it!

He needed the job, the lab, the access to the facilities, and he needed to save his reputation. He couldn't just tell her what he thought of her, that she was just a parasitic public servant whose only power was to say "No!" instead of saying "Yes, Sir!" like all servants do.

His mind drifted back forty years, when he was sent to the Principal after having held a political meeting and spoken through a handheld megaphone in front of three hundred students. It was the same feeling. He was proud of himself, and grey, dusty zombies were trying to turn this pride into shame. He then drew two small circles on the butter-smeared rusk with the honey tube, then a mouth and some curls on top. These were Madame Lavenue's goggles, the ones she permanently wore to survive in her file aquarium on the second floor of the Federal Ministry.

Then the words of Dickerdon sounded in his ears, the very ones he had made sure to regularly mock, because they were so true:

"Our biggest enemy, to all of us who belong to the crowd of creative and above-average intelligent people, is the envy of the mediocre. Instead of rejoicing at something new and great, they get hit twice, first by fright and then by a feeling of being worthless!"

For the first time, Tenace didn't mock Dickerdon's litany; rather, it was his salvation. Dickerdon dropped out of University and he, Tenace, was a Doctor, a certified representative of knowledge and intelligence. His eyes dropped to the rusks and Madame Lavenue's face became real. She started talking:

— Mr Fleming, I don't want to see such a mess in your lab. You can't leave everything mouldering on like that while you take days off! This is not the way to make discoveries!

Tenace first laughed, and then in an outburst of rage he punched Madame Lavenue right in the face. He stood still for a while near the kitchen sink, gazing through the window. Rusk was glued to his fingers like bad memories. It was dawn on the lawn but he wished it was dusk, so he could fall back into the night and forget. He turned on the warm water tap to slowly melt the sticky honey off his fingers.

He drove. The engine kept him company like a big warm bear grunting at each end of a curve, not the British Petroleum lion though; it was fifty years dead now. He rejoiced at not having bought one of those hybrid or electrical cars which go dumb as a fish at a red light. It would surely have made him feel even more vulnerable and lonely in this morning grey desert. He even enjoyed each asperity, each stone on the road, as they shook his knuckles and vertebras to remind him he was alive.

He had plenty of time to cook up a strategy, rehearse his sentences, prepare the answers to the most obvious questions. It would have been the right thing to do, but Tenace was not in the mood for doing the right things. He'd had enough of this; he was in the mood for pulling the table cloth down to the floor and throwing all the guests out. Madame Lavenue's predictable petty speech and list of rules he had probably broken would go down with the cutlery and the Sunday mint-sauced lamb. His last conscious thought was that Lavenue was not going to stop him. After that, he fell into a hypnotic motorised coma that barely enabled him to drive. That was it for the strategy.

She didn't await him with a copy of "The Daily Rubbish" spread across her desk, headlined: "A new Doctor Frankenstein in our State Hospital", nor did she stand up facing the window, sadistically planning the instant when she would turn around and spit it out. Instead, she calmly sat at her desk with hardly any sign of anger and opened her mouth.

At first, it seemed to Tenace that no words came out of it, she just kept on opening and closing her mouth like a fish gobbling in an aquarium, then Tenace started to hear words:

— Dr Tenace, it is a bit of a coincidence that within a week, seven of your patients have recovered from a prolonged coma. I'm sure you have an explanation for this other than blue aspirin pills. I am very eager to listen to you.

Tenace waited, but it seemed like this time no words wanted to come out of his mouth. He looked at the big bookshelf panel Madame Lavenue had on display, full of books ordered by colour it seemed, one metre of red, half a metre of brown and the other way around on the shelf underneath.

— God, Mrs Lavenue! he finally uttered.

She stared at him, expressionless, and lit a cigarette.

— God, or the Devil, Dr Tenace?

— Aren't they both sides of the same thing?

— For wicked doctors like you Mr Tenace, definitely not for me!

Tenace smiled slightly and his gaze suddenly froze as he was staring at a point obviously behind her, and in a low monotonous voice he asked:

— For you as the Head of the Ministry of Federal Health --

— Federal Ministry of Health! she interrupted.

— Or for you as Mrs Lavenue?

— Dr Tenace, I'll tell you, I, Ignace Lavenue, am totally revolted by your experiments and my dearest wish would be to beam you with the soul of a dog so that you can sit and bark next to your patients for the rest your days. What you have been doing is obnoxious!

Tenace was petrified. That bit about the dog hit him. He still managed to stutter:

— Beam? How do you know?

He felt himself shrinking into his own body, unable to react, to compose himself. He was the little boy again being told off by the headmistress for having been caught kissing a girl under the bed during a school trip. He just stammered:

— I am... I am... without being able to finish.

But then, Mrs Lavenue's myopic eyes, so small behind her huge goggles that she surely reads the paper holding it behind her neck, suddenly flip-flopped within her aquarium and a small mysterious smile appeared on her lips.

— But, as a doctor, Mr Tenace, I am highly interested, actually fascinated from what I know of this little hobby of yours, which happens to turn out into a *Meisterwerk*!

By then, Madame Lavenue was shouting. She had lost control of herself a split second and that split second was enough for Tenace. He couldn't believe it. He was trying to shrink the emotional distance he had so painfully built up between him and her, trying to catch up with the full savour of her words.

— I am even proud of you, James!

Madame Lavenue paced up and down her office, as excited as Tenace was perplexed. Proud! The compliment melted him. What? Had he heard correctly? He was a good little boy after all?

He would have fished for some more, if it hadn't smelled fishy. And then, as in a perfect Hollywood story revised by Syd Field, the third plot point came:

— However Dr Tenace, as a Head of the Ministry of Federal Health, as you put it, I cannot tolerate that!

There she screamed so vigorously that there was

no doubt that she meant it:

— You have one month, and I am very generous, to dismantle your ZOB and remove it from the clinic.

— ZEP, Mrs Lavenue.

— And if there is one more "resuscitation" that I hear of, that I hear of, she repeated in an ambiguous manner, you'll have to beam yourself into another doctor at the clinic if you still want to work there!

Something uncontrollable happened in his mind. Without being able to stop it, he spoke in a voice he did not recognise as his own, words that he thought someone else had put together, but words which would reveal themselves as extremely useful later on:

— Mrs Lavenue, it's too late. They are all on their way!

She looked at him in a mixture of exasperation and admiration.

Chapter 43: Resuscitation

Of course, it was a lie. A lie only the Devil could have shoved into Tenace's mouth, a very handy lie like lies always are. It was only after a quarter of an hour drive, crossing the forest on Marrow Road that Tenace realised that this little paragraph of his was no less than a *laissez-passer*, no doubt a forged one, for the little enterprise he had in mind.

And like an Englishman shortly before eleven o'clock, gulping down all the beer he can at the call "last orders", he beamed all the patients of his department in the very week following his meeting with Madame Lavenue.

To his utter satisfaction, 67 percent of them regained their spirits, well, the spirits of their nails. With their memories, that was another story. He'd need to work a little more on that but he had no time. Lavenue's fault. Another doctor would have probably postponed the therapy, unwilling to take the risk of bringing the creatures back to life with their pasts left behind. But Tenace hurried them on the train as if it was the last one, with or without their suitcases. Possibly he even thought it was better that way because he himself sometimes wished he had no such luggage as his past.

Was he doing them a favour? He perhaps had a favourite answer to this question but right then, he did not really care. He kept on loading them on the train, one batch after the other, end station: Lostness, one stop. He was not Mengele or that Russian doctor from Bulgakov's dog's life novel. He was just the Station Master, with no cap on, in the cold night of Science. What would become of them was none of his business. It was the nurse's business to assist them, to dry their tears and take them by the hand, which was more interesting than changing the nappies of vegetables. He still had this outdated frame of mind as to the role of women, hug and console the wounded while the unwounded warriors would wound the ones of the other tribe.

It was Friday now and though Tenace had ordered a party to celebrate his success, he had one more thing to do. He had dodged all the nurses by telling them the story of his magic pill, results of years of research. The pill was nothing else than an aspirin tinted with methylene blue. He had made sure the nurses administrated the pill to the patients on the evening he'd take them to the ZEP, and anyway the ZEP did give a bit of a headache.

After he had done the last patient, Mr Robertson, all alone this time because Ralf had gotten scared, Tenace set out on the most difficult part his project. It is possible that this part was the very motivation for all his research. He wanted to understand himself, his depressive and self-loathing cycles, the mountains of guilt he regularly had to climb. He was convinced they had something to do with his childhood, his oblivious childhood, but the secret of his childhood lay in a grave, in the grave of his mother half a mile away, down in the cemetery below the clinic. He wanted to watch the forgotten film of her life, to understand what had indelibly marked him for life. This film was not referenced in IMDb but was engraved in the bones and nails of the remains of his mother, or so he thought, and he intended to get them.

He set out shortly before 6 pm with his pickaxe and shovel. He did not ask for the moon to be full, but it was full, and the dogs howled in the night, just like in all horror movies of this kind. Though it was a short walk to the graveyard, when he knelt down in front of the grave, he was exhausted. Sure, he'd had to climb over the wall and had sung "Jack and Jill went up the hill" on up to the top of it, since the undertaker had judged it wise to lock the little iron gate that leads to the clinic's park, after what had happened a month ago, but that was not reason enough for him to be so knacked.

Tenace was exhausted because he was afraid, and that fear was draining every bit of strength he had in his body and soul. He was afraid of what he was going to discover, not so much in the grave but in the nails that he would find there.

Years of suffering and bad memories were draining out through each pore of his skin, he was panting and his head ached. He was going to confront her, not on her deathbed but in her grave. Better late than never. He was drowned in sweat.

The first blow did not achieve anything except a spark. The sound of a motorcycle made him pause. As it drove away he realised how stupid it was to hit the stone. He plunged the long arm of the pickaxe into the earth at the side of the stone and pulled the stick towards him. He did it eleven times all around the stone and it finally moved. He thought he heard someone whistle, so he forced himself to breathe deeply to calm down, then without warning, he fell on the tombstone head first. When he regained consciousness, he was so wet with sweat that he felt cold. Those engraved letters slapped him in the face again because they seemed to be written for him to read in this very moment:

"Let fame, that all hunt after in their lives, Live register'd upon our brazen tombs!"

Someone had made the mistake of adding an exclamation mark. The tomb was definitely not brazen but of some cheap concrete. He heard the wind stroke the trees behind him like the breath of some gigantic creature. Frightened, he grabbed his flask, the same flask he had taken along while burying his dog. And then, in an immense concentration of strength, he turned the tombstone over. Worms of all sizes and shapes wiggled under the moonlight. He felt nauseated. Were they the guardians of the secret? He took another sip to warm up his frozen heart, but that didn't help much.

— Mother! Mother! What did you hide from me? What secret did you take along to your grave? I am here to bring it back to light!

And the dogs howled again. Tenace was panting more than ever, disgusted, furious and afraid. He dumped the pickaxe and grabbed the shovel.

— Mother! I am going to cut that infernal chain of

traumas that we inflict on our children. I don't want my son to inherit any of your self-destruction drive. I want to know what was with you!

Tenace plunged the shovel into the nest of worms again.

— I shall disrupt this chain!

But then there were more silvery worms wiggling on the damp earth and Tenace wept. Though there was no need to light any of the candles he had brought along, since the clouds had gone, Tenace stabbed them into the earth between the worms in a circle and lit them. A re-birthday cake, he thought, watching the last warriors dancing under the candle lights. He then started to dig and this was no more a piece of cake. After thirty minutes of swinging the shovel, he finally reached the coffin. Though Tenace was tall, his head barely reached the level of the ground above.

There was a metal handle on the coffin, like on house doors. He lifted and banged it on the coffin wood three times. He giggled, turned towards an invisible camera and said:

— Knock! Knock! Who is there? Ma, Pa, I'm paying you a visit!

— But the knocks on the coffin had completed what the combination of time, humidity and worms had done to the wood. They transformed the remains of its fibres into wet dust. The last knock went through and opened a hole through which Tenace could see the skeleton.

Boy! That was a change from the last time he had seen her lying in her coffin some forty-five years ago. He stuffed two candles in the eye sockets because they would stay there, and started to enlarge the hole first with the shovel then as he noticed the wood was like butter, with his own hands. His eyes swayed across the skeleton.

He had never seen her naked and now she was more than bare. He had intended to take a bone sample, but to his surprise, the nails were still there, just a little longer. Nails don't grow when you are dead. It suited him because the prospect of amputating the skeleton revolted him. He was suddenly disturbed by some grunting noise above, and before the adrenaline had completely reached his heart, he saw a Doberman's head snarling at him from the edge of the grave. The bastard jumped in, snapped up a femur and with prodigious strength managed to jump out using Tenace's back as a ladder. At the same time, his mobile phone rang. It was Edmund and he was drunk:

— What's that with the bone James? I can't do that, the probe is too small. I never did bones, James.

Tenace, turning over some of his mother's nails in his left hand, said:

— It's alright Edmund; it's nails again, but I need it flash Edmund, tonight!

And then Tenace could hear the giggle of a woman on the line.

— Tonight? You got to be kidding. It's Friday

night. I'm off!

Tenace's face warped into a devilish grin, his eyes went astray and big. His mouth deformed itself, as driven by intense pain and he said in a cavernous voice, which frightened himself even more than Edmund:

— Edmund, you know! Your son can start his training at the palliative department next week!

There was silence on the line. Edmund took time to understand, but he finally did. Crows were circling above the graveyard and then Edmund's timid voice, suddenly sobered up, fried down the line:

— Ok James, exceptionally! Then the voice went slurry again:

— 'Cause you're a great doctor!

Edmund was obviously still fighting to get his spirits back and ready for the job, but Tenace was not much better. Though definitely more sober, he did look like a cheap zombie from a B-movie out for a spin among the livings. His head and hands were dark, like the mud he had been ploughing, only dried out. The right sleeve of his felt blazer was burnt and big wax spots decorated his trousers between his thighs. He handed Edmund three nails, still his favourite number, but this time there was no plastic bag. They came straight from his pocket. Edmund's eyes bulged out of their sockets, to complete the impression of utter fear that already emanated from his entire being after the quick look he had given Tenace. Edmund did not want to know, and in particular, he did not want to know where Tenace had been.

— You stink, James!

— You do too, Edmund!

— Well, it's Friday night.

— No, I don't mean the booze but that cheap brothel perfume!

Edmund looked away, and if there had been a mirror on the side Edmund was looking, he would have seen a slight shadow of shame on his own face.

— Edmund! You don't know how grateful I am. It's the best thing you can do for me. I'll tell you why later if God allows.

Edmund turned around, suddenly worried, and rushed to the sink to clean the nails.

— Where on Earth did you get these from?

It seemed again like Edmund knew, knew a hell of a lot more, that the nails had come from under the earth but he kept his mind as silent as the grave he guessed it came from. When Edmund tapped on his shoulder, Tenace was in the middle of a nightmare. He was skiing right against a tree and couldn't avoid it. He was about to hit it with his shoulder and Edmund's pat probably spared him the full dimension of the impact against the tree. But then again, he could not remember having ever experienced physical pain in dreams. Edmund handed him another of those hard discs.

— Spooky DNA for spooky Doctor!

Although it was past 9 pm, Tenace felt an acute sense of urgency. He wanted to know before the party! He rushed to his lab, shoved the disc in and lit a cigarette, waiting for ZOE3 to spit out the Eigenfractal of his mother. He put one of his favourite vinyls on the record player: PIL, and puffed smoke out the window towards the moon. When ZOE3 beeped, he slowly walked towards the screen to read: Eigenfractal reconstructed. Tenace then typed a date: 4th of April 1968, the date of his tenth birthday, just a guess that it was a relevant time, and got ready. ZOE3 was now calculating the multi-signals up to that time, letting the Eigenfractal digitally breed in its silicon wafers. He lay down on the table-bed of his ZEP, awaiting the effect of his shot. After he had locked the helmet, he closed his eyes.

Chapter 44: Happy Birthday

It is a very strange experience to suddenly have the consciousness of someone else, especially someone you know or have known, like your own mother. You start by feeling completely lost and frightened, a bit like you were on a mescaline trip, except that no one is deformed, your surrounding is not warped into an Escher world, and you don't stare at a white wall for hours, fascinated by its asperities becoming alive in your sight.

Tenace's mind oscillated between his own consciousness and what must have been his mother's. He was flooded by memories, but it was not clear where these came from. According to his own theory, neither the Eigenfractal nor the multi-signal it generated and which was frying his brain right now did comprise memories. They comprised just a state of mind, a mood so to say. Hence, and this is at least how he explained the phenomena later: what he saw and felt during the ZEP session must have come from his own memory, just lit up alternatively by his mother's consciousness and when its energy got lower in the chosen time window, by his own consciousness that would then resurface. A state probably quite schizophrenic, and somehow similar to that of a child confronted with the strong will of an adult succeeding in imposing his view on him. At first, Tenace felt seasick in that boat, recurrently doubting of his identities to the point of rejecting both. It would have been painful to watch his body convulse, because it looked as if he had been tortured by electric currents, which is exactly what happened though with much less amperage, but there was no one to watch.

Eventually he became calm, possibly too calm. He lay there immobile, staring at the ceiling of the ZEP in a state close to catharsis.

He saw a long room with a wooden floor and a low white ceiling. The wall facing the three windows was full of books, some piled, some standing on the shelves. It was dusk, and you could tell from the perspective of the branches swaying in front of the milky-red background of clouds, a few metres away from the window, that the room was on the first floor. Next to the middle window was a grey wooden desk with legs made of various iron circles welded together like the Olympic logo. A big dark-green long-haired Berber carpet lay in front of the desk along the bookshelf. It must have been summer because the middle window was open. Sounds of someone chopping wood down below came clear and loud.

On the desk was a typewriter. Written in big silvery letters was: "Royal de Luxe". For some strange reason, Tenace's perspective was about 1.30 metres above the ground, and it moved forward and backward, then along the books. He heard the strokes of the letters on the paper, but there was no one sitting behind the desk. Then suddenly he must have been sitting at the desk himself, because his nose was so close to the sheet of paper that he could smell the rubber roll. He suddenly fell ill at ease, tense, and he sensed the immense inner pressure to type. He was suddenly looking for words to prolong the sentence typed on the paper. He was typing!

It must have been a story he knew, because the sentences were familiar. He typed as if he knew the text by heart. He realised it was the manuscript of an unfinished novel his mother had written. He had read it years ago. The words were alive, like little animals; the "I's" had an eye on their stem, the "o's" were like the mouths of fish gobbling water and the "m's" were gnawing. That he was sure of. Then the whole room went down or his perspective rose, whichever, but the typewriter was still in front of his nose, floating under the ceiling with him, and the words now shouted at him. Then the room whirled around him but his nose was still stuck to the paper. He was now rolling and tumbling together with the machine. He heard mother shout:

— It's all rubbish. I should do the dishes. But there are no dishes. They're all in the dishwasher.

A smell of port wine reached Tenace's nostrils.

The Thai bells rang outside as the wind struck them, soon followed by the hacks on the logs like the drums of an orchestra. Little Tenace glimpsed timidly through the window and saw a man hacking some logs. Five hens were picking at the sparse grass. Suddenly little Tenace was projected back to the door he came through. He could see his mother standing up in front of the desk now. She looked furious, both hands on the sides of the typewriter this time, long white hands with red nails scratching the entrails of the typewriter and it started bleeding or was it her hands? Then he saw the paper again, with a yellow undertone and the hammers of the letters banged on it like a machine gun that made little Tenace's back arch as the letters paraded in rhythm before his eyes like soldiers:

"I thought I had bred eagles but they are just poultry; not even, just beheaded hens!" He read.

This time little Tenace bent forward, for his stomach ached. His mother's face had warped into an ugly mixture of hatred, contempt and despair as she stared at him, repeating the written text:

— I thought I had bred eagles but they are just poultry; not even, just beheaded hens!

And adding in a mutter:

— I gave up my career for you!

Little Tenace became even smaller than he was. He remembered the first sentence, he had heard it once and that was once too many. He didn't understand why she was saying that to him. He was so small, after all, and he had always had good marks at school, at least for him. An intense feeling of guilt invaded him; he became a tree for a second, a dry and broken tree struck by her lightning. He could not move, nor cry nor breathe. He neither wanted to be an eagle or a hen; he just wanted to go back to his Scalextric race track and see if the sidecar would win against the BRM this time. He felt tears run down his cheek but he wasn't crying. No, he wasn't! Then he realised he'd never be an eagle even if he wanted to, because she had just decreed so and he didn't want to disobey.

Maybe she would love him if he didn't disobey. So he'd remain a hen, and endure her contempt for not becoming an eagle, just to be loved.

That was now written in his spine; the letters had burned their imprints in his marrow like the glowing iron on the back of a sheep.

Then she raised the typewriter above her head and its blood dripped on her white robe. Suddenly little Tenace's self-pity turned into rage. His entrails caught fire and he needed to spit it out like a dragon. He realised, or perhaps it was grown-up Tenace who realised: It was a double bind! Whatever you did, it would be wrong! It was like being a successful communist entrepreneur.

Wrong to remain mediocre and wrong to surpass her. It was meant to make you stop, forever tortured, torn between ambition and modesty. This was the beheading! For a split second, Tenace caught that. His body wiggled on the ZEP bed like a fish heading straight from the hook to the grill. He shouted:

— You can't do that! You can't project your own ambition on us! You can't load us with the mission of reaching the dreams of greatness you never reached! We can't finish your unfinished plays!

Her arms weakened. She tried to put the typewriter on the desk, but she must have got the distance wrong because it fell on it with a big thump. Now she was abundantly weeping, as silently as Tenace had done, and the tears mixed with the blood on her robe and it looked like a beautiful aquarelle.

— My father wanted me to...

He interrupted her:

— He gave you the bug, and you're giving it to us! I want to break this chain. This is what I came for!

She looked at her 10-year-old boy, amused:

— This is what you came for?

She picked up a Senior Service and little Tenace finally spat his fire but it didn't light it. He said in his ten-year-old voice:

— You don't want us to become eagles because you failed becoming one! And if we happened to succeed, you'd feel as small as a sparrow, and that's why you want to make sure we never succeed by seeding this sick plant in our heads!

In rage, but fully shocked by his own words, little Tenace wanted to hug her; he opened his arms but there was no one there.

— Just like your father! he managed to add, closing his eyes.

His mother had lifted the typewriter again, and when Tenace reopened his eyes, she stood in front of the window and threw the Royal de Luxe through it.

It fell like a bombshell. Little Tenace flew to the ceiling like Peter Pan and over his mother's shoulders, he saw a man looking up and shouting but he could not hear him. He wore a beige raglan raincoat and Tyrolean hat, an ax in his hand. It was his father. The typewriter had just missed his head by an inch, and lay there half open at the tip of his toes.

Six beheaded hens were stumbling around between the chopped wood while blood still gushed out of their necks.

Then his mother turned around and her look thrust little Tenace back to the door again. There were more tears than blood on her dress now, and the aquarelle had turned into "fileto rosso".

Happy birthday, James! she said with a genuine smile, and her twisted body turned into marble beige.

Chapter 45: The Party

When Tenace came back to his own consciousness, he was shattered. The message he had received was no new message. Tenace had brewed equivalent conclusions his whole life, from books, talks and his own reflections. What was startling is that this time, it came straight from his own mother. It wasn't just another reflection in a mirror; it was the original. He had reached the centre of the mirror maze he'd been trapped in his entire life, and it was high time to get out.

Tenace slowly removed the fixing helmet, then sat on the ZEP bed like a kid on a bench and remained there holding his head between his hands a few minutes. Every 30 seconds, ZOE3 beeped in Morse code: ti tati tatiti or . -. -.. which, as a former transmission Officer in the Army, he instinctively understood: E N D.

He finally stood up. His body started to shake, and he gestured as if to remove invisible dust from his skin. He had not turned the lights on and the only glow came from ZOE3's screen. He rushed to the back room where all the disks and tapes were stored. He then started to pull out the two-inch tape reels which dated from the very beginning of his project, when he had broken in to the AMPEX museum to steal a recorder. On those were recorded the first multi-signal waves. He opened the reel boxes and started to unwind the tapes, one box after the other. He then went to the half-inch SONY tapes. These comprised not data but videos, black-and-white videos of the time he was a student, when the first semi-professional video recorders came on the market. He remembered the "Portapack", a 20kg, reel-to-reel portable video recorder flanked with a huge pistol-like camera. He recalled how he and his friend Rock had walked around the city, pretending to be a TV team. Their favourite interviews were the ones of female students outside the city library, asking them what they did when they were horny on the library chairs and whether it was compatible with learning for exams.

He also remembered distributing umbrellas on a bright sunny day to incredulous passers-by unaware of the camera. He saw the faces of the unlucky ones who had refused to take an umbrella and were suddenly soaked from the contents of the bucket which had then been spilled over their heads from the third floor of the oldest house of the narrow Brunngasse. But he kept on pulling the tapes out.

He remembered how he and Rock had afterwards hidden in the toilets of the nearby pub, fearing the police. Then this old woman popped up into his face, exactly as she had done thirty years ago at the sight of the camera, exposing her Auschwitz prisoner tattoo to the barrel of the Vidicon pistol, in front of the biggest bank of Switzerland.

He remembered his past, and wanted to throw it away. He would not put these tapes together to make a documentary, he would just pull them out of their boxes. He was not going to be an eagle; he would destroy what he had done, like a writer burns his novel or a poet lets the wind blow the pages away into the sea. Tenace enjoyed it, fanatically pulling the tapes till they broke. But they didn't break. He was just mad. Mad because he feared that his life would never belong to him. He had been a puppet. His past had never belonged to him, but neither would his future.

He had wanted to be a writer in his younger years but had realised that he had just wanted to please his mother. Then he had switched and decided to be a scientist. But he had then realised he was studying physics just to annoy his mother and that he was just as tangled in her wires as before. So he had decided to become a doctor and he had liked it. But again, that was following the footsteps of his father Rudolph and he would keep on suspecting that he was tangled in his wires now. Nothing would ever be his. All that he had envisaged was tainted, occupied, already rented. His desires had been hijacked. He could never free himself from the fear that whatever he did, he was possibly doing it to please someone else, and that was his despair.

However, the reason why he was now destroying what he had done was not so much this despair but the effect of the demon who had just visited him, the one shouting:

— You shall never be an Eagle!

By now the back room was full of magnetic tapes, which built up to a dark brown cloud as high as his head. Tenace was still pulling the wires of his past out of the boxes, to tread on it, soaked in his own tears, but his energy slowly faded, and strangely enough, he had not touched any of the hard disks containing the most recent and useful data and programs.

Eventually, he calmed down; perhaps what pulled him out of this trip were the cries of the crows outside. He came back to reality. The "party" must have started already. His duties called him. To carry on like this would have probably led him to Block 17, the "loonies" block. His fit was over now and he nicely resigned himself to go to the party he had launched, to celebrate his success, a success he was not even in a state to enjoy, haunted by this hereditary perfectionism that constantly whispered in his mind:

— This is not enough!

He still had tapes all around his neck and shoulders and a consistent topping on his head as well. It even looked like a bird's nest. 11 pm, time to go. When he left the lab, a crow flew from behind and tried to land on his head. It missed the landing but hit his skull with its claws. It then shrieked, flew on, gained some height and chose a tree instead.

The puppet theatre had never been so full. It looked like in the photographs that hung in the upper galleries of the room, except that this time no strings were attached to the puppets. They were not only more numerous but also much more alive than in the silver gelatine collection. Ralf was at the control desk, shifting the knobs up and down, secluded from the crowd by two gigantic headphones, between which his head looked small and lost. This way, he could have it as loud as it pleased him, but since the music he had to disc jockey was by no means his favourite brand, he had it just loud enough to perform the beat match adequately.

Tenace joined in, wrapped in the magnetic tapes.

— Lovely party streamers! said Miss Ferguson, standing at the doorway.

— Where did you get those?

Tenace did not bother to answer, as he had just spotted someone in the crowd he had not invited nor wanted to see: Mrs Lavenue. She seemed utterly pleased, talking to Edmund, and they were both laughing, both holding a glass, which by the colour of it could have been an Aperol Spritz. Something the Italians never drink after five in the afternoon. Tenace went straight to her, stretching out his hand:

— So nice of you to have come!

— Indeed! she answered. I was so touched by the fact that you reckoned my presence so natural as to not even bother sending me an invitation!

Edmund's eyes turned into interrogation marks and Tenace swallowed.

— I was so afraid you'd decline, he said, hardly repressing a ten-year-old's smirk.

It could not be her first Aperol Spritz because she went on:

— Fantastic, James! And they can talk! I have just had a conversation with Mr. Mueller, he is fine. It is impressive. I like your hat.

All these people; so much noise. Tenace wanted to switch the film off but he couldn't find the remote control. He moved on, not even answering. You could tell he was looking for someone, shaking hands, absent-minded, overhearing the congratulations, bumping into some his patients. He needed a drink and none of what was offered to him by the waiters was to his taste. Face after face, handshake after handshake, he moved through the crowd towards the bathroom, where he had put a dozen of bottles of champagne in the bathtub with ice. He felt slightly ashamed that it was sort of kept secret. He felt like a guest stealing the best bits at the party, although he was the guy who was inviting. He moved slowly towards his target, obsessed by the champagne, trying not to act suspicious, convinced everyone was thinking: - Tenace is going to get some champagne! He was now in the grey corridor and already saw the cold neon light of the bathroom, relieved that no one had noticed him. He walked in, having already spotted the bottle of Veuve Cliquot Ponsardin Brut, not the best but better than any sparkling wine, with its low level of sugar and bubbles.

— The bubbles are the best in champagne, like the holes in Emmantaler cheese, he caught himself muttering.

Then he sensed someone at his back and turned around: There were ten people, obviously with the same thought in mind, since they were all following him in a row.

By the time he came back to the crowd, he had gulped down half of the bottle. It was his ex-wife he had been looking for, and she wasn't there. He retreated again towards the corridor to call her. He wanted to show her his achievement, to show her that all the work and research he had started in the last years of their marriage had come to an end and that it was not just a "little chichi" of his to get away from her, as she used to put it. It was serious business, his 'meaning of life', but she didn't pick up.

When he came back on stage, he spotted another person he had not invited, but this one was someone he did not want to see at all: Frangier!

Frangier stood by the doorway and was talking to Lavenue. He had not even bothered to take his police hat off his bloated head! Tenace's heart missed a rev. He had more than a vague idea why Frangier was here, and the fact that he was talking to his boss was the most unpleasant thing that could happen to Tenace. He started to panic. He tried to calm down, to master his thoughts, repeating to himself that there is no "objective reality"; it was just the way you looked at it, and if you looked at it the bad way, it became bad, because you made your own reality. Strengthened by these sparks of "radical constructivism", he walked up to Frangier, resolutely intending to kick the bastard out of there.

— I can't recall having invited you to my party, Officer!

— Absolutely right, Dr Tenace, I am not a guest. I am on duty! And you know very well what kind of duty I am on.

— Still curious about who shat on the graves?

You are not at the relevant location, Mr Frangier. The graveyard and its management is four hundred metres down below, and it is not administrated by Falkennest, except that our patients are too often, and this I regret, good customers of it.

— It is precisely about one of those "customers" as you put it, Dr Tenace, that I am here.

Tenace's stomach took off like he was on a rollercoaster but there was no fun at the fair.

— Officer, I really appreciate your tenacity and involvement and wish all the personnel at Falkennest would follow your example, but Mrs Van Brandstaetten died on a Wednesday night, and you very well know it, because she's on the group photograph I'm in the habit of taking every first Wednesday of the month.

— She is indeed in the picture, Dr Tenace.

Frangier paused, looking straight into Tenace's eyes. Madame Lavenue had stopped smiling and Tenace was struggling to conceal the fear that had invaded his entire body. Ill at ease but pragmatic, Madame Lavenue offered: Let's have a look at the photograph!

And all three walked up to the upper gallery and soon enough stood in front of it. Perplexed, Madame Lavenue turned to Tenace and asked:

— Why is this picture black and white? All the other ones are colour.

— I love black and white, Madame Lavenue.

Photography is my hobby. It makes them all so much more alive, don't you think?

— Indeed it does! interrupted Frangier.

— Especially Mrs Van Brandstaetten, so much more alive...! I wish to see the negative, Dr Tenace! he added, and it sounded like an order.

Trapped and despairing, Tenace attempted a last escape:

— But the negative is in colour, Mr Frangier.

— Precisely, Dr Tenace, Mrs Van Brandstaetten has beautiful eyes and I'd like to know what colour they were... He paused and looked straight at Dr Tenace's face, then finished:

— on Wednesday...

Tenace's "radical constructivism" had evaporated like a drop of water on a hot stone. Completely panicked, he managed to wave Ralf over. Mrs Lavenue intervened:

— On Wednesday? Wasn't the picture taken on Wednesday?

— Oh, I have no doubt about it, added Frangier, his eyes still hooked onto Tenace's.

As Tenace had foreseen it, Ralf reluctantly left his mixing desk, and when asked by Tenace to fetch the negative, he bluntly refused, saying he was in charge of the music. Tenace's plan had worked.

— I'll go and get it then!

Frangier gave him a suspicious look. The thing he instinctively wanted to do was to handcuff Tenace immediately but instead he felt compelled to say, and that was his mistake:

— Please do so!

Tenace couldn't wait, and he left the two immediately, disappeared into the corridor leading to his office, grabbed his trench coat and rushed outside to his car to never come back.

It was not until his car had reached the speed of 140kmh on the main road to Zinkow that he realised he had made a huge mistake: He had not taken the negative with him! But it was too late.

While the trees were zapping by left and right, whipped by Tenace's headlights, Frangier was calmly scrutinising with a huge magnifying glass the negative he had finally ordered Ralf to bring. He went straight to the point. The picture had been taken with flashlights and all the patients around the middle of the picture showed the typical red eyes except Mrs Van Brandstaetten, though standing right in the centre of the picture. Her eyes were not red!

— Do you know why her eyes aren't red, Madame Lavenue? Because Mrs Van Brandstaetten was already dead!

Madame Lavenue, who had studied medicine, though that was forty years ago, should have known why, but she none the less had no clue. Perhaps it was the alcohol that made her forget the basics of blood circulation.

— Because there is no blood in her retina anymore! said Frangier.

- And the flashlight, which reflects back from her retina towards the lens, is no longer tinted with the red of the haemoglobin, like with any living creature on earth including the myxomatous rabbits on the road. I happened to notice this when I was a simple traffic officer and had to snapshot victims on the highway, Madame Lavenue.

— Is this why the print is black and white? To conceal it?

— Yes Madame! Dead people don't have red eyes!

Chapter 46: Escargots de Bourgogne

When Sarah Schein finally closed the door of the green Jaguar Mk II, actually Tenace's car, which she had managed to extort from him during their divorce, thanks to her smart lawyer, she was already late.

She had wanted to be elegant and conceal the work of age and sorrow on her face. It had cost her more than two hours of hard work in front of the mirror, and at least a hundred Swiss Francs worth of rejuvenating creams and make-up before the little voice in the back of her head would finally tell her she is now the most enticing female creature of Marrow Forest.

She had decided to attend the party. But it was not to rejoice at her ex-husband's success; she wasn't really in a position to seize the medical meaning of Tenace's discovery, and if she had been, she would have been too envious to celebrate. No, she had decided to attend as one goes to a movie or a street parade, just because it was an event one should not miss. It pulled her out of her inactive and monotonous life and she'd have something to talk about for the next three weeks. You never know. Of course, she wouldn't miss a chance to poke at her ex-husband if he did not pay attention, and she knew him well enough to bet he wouldn't.

But now she was late, and that annoyed her. Luckily, that stupid old car she had confiscated just because her ex-husband loved it so much, started right away. She intended to catch up with some of the lost hours by giving the engine a good kick in the ass. She drove fast for a while until this stupid lorry showed up, just as she got out of town, on that little road leading to the ponds with a continuous white line in the middle telling you not to overtake. That lorry was a real snail itself, she thought after having read "Escargots de Bourgogne" in faded red letters at least a hundred times on the back of it.

She didn't dare to overtake, but every now and then she would start an overtake manoeuvre just to have a look, since the snail-in-chief would not react to her honky requests to speed up or let her by.

She looked at her second hand Jaeger-Lecoultre Reverso watch but it was reversed. It particularly annoyed her that someone could glance at her expensive timepiece without having paid for it. It was expencive time and it was her's, but this time it annoyed her even more that she had to fiddle with it while at the wheel to check how late she was.

Fleeing was the dumbest thing he could have done. But the panic that had seized Tenace had short-circuited his neo-cortex and his reptilian brain had taken over. He should have destroyed the negative, a matter of seconds, and come back to Frangier with an innocent and sorry smile and Frangier's suspicion would have turned into wrath but would have remained a vague divagation that no jury in the world would have taken seriously. But he hadn't done that; instead, he had served him the rope to hang him, and on a silver platter, most probably an unconscious manifestation of Thanatos, as Freud would put it. The same drive that makes the assassin always returns to the locus of the crime.

In Tenace's case it was perhaps a little more complex. Deep inside, he felt right. The death of Mrs Van Brandstaetten was an accident, but it was nothing in the light of the tremendous discovery and gift he believed he'd made to mankind. Given that Mrs Van Brandstaetten was brain-dead, Tenace considered the death of her body merely a relieving formality. This is why he had kept on playing the game. He was utterly convinced that he was not a criminal and had nothing to hide. But he had, and by dwelling on this contradiction, it got him, like it gets all of us, hesitating until the last second between right and left, between right and wrong, to end up hitting the signpost between the two roads, the forehead shattering the windscreen in a big bloody thump. Had Tenace been a criminal, he would have carefully planned his moves, and would not be driving down the road to Zinkow now at nearly 140 km/h. That's the drama; they always catch the innocents, the weak. The real bastards are still at the party. Justice has never been rightfulness but just an extended robotic arm of power.

Tenace had not a clue of what he was doing. He was just fleeing, tetanized at the driving wheel, his foot threatening to pop out through the brittle plastic ground of his Mehari, just below the gas pedal. He was just flunking it all, once again, like it was written in the holy book of his childhood.

He was approaching the bridge now, the bridge

that stretches over the ponds, and that bloody car down the road would not dim its headlights. It ached under his skull. He closed one eye, like he always does, to at least have one that could see something after the blinding was over. Perhaps he should slow down, he thought, but he didn't, he decided to slow down after the bridge. He had to get over the bridge, then he would be safe, he would then be in Zinkow, the city where you can hide and consider what your next move should be. So he squeezed down on the gas pedal even more, though there was nothing left to squeeze. He felt free, the old walls of the bridge now clearly focused on his retinas, he could even see the moss on each stone. He was crossing the frontier! He felt exhilarated and the face of Frangier in his back mirror faded away. He was free!

And suddenly this blinding lorry coming up to him replicates itself, as it now has four headlights. His vision is impaired. He's hallucinating. It must be an optical illusion triggered by his lack of sleep. He has nearly reached the small bridge over the first pond now, but the second set of headlights is still there, lower than the first; it's not a reflection, not a replica, no mirage, but another car, overtaking the lorry on the bridge!

This was Tenace's last thought. There was a terrible crash that he only heard the first movement of, then he felt an acute pain on his forehead and all went briefly red. He was now flying, and the cool wind whistled at his ears, then it was all silence, but Tenace was no longer there to report on it.

When Tenace regained consciousness, well, what he thought was consciousness, he was hovering fifty metres above the bridge, among the crows. Beneath him were a flashing ambulance, two car wrecks, a white lorry leaning on its side and another car he could not identify. Then he spotted two bodies, one in the high grass on the side of the road, the other one right in the middle of it thirty meters past the bridge. The blinking light of an ambulance threw stroboscopic shadows on the road. Two men were leaning over the body in the grass. The lorry had its hatch open and boxes lay spread all around. Tenace dove to the body in the grass. He recognised his wife in spite of the oxygen mask, but he felt no emotion, neither sadness nor shock. He asked the medic if she was alive but no one answered.

He flew over to the MK II or what was left of it. A snail had climbed on the silver feline figurehead. Tenace did not smile; it all seemed normal to him. Than he slid to the other body over columns of snails on their way to freedom. He recognised his own trench coat, though it was soaked in blood. A good match for the last trench, he thought with a smirk. The skull was fractured right across the forehead; the eyes were red but were astray. Tenace wasn't sad, nor did he feel sorry for the disfigured and dismembered body that he recognised as his own. He was immensely calm. Then two men shifted his body onto a litter and carried it towards a car. It was no ambulance; it was dark, and all the back windows were covered with dark red velvet curtains from within, the same dark red that soaked his trench coat. He went up again, and felt someone behind him. He whirled around, and there was his wife, among the crows. She looked as transparent as him but she seemed so serene. Puzzled, he looked down again towards her body and it was still there. Suddenly an intense drive to live seized him. He dove down like a bird of prey towards her corpse, as if he had checked that hers had a better chance to survive than his. He melted into it, hoping it would let him in, if he'd pay the rent that is, to remain alive.

The news of Doctor Tenace's death had spread like a fire. It was all over the local papers and even in the first national one. From "Frankenstein died in a car crash" to "Will Tenastein resuscitate himself?". The Daily Gossips even titled it, "Dr Tenace's last victim". Alone out there was the alternative weekly magazine "The Marrow Tinkers", which had a laudatory column about Tenace's medical breakthrough. But that was no surprise, as Dickerdon was the chief editor's friend and had been the co-founder of the paper fifteen years ago.

Sarah Schein had finally been moved to Block 15, since she had not recovered well at all from the deep coma she fell into after the crash. Tenace had died on the spot, completely unresponsive to any of the emergency measures applied. His body had been stored in one of the drawers of morgue 15. According to his testament, it was to be conserved six months after his death in a cold chamber before being buried. Edmund and his wife had taken little Bob to their house. Both Edmund and his wife Karina had done all they could to cheer him up but it didn't help much. Little Bob would hardly talk, and spent hours staring at various computer games after school. That depressed Edmund so much, who had himself lost his father in WWII at about the same age, that he also started to spend hours in front of a computer after work. A masculine trait it seems, except that it was not for gaming, it was ZOE3. Edmund and Dickerdon spent many nights looking at Tenace's work and program, both obsessed by the idea of continuing his work.

Chapter 47: Valerian

It was about 8.30 pm and Edmund was still in his laboratory. He had nothing to do there except to wait, and he hated it. Tidying up his office did not take long because his office was tidy enough, and he was not of the manic fraction. He had no work to do either. It had been very calm anyway the last few months, the only sign of life being sampling nails for Dr Tenace, but that which had filled the past three weeks had died, just as Tenace did, since he had been the contractor.

Edmund was definitely no workaholic. Of all the 'holics, his choice had fallen on a more native casus of the declination, but that was not on the list tonight because he had something else on the list that required absolute sobriety. So Edmund had no other choice than to finally open the dinner-box he had filled with his own favourite cooking: lentils with princess beans, spiced with onions, tomatoes and French garlic saucisson. He unscrewed the metal cylinder lid and inhaled the fumes through his great nostrils, which if you had looked at them from the tin's perspective would have looked like sunglasses. Obviously satisfied by the smell of his meal, he poured it into his white plate and unscrewed the top of his quarter-litre red wine bottle he had saved from his flight back from Karpathos in September.

He was just about to put the first spoonful into his mouth, his senses all set for the enjoyable experience, when he heard steps in the staircase. Nobody ever takes the stairs in Falkennest.

Edmund thought it was the watchman and he hoped he wouldn't check his office, so he turned the little desk lamp off. But the steps got nearer and louder and there was a knock on the door and another one. Worried, Edmund was about to answer when the door opened. Dickerdon stood at the doorstep.

— Let's go, he said to Edmund in a boss-like tone.

— How the hell did you get in here? We were supposed to meet at the ZEP at 9 pm!

— I know a lot of ways in here! Let's go!

Edmund wanted to finish his supper, that was for sure, but something in Dickerdon's manner was so dominating, so strong, that he did not dare to mention his supper. He was the one who had pulled Dickerdon into this; he needed him. He had the knowledge, since he had developed some of the programs with Tenace. It was Edmund's idea after all, even if Dickerdon had sounded enthusiastic about it when he had sought his help. Edmund was dependent on him, so he stood up, nonetheless managing to stuff three spoons full of his princess beans and lentils into his hungry mouth, and off they went.

Edmund followed Dickerdon. They went the same way he had come in. In front of the D15 staircase, Dickerdon stopped, and Edmund went up two floors. He walked into Tenace's office and straight to an almond-green sealed plastic bag. These were Tenace's belongings on the night of the accident. He ripped the seal off, fiddled a while, pulled out a bunch of keys and walked out the same way. Dickerdon was waiting for him in the dark. Edmund knew about the cellars, but part of the way was unknown to him, especially the underground passage leading from the Falkennest cellars to the ZEP's dwellings. Edmund shivered one more time when passing in front of Morgue 15 where Tenace was temporary conserved.

Edmund himself did not know how he got that crazy idea of trying to bring Mrs Tenace back to consciousness using her ex-husband's latest discovery. One thing is sure, he was so sad for the little boy who had lost his mother even if her body remained alive, that it is very probable his sadness had triggered this adventurous endeavour in Edmund's mind, and now he was following Dickerdon's green Wellingtons. It is also possible that he was obeying Tenace's will. A will that Tenace had seeded in Edmund's mind, like parents in their childrens' minds, while peering into his eyes like he used to do. Tenace had written a testament according to which he was to be kept in the freezer for a while in case of death, which was weird enough to envisage that he might have made other testaments, unwritten ones, in peoples' minds, people like Dickerdon and Edmund...

Dickerdon acted as if he was born in the ZEP. He had ZOE3 up in less than a minute and had found Mrs Tenace's Eigenfractal file within the following minute. Edmund remembered when he had sampled out Tenace's ex-wife's nails about six weeks ago. The certainty that such a file existed had definitely helped them to find it. They turned the ZEP on, loaded Mrs Tenace's

Eigenfractal as input in the multi-signal generator, and set the time of this generation to the time they had planned to bring Mrs Tenace on the ZEP bed: 11 pm.

Now ZOE3 was generating the multi-signals, and it would take around an hour, because Dickerdon had decided to beam her with three hours of her own consciousness instead of the half an hour Tenace used to do. This is why he had shown up earlier than agreed.

They had to hurry, they were a little tight on the schedule, it was 10.45 and they wanted the ZEP signals to be synchronised with real time. That was Dickerdon's sine qua non idea. He had fought with Tenace about it but Tenace had not cared, he had not believed such a synchronicity had any advantage and he had never bothered about it. But Dickerdon did, and Dickerdon was the boss now. So they hurried to Mrs Ex-Tenace and she looked at them like a sickly calf, her lost eyes as much astray as her hands, instinctively knowing what was going to happen to her, the same despair and resignation. Only the grunts were missing, but these would come afterwards. They put her on the litter and headed off to the ZEP.

They were both extremely nervous, as neither of them were doctors, but aside from the fact that they had not brought the oxygen mask nor the defibrillator, it seems that they knew their business as if they had been doing it over and over again for the last fifty years, especially Dickerdon, who manoeuvred the fixing helmet as if it had been his own grass mower. Part of this is certainly to be explained by the fact that Dickerdon had stolen Tenace's diary where the latter had written all the protocols he had used for his ZEP sessions.

So when Mrs Tenace was about to wake up after the hree-hour irradiation of her own cybernetic consciousness, they gave her the drink that was prescribed in the diary as soon as she could speak and that drink was something much more efficient than Valerian and back she was, in her own bed, except this time she was snoring, suspiciously snoring.

On the morning of the twelfth day after the accident, Sarah Schein woke up from coma. She opened her eyes then closed them again. There was something odd about her body. It felt different, it seemed to have a different volume: smaller, lighter. She raised her arms and they responded much faster, as if they were shorter. She did the same with her legs and felt the same. She moved her hand towards her crotch and then quickly to her breast, shrieked and wanted to jump out of her bed. But she was too weak, and only managed to sit on its side. An expression of disorientation close to panic invaded her face.

She remained in this position for a while, her body leaning forward, seemingly staring at her knees. But her eyes were not focusing; she was absent. Then slowly she raised her head and her look reached her image in the mirror. There, she attentively observed herself, making faces, raising one arm after the other as she would have if seeing her body for the first time. Then she started to laugh. It was more a hysterical laughter, turning her head right and left like a dog at the rear window of a car, except that this dog was snarling. She uttered a few words that were not very ladylike and her voice had at times a much deeper pitch and a more guttural intonation. She then gathered the energy to stand up and to walk towards the mirror. When she had reached it, she started to kiss her own image on the lips. Then, she stepped backwards and punched it. It was a miracle that the mirror did not break.

Then she put on a smirk very untypical of her. This smirk looked more like Tenace's smirk. She then popped her breasts out of the night gown. They were no voluptuous breasts, rather flat actually, like two fried eggs in a pan. With one hand, she started to lasciviously massage and squeeze the left breast, grunting with pleasure, but that grunt was too masculine to be hers and then suddenly, the other hand started to hit the first hand and tried to rip it off the left breast accompanied by shrieks that drowned out the grunts.

Eventually, the first hand gave up and escaped to another part of her body, down below. The grunts got louder and longer and her face melted into an unambiguous expression betraying an intense sexual pleasure. Then the grunts were interspersed with shrieks and the other hand came down as well, but again, it was to rip the first hand away from the crotch. Her whole body jerked. It looked like she was fighting against herself or fighting with someone within her.

Doctor Tenace was back again! He was in his ex-wife's body, trying to enjoy the body which had been refused to him through twenty long years of an abstinent marriage. The fight went on for quite a while, but the shrieks became weaker and rarer. Finally you could only hear the grunts and it sounded like Tenace's grunt. Tenace had fully conquered his ex-wife's body!

Had his soul hijacked his ex-wife's body as they were both dying on the road? It is hard to believe in such a deus ex machina plot point and this is precisely why Tenace-Schein, who was not a slow thinker, decided to conceal this fact, and from then on, did all he could to speak with a higher pitch, damp his brusque, manly gestures, and put on a Sarah Schein as feminine as he could. When the nurse finally came, alerted by the grunts and shrieks, Tenace-Schein reached for the most feminine smile in his collection to request his make-up, except he made a mess out of it and the nurse had to redo it all, secretly blaming Sarah's clumsiness on the sequels of the crash.

The news that Sarah Schein had come back from coma spread as fast as Tenace's death. The first to visit Sarah was Edmund. They hugged each other so that even the Tenace in her started to get jealous. But when they looked each other in the eyes after the embrace, there was something strange in her eyes, a thankfulness or a complicity as if they both performed a "coup" together that no one was supposed to know about. But this complicity was only in Sarah's eyes, or should I now say Tenace's eyes. Edmund was puzzled. He walked out backwards, facing Sarah and if you looked at him observantly, you would have noticed a slight shiver and glimpses of terror behind his glasses.

It was not what he had expected.

Chapter 48: Papa

It is not clear whose idea it was, probably the vicar's, because it was not written in Tenace's testament. There was a mourning morning for Dr Tenace, not at the clinic's chapel though, but at Morgue 15.

They had just pulled the drawer out. Two black cubes on each side of it, each with a pot of flowers on it, did not manage to render the room adequate for the ceremony. Half of the clinic's personnel was there, although it is not clear if some of them weren't there just to take a break.

Little Bob was there, and he had tears in his eyes. He stayed near his father's corpse the whole time, looking at him, changing sides, looking at the people looking at him, and looking at him again. He had noticed the snail on his lower arm. All frozen and stuck to it, hit by a wave of cold, in its ascent to the top. He had seen frozen snails before, but none like that; rather in their shells, sunk in butter. His mother liked them so much. The snail had its horns proudly erected like a male climbing up Mount Venus.

Dickerdon, Edmund, Madame Lavenue, Ralf, nearly all the nurses, and half of Tenace's patients attended the ceremony, including the being that was commonly referred to as Mrs Sarah Schein. Every now and then she kept trying to hold Bob's hand, but Bob regularly withdrew his hand.

The Tenace in Sarah's body stared at his dead body and was appalled at the sight of the massive head injury that the undertakers had not quite managed to conceal. It is a strange feeling to mourn one's own self. So Tenace-Schein left that task to the others and secretly enjoyed the fervour that was on display in all the participants, even in Frangier, who for once had not come in his police uniform. What touched Tenace the most was the deep sadness of his own son. He had all the pain in the world refraining himself from hugging his own son to tell him he was still alive though in his mother's body. It is not even sure that it would have relieved his son because then it would have been clear to him that he had lost his mother. But little Bob felt anyway that he had lost his mother because this mother that looked like his mother did not really behave like his mother, and little Bob perceived much better than most adults that there was something strange about his mother, because children feel more and think less.

There might have been two adults though who could have been on the same wavelength as Bob, and these were Dickerdon and Edmund, but it was for them so monstrous that they did not want to face it.

Though he had initiated it, the vicar had refused to attend the ceremony, pretexting another ceremony that unexpectedly took place at the same time. In reality Tenace's activities has repulsed him so much that he felt the Church could not participate in mourning of a man who had made a pact with Satan.

This is why the oration was to be spoken by Mrs Tenace-Schein herself. Sarah Schein pulled out a sheet of paper from her bosoms and started to read in a tense voice the speech she had written herself:

— The medical and scientific community has just lost a great spirit. A man who has devoted his life to medicine, a man who has since very young followed the footsteps of his father, Dr Rudolph, who some of you will remember. He was the first doctor who managed to revive human beings long after the usual twenty minutes after the heart had ceased to beat. His method was not everyone's cup of tea and he had a long and hard time trying to convince his peers of the pertinence of his method. Today, his work is still subject to great controversy.

Sarah paused. Edmund and most of Tenace's colleagues looked at Mrs Schein intrigued and ill at ease. They wondered how she knew about this chapter. Sarah continued:

— Dr Rudolph's method has nearly fallen into oblivion, not so much because of this controversy but because all the patients he had so revived lacked something fundamental in life: consciousness. They were alive like melons and cucurbitaceae are alive, but no spark of a soul would ever flash out of their homeostatic organisms.

There, Dr Welling raised his eyebrows and Edmund coughed, both very intrigued by the specific vocabulary used by Mrs Schein.

— This explains why the work of Dr Tenace's father remains as an unpublished manuscript in Falkennest's medical library.

As Sarah said those words, there was suddenly a guttural tone in her voice. It was now apparent that she wasn't reading her paper anymore, if she had ever read it.

— But today, thanks to Dr Tenace's work, the way that looked like a dead end seems clear again. My ex-husband found the way to make such patients regain consciousness and though there is still work to do to re-establish memory, we can consider his work as a gigantic step for mankind.

There was a repressed indignation in the left part of the assembly, mostly populated by members of the parish, and Mrs Schein's confident tone slightly vacillated.

— I admit not having measured the importance and pertinence of my ex-husband's work at the time, mostly preoccupied by our family life and what I reckoned as neglect of it by my ex-husband, since he was so obsessed by his research. But now I realise, it was worth it and I regret not having given him full support. Mrs Schein then started to sob:

— I was just an egoistic bitch, jealous of my husband, hurt that he had something more important to do than take care of me. Sarah Schein's eyes went suddenly astray and a convulsive deformation appeared on her mouth. She then jerked violently, stamped the floor and her voice became suddenly totally masculine:

— I wish Dr Rudolph were still be around to resuscitate the carcass of his son!

Mrs Ferguson shrieked.

— And I wish someone were sufficiently acquainted with Dr Tenace's technique to beam such a moronic living organism back to consciousness so that Dr Tenace could continue his work!

There, Mrs Schein looked and spoke like Dr Tenace himself. Little Bob jumped back. There was an uproar in the assembly.

The mourners were paralysed with horror. Little Bob looked at his mother and although you could not hear a word, you could read on his lips:

— Papa!

Chapter 49: Kosher Tenace

What was just a little seed in Tenace-Schein's mind during the ceremony had grown to a massive tree in his brain, and if ideas were visible, you would see huge oak branches popping out of the skull four metres high and wide.

Tenace-Schein was madly obsessed with the idea of resuscitating his own frozen carcass. There he lay, in bed, reading his father's manuscript for the fourth time in a row. The basic principle was to get the old blood out, because it contained all the toxic substances that inhibited cell life. At that time, telomerase, the very substance that helps cell replication, had not yet been discovered. Tenace deduced that the toxic substances in the blood Rudolph had suspected, were nothing other than substances disrupting the telomerase.

The best strategy against that, according to Rudolph, was to reactivate the heart first according to his principle. That was the easiest part. It necessitated opening the thorax, draining the heart of all old blood by repeatedly squeezing it and soaking it with fresh blood, and then applying the electro-stimulator to it till it started beating again. This would not always happen, and Dr Rudolph in a footnote had explained that in some cases he had to press a pig's healthy and functioning heart close to the dead heart for it to work.

This was due, according to Rudolph, to the electromagnetic field of the pig's heart, which would induce a synchronous electromagnetic field in the dead heart and, together with the synchronous electric currents from the stimulator, trigger the revival of the heart. The footnote reminded Tenace of his first experiments with the multi-signals on the cat and of the Russian professor's experiments. When the heart was going, it could be used as a pump to drain the old blood out and bring the new blood in.

But this was a critical phase, because the old blood was toxic to the newly-reborn heart. This is why Rudolph recommended to drain the corpse as much as possible with an external pump beforehand, just like the Russian professor did to his dog.

When the entire body was finally completely imbibed with fresh blood, there was a chance that the lungs would start to function again if assisted with oxygen supply and a pneumothorax. If the lungs went on working, there was a good chance that one by one all the other organs would come to life again, till it could be said that the entire body was organically alive.

From that night on, Sarah Tenace-Schein spent all the following nights gathering the necessary equipment, from pneumothorax to exo-heart prosthesis to fresh blood of his own group, stealing stuff at night from the clinic and from Tenace's father's instruments that Tenace had kept in his cellar. He brought it all to the ZEP's rooms.

Sarah Schein-Tenace did all this herself at night,

except when she asked Dickerdon to buy a pig from one of the local farmers and bring it to the ZEP on the night she had planned the operation.

Dickerdon and Edmund knew that it was Tenace living in Sarah Schein's body. It was their mistake. They had beamed Tenace's Eigenfractal into her, thinking Tenace had named her file 'Tenace', not realising that Tenace had renamed her file Schein.

On that Saturday night, everything was ready for the operation, much too ready, because the pig was squealing in the ZEP's anteroom, possibly because Dickerdon had forgotten the sedative shot.

Tenace-Schein had to go. It was a bit early, but that dammed pig was squealing. He went directly to the ZEP and that stupid pig had shat all over the place. Tenace had asked Dickerdon to tie its legs after the sedation but Dickerdon had done none of it. As Tenace-Schein walked in, the pig was ready for a fight, it seemed, looking at Tenace-Schein like a bull in a corrida. Tenace-Schein was quite afraid.

He decided to try to appease it by talking gently to it but that did not work, as if the pig knew it was going to be slaughtered. As the pig wouldn't calm down, Tenace-Schein changed strategy. He spotted the shovel, still muddy from the graveyard expedition, seized it and hit the pig on the temple like an expert golfer. That was it, for the squealing. He then rushed to the syringe that Dickerdon had left on the table three quarters full, and hoping it had the right mixture in it, gave his first injection to the animal. The pig rolled down onto his side, appeased at last.

Tenace-Schein, still in his dressing gown, proceeded to Morgue 15 all alone. Dr Tenace's corpse was nearly at room temperature when he opened the drawer thanks to the precaution Tenace-Schein had taken to turn off the freezer the night before. He did not need to stick a thermometer up his bum to know that. It was now midnight again and loading the corpse onto the litter carriage was not a piece of cake, not so much because of the weight of a corpse, but because it felt so strange and horrible to deal with a body that had been your own for over fifty years.

From then on Tenace-Schein cannot remember very well what happened. He performed all the tasks like a robot, as if some foreign entity were steering him through the delicate surgery he had to accomplish. It was like in a nightmare. He cannot recall what was worse: pulling out this poor pig's heart and immersing it into his provisional biotope or opening his own thorax, that is, Dr Tenace's thorax.

It was bloody and smelly. As a safety measure, he had put the pig's heart into a plastic bag before laying it close to his/Tenace's heart, to avoid any contamination. He can't remember all the details. How long had he squeezed his own heart and how long had he soaked it with the fresh blood? When had he started the electro-stimulation? He just remembered the obnoxious smell of burnt flesh, probably from the current he had applied to the heart. At one point he thought he'd have a heart attack himself. It was not working. That bloody heart would not pump. He thought he was crazy, crazy to have believed for one second in that fairy tale of his father's. He was desperate. It was just a bloody joke and he was just a butcher. He took his head in his red hands and sobbed.

It was over now; he would never recuperate his own body, he would have to continue his life as his ex-wife. Oh, how foolish he had been. The beeps of the electro-stimulator faded and he faded away as well.

When he recovered, something was tickling his nostrils. Like a wiggling frog-leg under current. It smelled of blood and roasted lamb. One eye opened, and he could only see the colour red. He then realised that his head had sunken onto his own heart and that wiggling flesh that was tickling his nostrils was his own heart! Tenace's heart was beating!

He could not believe it, he could not refrain from crying, a long victorious cry, half overwhelmed by the noise of the rain outside, which was now heavy on the roof.

Tenace-Schein was a doctor again, a mechanical doctor. He proceeded with the steps he had learned by heart during the preceding nights: turn on the second exo-heart prosthesis, turn on the pneumothorax, the oxygen supply and wait, wait.

Tenace-Schein was in a dream now. His remaining attention concentrated on the surface of the breast to detect any endo-motion. It reminded him of the birth of his own child, waiting for the head to pop out of the uterus, except he was his own child now, a big and already old one.

Then someone knocked at the door. Tenace-Schein shivered. He prayed. He who was an atheist prayed that he had misheard, that it was just the wind.

Dickerdon came in. He remained totally indifferent to the scene. Completely calm and detached, not even bothered by the blood or the smell or even the meaning of what was happening, he just asked in a low and monotonous voice:

— May I have the pig now?

Tenace could not believe it. He looked at him completely puzzled, and said:

— Get the hell out of here with or without the pig!

Dickerdon loaded the pig on his bright shoulders and humped off.

Still gazing at the door, another strange noise caught his attention. It sounded like... a breath. His slowly turned his eyes to the corpse's chest: It was no corpse anymore. It was breathing!

Chapter 50: Just the Two of Us

At 2 o'clock in the morning, its body temperature had finally reached 37 degrees. Tenace-Schein called Edmund again. Edmund had been warned that he would be witness to something extraordinary. But no one could ever been prepared for something like that, and when Edmund got to the ZEP and was shown the evil deed, he freaked out and fainted.

Tenace-Schein had no other choice than to have someone attend Tenace day and night until the wound had healed and the state stabilised, and that someone had to be devoted to Tenace. Edmund was the only mate having both this devotion and the medical know-how to fulfil this secret task. Tenace-Schein could not do this, as she had to remain a patient in Block 13.

A fortnight later, Tenace's condition had greatly improved. The intravenous supply had been switched progressively to normal food, since the digestive tract had recovered as well, and both Tenace and Tenace-Schein were now ready for the ultimate phase of this mad enterprise: beaming conscious-less Tenace with Tenace's Eigenfractal.

It was Sunday night again. Tenace-Schein had loaded Tenace on the ZEP bed for a beam. This time Tenace-Schein had opted for a direct beam, so he had placed himself at the other focus of the ZEP to replicate himself directly instead of using his file. This had the advantage of beaming in the most up-to-date Tenace Consciousness, which now resided in Tenace-Schein's mind. Tenace-Schein had planned a 3-hour session to yield the most faithful replica.

There is nothing to report on this now rather routine session. The interesting part is what happened at the end of it. Two different bodies, Tenace and Tenace-Schein had the same consciousness.

When Tenace-Schein left the ZEP bed, she had the feeling she was living in Tenace's body. When she observed Tenace removing the fixing helmet, she had the feeling she was out of her body and in Tenace's body. As she looked at him removing the helmet lock, she was feeling that the helmet was on her face, except that her face was ten metres away, at the other focus of the ZEP. She felt her leg muscles straightening her body up as Tenace was trying to stand up. She felt herself saying: What am I doing here? Except the person saying this was this man at the other side of the ZEP. She walked up to him, except that she was seeing herself walking up to her. She realised there was only one consciousness, dispersed in two bodies, and that was weird. She felt very strange. No! He felt strange. He was two! No, she was two! They got close to each other and she was seeing herself. Was it double consciousness? It was unbearable, to feel her own self in another body. She shrieked. He cried. They met, they were one, yet two. This is when they realised or he or she realised, one of them was too much, and one of them had to disappear because you cannot live seasick for the rest of your life. But who should disappear?

She hugged him or he hugged her, but when he stroked her cheek, he felt her stroking his cheek. Who was Tenace now? Her or him? Who was going to kill who? They were both Tenace. And they both answered the unspoken question:

— We are immortal; only the Self dies.

And since there was only one consciousness reigning above both bodies, that consciousness decided SHE had to disappear because this consciousness was Tenace's consciousness, who wanted to live in his own body.

So HE decided SHE would lie in the ZEP again and he would beam her with the zero file, the file of the comatose.

It was sad to commit suicide, to kill oneself and see oneself plunge into the night. Tenace moved her body down to Focus one, walked to ZOE3, selected the Zero file and ignited the beam.

His consciousness was still split between her body and his, but gradually the feeling of her body faded, and the feeling of his body focused on his own body, until he was one again. His consciousness reached clarity again, Tenace again, only Tenace-and-her faded completely. Sarah Tenace-Schein was Sarah Schein again, probably, back in the night of coma.

That felt good. Tenace was Tenace again, Tenace and only Tenace, in his own old body, slightly disfigured though after that bloody car-crash, but he was good old Tenace again.

He was knacked and the scars on his thorax still hurt. Now that her body was separated from his consciousness, it was possible to beam her with her own consciousness and repair the mistake that Dickerdon and Edmund had made. Tenace was already looking for her own file on ZOE3. He felt something strange in the air. He walked to her at Focus 1. She was not only comatose, she was dead. Tenace did not understand. Why did the zero file kill her? He felt guilty, but just for a split second, like a doctor who did not manage to save a patient's life. Tenace knew that routine.

Use old Rudolph's method to make her heart beat again? That was on his mind till he heard Frangier's voice outside:

— Police! Open the door at once!

Tenace did not hesitate. He loaded Sarah on his shoulders and went out through the back door.

Chapter 51: Good Old Edmund Rosegarden

When they wanted to bury Dr Tenace after the six months following his death had elapsed, they were very surprised to find Sarah Schein-Tenace in the drawer at Morgue 15, but at least they had a small consolation: they now knew where she was.

I wouldn't have been able to tell you this story, had I not met this man in a French hotel resort in Guadeloupe in 2003. He had a terrible toothache as he sat down at the table next to mine on that Sunday morning.

I happened to know of a French dentist: François Adam, on the main street in Port-au-Prince, an old friend of mine with whom I went to primary school in Saint Maur near Paris.

When I met this man again at dinner the same day, he told me that on the same floor, there was another doctor's surgery. He saw a man walk into it whose gait and habitus reminded him of someone he had known intimately. He walked up to the door and read the brazen plate affixed to it:

Dr Tenace: *Soul transfer and reincarnation...*

This man's name was Edmund, Edmund Rosegarden.

If you liked it, write a line on Goodreads and/or Amazon and visit the author's webpage at:

www.ybernas.de

Printed in Great Britain
by Amazon